Sorcha could not explain her reaction to Alan Cameron.

Of all the men here, he was the most dangerous to her. God forbid she slip up and err in front of him. What had James said about him? Ah, aye, he was a tracker. He found and sorted clues to find missing things and people.

All the enjoyment she'd felt during the last few hours soured as she realized he was the worst possible man for her to spend too much time around. Her inexperience with men while under her father's protection had left her with little knowledge of how to protect herself from him.

Sorcha understood the danger of him. Of his appeal. Of his smile. Of the way he met her gaze and stared back. But, for tonight, she would allow herself the weakness of savoring those few special moments during which he'd been with her.

Author Note

When I was researching and found information about the more than three centuries long feud between two powerful Scottish clans—the Mackintoshes and the Camerons—I knew I'd found a wonderful source of stories. That was how A Highland Feuding began—as a way to share so many generations, so many locations and so much history with readers.

Alan Cameron appeared in the first book in this series, *Stolen by the Highlander*, as a young man, and even tried to be the hero in *Kidnapped by the Highland Rogue*. I took that as a message that Alan needed to be a hero in his own right. So here is his story. Though you will find some familiar faces, there are some intriguing new ones that may show up in their own stories, too.

Sorcha MacMillan is a woman lost who must not be found and, of course, there's nothing more enticing to a man experienced in finding things than that. Drawn in by her vulnerability, Alan reveals many of his own secrets in this story as he seeks out Sorcha's truth.

I hope you enjoy *Claiming His Highland Bride*!

PS—On a wonderful trip to Scotland I had the chance to visit Cameron lands and the Clan Museum. Let's just say that my visit and sightseeing and research have inspired many stories. See you soon!

Claiming His Highland Bride

TERRI BRISBIN

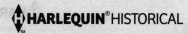

Recycling programs
for this product may
not exist in your area.

ISBN-13: 978-1-335-46758-4

Claiming His Highland Bride

Copyright © 2017 by Theresa S. Brisbin

HARLEQUIN®
www.Harlequin.com

Printed in U.S.A.

Terri Brisbin is wife to one, mother of three and dental hygienist to hundreds when not living the life of a glamorous romance author. She was born, raised and is still living in the southern New Jersey suburbs. Terri's love of history led her to write time-travel romances and historical romances set in Scotland and England.

Books by Terri Brisbin

Harlequin Historical
and Harlequin Historical *Undone!* ebook

A Highland Feuding

Stolen by the Highlander
The Highlander's Runaway Bride
Kidnapped by the Highland Rogue
Claiming His Highland Bride

The MacLerie Clan

Taming the Highlander
Surrender to the Highlander
Possessed by the Highlander
Taming the Highland Rogue (Undone!)
The Highlander's Stolen Touch
At the Highlander's Mercy
The Highlander's Dangerous Temptation
Yield to the Highlander

Visit the Author Profile page
at Harlequin.com for more titles.

These last twelve to eighteen months have been some of the hardest in my entire life, but the bright, shining moments in the darkness have been my grandbabies. Brisbin Princesses Alexis and Sydney and our new Brisbin Princes, Bryce and Chandler, have brought joy to me when I needed it the most.

To my grandchildren—Alexis, Sydney, Bryce and Chandler—I wish you happiness, health, success and lots of family and friends around you all the time! But mostly, I wish you lots of love...and books!

Prologue

Castle Sween, Lands of Knap, Argyll,
Scotland—summer, ad 1370

'Sorcha, come and sit with me a while.'

Sorcha glanced over at her mother's companion for permission before approaching her bed. Anna nodded, so Sorcha climbed up on the high rope-strung mattress, having a care not to sit too close. Her mother had been ill and failing for years, but the last few weeks had brought a sunken and grey look to her face. From Anna's grim expression and her mother's glassy, weak gaze, Sorcha understood that Erca MacNeill had little time left living on this earth.

Sliding a bit closer and reaching out to touch her mother's hand, Sorcha found it difficult to speak. Her throat tightened and clogged with tears as she understood this might be their last conversation. With a slight movement of her eyes, her mother dismissed Anna and soon the silence was disturbed only by the sound of laboured breathing.

'Honour,' her mother whispered before coughing.

When she regained her breath, she struggled to say two more words, two words Sorcha knew would follow. 'Loyalty. Courage.' More rough, deep coughing that produced blood filled the chamber. Even when she tried to hush her mother from trying to speak, the woman shook her head and forced herself to continue.

'Mother, I pray you, do not speak,' she urged, as she leaned closer. Careful not to press against her mother's frail body, Sorcha felt the tears tracking down her own cheeks.

'Honour. Loyalty. Courage, Sorcha,' her mother whispered, tugging her hand to bring her closer still. 'Women know it. Women live it.'

'Aye, Mother.' She nodded and promised, hoping it would quiet her mother's spirit and struggles. 'I will live it. As you taught me.'

'You father has none. He follows a path that will lead to our destruction and your death.'

Her mother's gaze cleared then and Sorcha saw a strength there she'd not seen in years. Her father made certain his wife was obedient and biddable, if not with harsh words and commands, then with his fists and other punishments. Yet just now Sorcha recognised something in her mother's eyes that had been long gone—defiance.

'Mother, you should rest now,' Sorcha began. The tight squeezing of her hand stopped her.

'I will not go to my death without protecting you, Sorcha. I will not allow him to sell you into a life of suffering and pain and destroy the rest. Not as I was. Not for gold. Not for power. Nor for this castle. I will not.'

The words admitted things that her mother had

never spoken of between them. Everyone knew the laird was a rough man, with little tenderness or mercy within him. Everyone whispered behind their hands that he beat his wife. Everyone guessed Erca MacNeill would die soon and that her daughter would be married off and gone soon. With that, his claim on Castle Sween would weaken. He had needed a son off Erca MacNeill and she'd denied him that.

What most were not privy to was the fact that her father was in talks with a powerful chieftain in the Highlands for Sorcha's hand in marriage. One who was surely powerful enough to shore up his claim against anyone who tried to push him out. But that was not the disturbing part of the rumours. Nay, there was something more. Something worse and more frightening to her.

She'd heard the gossip about the harsh lord whose past wives had met unhappy ends, but they'd only been rumours. As a dutiful daughter who understood her place and her value to her clan, she'd wait on her father's word about her future. Though now, with her mother's warning and declaration fresh, she wondered if the stories were true and if there were more to this than she knew.

One glance at the frail and failing woman on the bed told Sorcha that refusing her mother's attempts to speak about it would exhaust her mother and upset her even more. So, Sorcha stroked her mother's hand and nodded.

'Tell me, Mother. What would you have me do?' She expected some ramblings about a woman's place and the choices ahead of her, but instead her mother spoke with clarity.

'You must be ready. It may be before I pass or just after. Someone will come in the light of day or dark of night. Someone you know I trust will bring you word.'

'Mother! I pray you not to say such things. You will recover...' In that moment, the sadness that entered her mother's eyes then, making them appear grey rather than blue, forced the truth upon her.

'Courage, Sorcha. You must be ready.'

'Ready for what? What do you wish me to do?'

Small beads of sweat gathered on her mother's brow and her upper lip. Her grip on Sorcha's hand tightened more than she thought possible with her mother's waning strength.

'You must run...'

Her mother collapsed then, releasing her hand. Sorcha called for Anna. The woman rushed into the chamber and brought a cup of something steaming and aromatic to the bedside. Sorcha slid away to give her room to minister to her mother. As she watched the servant tend to her, Sorcha thought on her mother's odd and disturbing words.

And how she had spoken them. Her mother had shown no such fortitude for weeks, not rising from her bed for over a fortnight. Yet her words and her grip revealed strength hidden somewhere deep within her and now coming out.

She must run?

As Anna assisted her mother in drinking some of the concoction, the words, a warning in truth, swirled inside her own thoughts. Run from here? Run to whom or where? When Anna stepped back, Sorcha understood her mother would and could answer nothing she would ask. The grey colour spread through her neck and face and she lay listlessly on the pillows, seeming now even smaller and frailer than just moments ago. But she must try.

'Where would you have me run, Mother? I know no one outside of our kith and kin here and none would help me and face Father's wrath.'

'My mother's family would aid you. One of my cousins is an abbess in the north, if you can reach her,' she managed to whisper. 'And I have other cousins, MacPhersons, who would give you refuge.'

'You would have me take holy vows?'

'It is one escape.' Her mother pushed herself up to sit then and waited as Anna arranged pillows to support her. 'Once done…'

Sorcha understood that not even her father could unravel vows taken to enter the religious life. Was that a better life to face than marriage? Staring at her mother's worn face and knowing her beaten-down spirit, Sorcha had to accept it might be.

'Anna.'

At her mother's whisper, her companion left her mother's side and walked over to a place behind the door. She touched and searched along the stones until she pulled a small one free. A small leather sack came free and Anna held it out to Sorcha.

'For you, my lady. Put it with the others and be ready as your mother instructed,' Anna said softly.

Sorcha could feel several pieces within the sack, more jewellery from the size and shape of them. Her mother or Anna had been giving her such things for the last several months with some plan in mind. Though she wanted to press both of the women for more knowledge of whatever they planned, the grim expressions of determination that now met her own gaze told her they would reveal nothing for now. She walked back to the bedside to take leave of her mother.

'Rest well, Mother,' she whispered, lifting her mother's hand and kissing it. 'I will see you on the morrow.' The only response was a single tear that trickled out of the corner of her mother's eye and down her face.

Sorcha nodded to Anna as she passed her and tucked the small sack up into her sleeve, hiding it from anyone who witnessed her outside this chamber. Once in her chamber, she dismissed her own maid and hid this sack with the other parcels and bundles her mother had given to her over the last months.

As night fell and the keep and the MacMillans there settled into their sleep, Sorcha could not find rest. Her mother's words and the other hushed words she'd heard whispered about Gilbert Cameron repeated in her thoughts, keeping her awake and adding to her confusion. Giving up the battle, she rose, lit a small tallow candle and brought out the things her mother had given her. If she organised and assessed them, mayhap she would find sleep?

She'd not kept a count of how many times her mother or Anna had given these to her, so Sorcha was surprised to discover fifteen such gifts. Though most contained small trinkets or coins, bits that could be used without drawing much attention, one ring was costly enough to raise concerns from anyone receiving it. Her mother had not worn it in years, but Sorcha remembered it as a gift passed down from her mother's mother. A thick and wide gold band covered in precious stones and gems. Something like this would be worth…a small fortune.

* * *

Stunned by this small treasure, Sorcha had found that sleep eluded her long after she'd bundled the items up and placed them back in their hidey-hole. As the sun rose and her sleepless night ended, Sorcha prayed that her mother would not die and that word of a need to flee would not come for a long time, if ever.

'If ever' did eventually come for Sorcha.

It did not come when her father approached her with the news of her betrothal to the chief of the Camerons. It did not come when she dared to utter her refusal, nor did it arrive when her father punished her for her disobedience in the matter of marriage.

It did, however, come in the dark of night.

Chapter One

Achnacarry Castle, Loch Arkaig Scotland

'It took you long enough to answer my summons.'

Gilbert Cameron's voice echoed from where he sat—at one end of the large hall—to the place where Alan stood near the entrance. Enough arrogance and anger filled that voice that anyone not needing to be in the hall for duty or interest scurried out through every possible doorway. No one wished the chieftain of Clan Cameron to turn his eye or his ire on them. As it now was on Alan.

'Uncle, I came as soon as I received word,' Alan said, walking forward. A few who yet remained nodded at him, careful not to let his uncle see their greeting. When he reached the place where his uncle sat, at a long table and in the high chair of the chieftain, Alan stopped and bowed. 'My lord.'

Alan detested his uncle, though he'd made a vow that not through word or deed or curses whispered under his breath would anyone know. The curses now were aimed at his own stupidity for, indeed, delaying before answering the call when it did come. No encounter between them ended well and probably never would. Not since his uncle had become chieftain. Truly though, not since Agneis had married Gilbert Cameron.

'Did The Mackintosh have you dancing to his tune then, Nephew?' Gilbert sneered out the words. 'So that you could not answer the call of your kin and chief in a timely manner?' A few snorts and chuckles echoed around them as some of his kin joined in his uncle's scorn.

'I was not in Glenlui, Uncle,' he explained in a half-truth. 'As soon as I received your message, I rode.' Alan watched his uncle's reaction to his softened and almost respectful tone and saw the moment that the man decided to move on from scorn to…

'I require your presence,' he said, tilting his head towards the small chamber near the corridor. 'Come.'

Alan followed his uncle and two others into the chamber used by the steward of Achnacarry Castle and waited for his uncle to sit. From the continued silence, he suspected the subject would not be to his liking.

'I need you to accompany me south towards Mac-Millan lands.'

'Knapdale is about four days' ride, when I travel alone.' He always travelled faster and better alone. Several questions sat on the edge of his tongue but he held them back, waiting for more about the task. Then Alan realised his uncle's words—*towards MacMillan lands*. 'Towards their lands or to them?'

'It seems I must go to meet my betrothed,' Gilbert said. Alan let out a breath and shook his head.

'Betrothed, Uncle? I did not ken you were marrying again.'

The thought of it roiled in his gut. Another woman put to the not-so-tender mercies of a cruel man who ruled with cold regard for anyone but himself. The icy gaze that felt upon Alan then told him he had overstepped once more. The only thing he could do was draw Gilbert's attention from his anger or sense of insult to the matter before them. 'As I said, four days.'

'Then, since I had to wait on your arrival, 'tis a good thing we will meet them halfway.' Gilbert nodded at the others. 'They should be near Ballachulish now and we can reach there in two days.' Gilbert paused when someone knocked on the closed door. 'Come.'

'My lord, they are ready.' The servant delivered his message and tugged the door closed behind his interruption.

'We leave now,' his uncle declared. 'Fill your skin and get some food.' With nothing else to say, Gilbert left the chamber. Alan stood for a moment as the surprising news sank in.

His uncle, the widower of two very young and now dead wives, had sought yet another. In secret. For, if The Mackintosh had known this news, he would have shared it or asked after it with Alan. And that sent a shiver of foreboding down Alan's spine. The old laird had been fierce and ruthless, but never had Alan not trusted him or his word. As he left the chamber and walked to the kitchen to replenish his supplies, he realised that was the problem now.

He did not trust his uncle.

Not for a moment.

Not to keep the clan's interests placed before his own.

Nor did he trust any young woman to his care.

Alan had not known Gilbert's first wife, Beatha, but he had known Agneis. They'd run the forests and swam the lochs together as children when she would not be left behind by the lads seeking childhood adventures. Mimicking their every action, she boldly claimed her place among them…until she reached the time when it was clear she was a young woman.

As she'd blossomed in body, Alan had even had a wee dream of marrying her, but their bond was too deep to allow him to think of her as anything but a friend. When news came that she was to be Gilbert's second wife, he was forbidden to speak to her again.

Agneis had not wanted to marry Gilbert, but since he was high in the esteem of the clan elders and his brother the chieftain, her father forced her to it. Two years, she'd lasted. The subtle marks of abuse became more blatant but no one took her husband to task for it. Alan had not been here, had not been here for her, and he blamed himself even now for her eventual death.

Turning the corner into the corridor that led to the kitchen, Alan nodded to several people along the way, trying to make the grim smile he kenned he wore into something less threatening. He yet had many friends among the kith and kin of Achnacarry Castle and did not wish to frighten them away during this short and rushed visit.

With his uncle waiting for him, Alan did not dawdle too long in the kitchen or in the chamber he used when here.

A scant quarter-hour later, he mounted a horse and rode out with the chieftain and his men. All were warriors and accomplished at travelling hard and fast and Alan's estimate of his own travelling time was not increased by much by their company.

Alan kept to himself during the two days on the road, as he always did around his uncle. His father's presence could have a moderating effect on the animosity between them, but Gilbert had made certain his father was away from Achnacarry as much as Alan was. By placing him in charge of Tor Castle in the southern part of their lands, it kept his father out of sight. As they crossed out of Cameron lands his uncle approached him.

'You will speak of this to no one,' Gilbert said. 'Nothing you hear or see. To no one. Unless I give you leave to do so.'

'Certainly, Uncle,' Alan said, nodding in agreement, still not sure of his purpose here. He was not high enough in the clan to need as a witness and not liked at all by his uncle. So, why had he been summoned then?

'Not even your beloved Mackintoshes.' There was so much more than disdain and dislike in his tone. Something else deeper and darker echoed there.

Alan nodded again. His uncle turned and walked away as quickly as he'd approached. Clearly, his task was done and he felt no need to speak to Alan otherwise. The comment, or command as it more felt to him, about the Mackintoshes worried him.

Something about this whole situation—a secret betrothal to the MacMillan heiress—did not feel right to him. There was no love lost between the MacMillans and the Mackintoshes or others in the Chattan Confederation. Or with the Camerons for that matter. So, why would his uncle tie himself and their clan to them? There had to be some benefit, even if just for himself and not the clan. Right now, Alan could not see it.

His father had been banished to Tor Castle though his uncle couched it in terms of loyalty and defence. When they passed by Tor without pause, Alan knew there was no one to question or from whom he could seek counsel. So, he would have to wait and see what happened when his uncle met with his betrothed. Would they return to Achnacarry or travel back to Knapdale? Would the marriage occur soon? He had many questions he dare not speak.

Any hope of getting answers were dashed the next morning as they reached the encampment of the Mac-Millans. A huge man wearing a grim, dark glare stood waiting for them as they approached. They drew to a stop a few yards from him and all remained mounted while his uncle climbed down and strode to the man.

There were no pleasantries spoken between them. No greetings exchanged or signs of familiarity or friendship. His uncle matched the man's stance, feet spread wide and arms crossed over his chest, and they spoke in tones so low no one could hear. Tension rippled in the air around them as the two chieftains spoke for some time, each one's voice getting more strident as the conversation continued. Alan studied the two men and realised that, of the two, his uncle was more at ease. Calmer. More focused. The MacMillan, who it surely must be, was agitated. Angry. Worried.

'Alan!'

He threw his leg over the horse's back and dropped to the ground. Well, if nothing else, he would now discover what had happened and his part to play. He strode to the two and bowed. 'Uncle. My lord.'

'It appears that there is a problem with The Mac-Millan's daughter,' his uncle said. Alan remained silent, for his uncle wanted to control how he spoke of this problem. And he had no doubt at all that whatever had happened was no surprise to Gilbert Cameron. So he waited. 'She has disappeared.'

Of all the things he could have dreamt of hearing that was not one of them. Alan glanced first at his uncle and then Lord MacMillan and knew one thing. His uncle was not surprised by this news. That played into the reason for his summons, Alan knew.

'How can I help?' he asked, carrying out the role he was meant to have.

'Your uncle speaks highly of your skills in finding those lost. She has been missing for nearly three days.'

There were many questions he wished to ask, all of them would be deemed impertinent or too personal, so he asked for that which he needed to begin his task.

'When did she go missing? Where was she?' Alan looked back at the encampment. They'd chosen a place by the river, on high enough ground to stay dry.

'She was seen last after we had our evening meal, three nights ago. She retired to her tent and her servant saw to her. The next morning, when she was called to break her fast, the tent was empty.'

Alan nodded. 'Take me there.' At the surprise on the chieftain's face at being given an order, Alan added, 'If you please, my lord.'

With a huff, the MacMillan laird turned and walked towards the tents and the river. They passed by several larger ones, reaching the last one that lay closest to the river. The noise of the rushing river grew as they approached it. How had the lady slept with this much noise? 'This one?' he asked in a near shout. 'Has anyone touched or moved anything? You have searched the area?' he asked, believing that the laird would have done that first.

'Aye, my men searched along the river and back to the last village. No sign of her.' As Alan lifted the edge of the tent's flap, the laird continued. 'Her maid said nothing is missing from her belongings and nothing seemed awry when my daughter retired for the night.'

'And no one else went missing at the same time? Could your daughter have gone off with one of your kin or other servants?' Alan asked.

He paused and stood blocking the entrance for he did not wish the laird to follow him inside. He wanted a chance to search for himself. A chieftain's daughter, a wealthy heiress, did not simply walk away from her father. There was every possibility that she had been kidnapped.

'Have you received any demands for her return?'

'You think she was taken?' his uncle asked before the other could. 'Who would do that?'

From his uncle's expression, he'd not thought of that possibility. Why not? The MacMillan's daughter stood as his only heir and would be worth a huge ransom. Alan narrowed his gaze, watching his uncle's eyes. His stomach clenched then, making him certain his uncle both knew more and was more involved than the woman's father might be.

Though he wanted to understand his uncle's part in this, right now he needed to look for signs so he could track the woman. Good God, he did not even know her name!

'My lord, what is she called? Your daughter? How many years has she?' he rattled off the questions quickly. He needed to know certain things now. 'How tall is she? Her hair and eyes—what colour are they?'

'Her name is Sorcha,' Hugh MacMillan said. There was no hint of affection or concern in his voice. 'She has ten and nine years and stands to my chest.' The chieftain marked her height on his chest then. 'Her hair is dark brown and her eyes are blue mostly.'

'I need some time to examine her belongings. How far downriver have your men searched?'

'Storms raged until late last night, so not far yet.'

'There were storms the night she disappeared?' Alan glanced at the swollen, raging river and suspected something other than kidnap then.

'Aye. Heavy rains, lightning.' The laird pointed over towards the river. 'A bridge upstream washed out yesterday. Some farmers said they'd never seen such storms or such a flow as it is now.'

Alan was filled with a strange sadness then, for he suspected the lass was not just missing but was, indeed, dead. If she left her tent for any reason and lost her way or her footing, she would have been washed away in a moment.

'I want to search her things,' he said. 'If you will gather the searchers, I would speak to them as well, my lord.'

Alan spent the next hours examining the woman's belongings, questioning her maid and the men who'd gone off searching for her and walking the course of the river for several miles himself. His uncle stood with a knowing look in his eyes and The MacMillan glared at him the entire time, giving no hint of warmth or true concern over his daughter's loss.

From the few bits of conversation he'd overheard between the two chieftains, Alan wondered which one was the more ruthless man. He also came to realise that the lass mattered not to either of them, but the marriage and the alliance did. That was all that seemed of importance to them.

By nightfall, Alan had finished his work and stood before the chieftains and their men to tell them what he'd discovered. The conclusion was not difficult— Sorcha MacMillan was dead. Something bothered him about it though. Though the others had missed the signs, he'd found them easily. Torn scraps of the gown she'd worn to bed. Bits of ribbons she used to tie her hair in braids. He'd even discovered one small braid of her hair entangled in the bushes near the river. Almost as though a path had been laid out before him there, leading him to one conclusion.

As his uncle and her father stood waiting on his words, Alan understood that less experienced searchers might not consider the signs he'd seen as easily found. Even without finding her body, for the strength and flow of the river might have carried that miles and miles down through the glen, he was certain of his findings.

'My Lord MacMillan,' he said quietly, holding out the ribbon he'd found, 'I fear that your daughter is dead.'

If Alan had expectations of an emotional display

or even a few kind words expressed over the loss of a beloved daughter, they did not come to fruition. If anything, the hard man turned harder still with an iciness in his gaze that had nothing to do with the chill weather around them. At his uncle's nod, the chieftain followed him away from their gathered men to a place a short distance from the tents. Although they turned and left quickly, it was not so quick that Alan missed the knowing smile on his uncle's face.

Gilbert Cameron was not displeased by this death.

Once more it would seem that his uncle would be the one benefitting by a young woman's death. As he waited on his uncle's orders, he offered up a quick prayer that *this* lass, like the ones before her, was in a better place than she would be as Gilbert's wife.

Chapter Two

Two weeks later—near Glenfinnan

Weariness and cold unlike anything she'd ever experienced sank into her bones and her soul. She'd followed Padruig for days and days, into the dark storm and away from her father. She had followed him across lochs and around them. Followed his unrelenting steps towards freedom.

And now she watched as some villagers buried him in the ground.

Sorcha had held on to hope, even in the terrible days after her mother's passing. Even when her father had forced her to accept the betrothal to the ruthless and brutal Cameron chieftain. Her mother had sworn there was a way to escape it, but now, at her weakest moment in the last two months, Sorcha was not able to find the strength to cling to that hope.

Tears she'd held in for so long threatened to spill and yet she could not allow the weakness to gain control over her. Sorcha knew that holding in her fears until she was safely at her destination was the only way she would survive. The burial completed, she nodded to those watching. They thought he was her father. She would not cry over her father, but they did not know that.

'What will ye do now, lass?' the miller's wife asked as she stood by the grave. 'Do ye hiv kith or kin nearby?'

'Nay,' she whispered as she shook her head. 'My mother's kin is out on Skye.' Padruig had revealed her mother's plan to her within hours of their escape from Ballachulish and it included fleeing to her mother's sister on Skye—and life in a convent. But she must not reveal that to anyone.

'Is that where ye were journeying to when he passed, then?' the woman asked. The concern lacing her tone and words removed some of the chill on Sorcha's heart. Coming from a stranger, it surprised her.

'Aye.'

'This road is the way there, so if ye bide awhile ye might find someone travelling there and go wi' them.' The woman, Coira, nodded and smiled. 'Ye wouldna want to travel on alone, lass.'

Sorcha shook her head and shrugged. She must decide how to proceed, but right now, it seemed any decision was not within her power to make. She needed to rest and clear her thoughts before taking another step towards…anywhere.

'Is there a place where I could stay here? Or nearby? I have some coins and could pay.' That did not include the fortune sewn into the hem and lining of her gown. She knew better than to reveal that kind of wealth to anyone, be they beneficent strangers or kin.

'Och!' Coira said, sliding her arm under and around Sorcha's then. 'Ye can stay wi' us, lass. There's always a place to sleep and a crust of bread to share with someone in need.'

'Your husband will not mind?' she asked. That husband had helped bury Padruig when Sorcha had discovered him dead this morn. 'He and the others have helped so much already.'

'Nay, Darach is kind-hearted under that gruff manner. Something about ye touched him, lass. Our first daughter would have been yer age now and I think he sees her in ye,' Coira admitted. So many bairns died too soon and theirs had been one. Her own mother had lost six bairns during carrying and their first years, so Sorcha understood the loss.

Sorcha followed the woman away from the graveyard to a small cottage that sat next to the millhouse there on the stream. Coira opened the door and bade her enter. Peat burned there in a hearth built into the one wall and she appreciated the warmth it gave off. Too many days on the road, exposed to the Highland winds and rain, had left her cold and damp. She moved to stand nearer to it and watched as the woman retrieved a pot from over the fire and poured some of its contents into a cup.

'Here now, lass,' she said. 'This will warm ye. Have ye eaten yet?'

'My thanks.' Sorcha accepted the cup and sipped the warm brew within. It was hot enough to spread the warmth through her and sweet, too. 'I did eat something.' She put the cup on the table there. 'I should get my bags and bring the horses here.'

As she turned, she lost her balance and swayed. Coira grabbed hold of her and guided her to a stool. Pushing her hair from her face, Sorcha fell hard on to it.

'Dinna fash, lass,' Coira said, bringing the cup to her. 'Drink and take a bit to rest.' The woman walked to the door and called out to someone. 'Kennan! Fetch the lass's horse and bags. See to them!'

'Kennan?' she asked, drinking down the last of the cup.

'Our son, the youngest,' Coira said, never pausing in her work as she moved from one task to another in the cottage. Folding this, pouring that, and so on. 'So, was yer father ailing for long?'

For a moment, Sorcha was confused, thinking of her true father instead of the man who'd been her mother's servant for decades. Then she shook her head. 'Nay, not ailing at all.'

She thought on the last days of their journey and realised Padruig had been tired. He'd complained of his arm and shoulder paining him yesterday and laughed about being an old man to ease her concern. Then last night before they slept, he mentioned that his stomach was unsettled. But those things could have been anything and she'd not connected them with an illness. The journey had been long and filled with tension and fear over being found and returned to her father. Her own stomach had been unsettled for days. Her arms ached from hours of controlling her horse on unfamiliar paths.

'Well, lass, sometimes the Almighty is being merciful to take someone quickly. 'Tis still quite a shock.'

Sorcha murmured some reply, unable to think of what to tell this woman who clearly only wanted to help her and offer her some measure of comfort over losing her father.

* * *

As the next hours passed, Sorcha realised that she'd never spent this much time with the common people who lived their lives outside her world of comfort and wealth.

Other than those who served them within Castle Sween, Sorcha never had much to do with people who did not live in the keep. Nor had she seen how they lived. Oh, she'd seen and passed cottages in the village before, but had not spent any real time there, observing their tasks and speaking like this. Her father had forbidden all but the most casual of conversations or visits, deeming them beneath the dignity of his daughter.

She watched as the others in the family arrived back after their chores and duties and greeted each other warmly. Though she'd done nothing to help, their hospitality was freely offered and gladly accepted. Coira brushed off any gratitude she tried to express. Soon, it was the darkest part of the night and Sorcha lay awake, considering her plight and the possibilities before her.

The next dawn found her still awake and with no firm plan of what to do. For now, she could remain here but that could not last for long. It would not take long before her inexperience at working or seeing to herself became apparent even to those people who were not looking too closely.

Sorcha walked along the river, trying to sort out her thoughts when the question occurred to her. When Coira came out to hang wet garments to dry, she approached and tried to help, following the woman's example. After twisting and then shaking out a few pieces of clothing, she asked her questions.

'How far are we from Skye?' she began. 'How many days to reach there?'

Coira paused in her work, placing her hands on her hips and staring off to the west as though she could see it from where she stood now.

''Twould take about three days to reach the shore. Then, across to the island and to your destination.' She turned and looked at Sorcha. 'Where on Skye do ye go?'

'Nigh to Portree.'

'Then add another day, and two if a storm blows in off the sea.'

Sorcha then thought on her other choice. Rather than rushing to the refuge of a convent, her mother had mentioned another cousin who'd married into the Mackintoshes. Mayhap she should go there and seek counsel about her choices?

'Do you know far it is to the village of the Mackintosh clan?'

'In Glenlui? Near Loch Arkaig?' Sorcha nodded. There were other Mackintoshes further north, for they were a large clan with many septs, but that was the one she needed to find. 'Not too far. Two days up the glen. Longer if ye go back out the way ye came in.'

She could not go back the other way. Padruig had explained that the Cameron lands sat between them and both the MacPhersons to the northeast and the Mackintoshes to the northwest. They had quickly, and with care, made their way around the Cameron lands to avoid any chance of her capture. Disguised as a merchant travelling with his daughter had shielded her from much scrutiny. The other factor that protected her was that no one knew The MacMillan's daughter or, if they did, they did not expect to see her here or now.

'Does anyone travel there?' she asked. 'My mother always spoke of her cousin who married a Mackintosh of Glenlui.' She needed an escort, for truly there was no way for her to make it there alone. Although Sorcha might be tired and heartbroken and losing hope, she was not so lacking in wits to try such a thing. 'I could hire them. Or exchange their escort for my father's horse.'

She saw the interest spark in Coira's gaze. Sorcha knew the importance of a horse, even if this one was a bit old and worn.

'Aye, I may ken someone,' Coira said.

Someone, indeed, for three days later, Sorcha bid farewell to the helpful people here and to Coira and rode north following Coira and Darach's eldest son Tomas. The woman had promised to have the priest say prayers over Padruig when next he passed through the village and that gave Sorcha some comfort knowing his soul would be blessed even if he'd not been shriven before his death. He'd been a good man, a faithful servant to her mother and a brave friend to help her escape, knowing his fate if they'd been captured.

Just over a week after Padruig's death, two months after her mother's and three weeks after her own, Sorcha arrived in Glenlui and stood before the cottage of her mother's cousin, Clara MacPherson, wife to James Mackintosh. After watching Tomas ride out of the village towards the glen, Sorcha knocked on the door and found Clara tending to her bairns inside.

At first, before Sorcha even had a chance to speak, Clara stared and blinked at her. Then she shook her head and examined her from head to toes before canting her head and shaking it once more.

'For a moment, I thought 'twas my mother's cousin Erca standing before me.' Clara studied her closely and laughed. 'You have her hair colouring and the shape of her face, but that chin is certainly not hers. Those eyes are a bit of both, are they not?' It took but a moment more for her expression to grow guarded. 'Why are you here, lass? Where is your mother?'

So, word had not spread yet? Out through the Mac-Millans to the MacNeills and MacPhersons? The Camerons surely knew it. Sorcha drew in a breath and tried to speak, but the words came not. The tears she'd somehow managed to control did though, breaking free and pouring down her face. Clara, bless her, did not need the words to understand. She drew Sorcha into her embrace and rocked with her, all the time murmuring words of sympathy and comfort.

'Come inside,' she said. 'We can speak of her and the reason why you are standing at my door.'

It took some time to calm the torrent of tears once it had begun. Sorcha sat in a chair in the corner while Clara made some tea and tended her three bairns. Wee Jamie, Wee Clara and Robbie clung to their mother's skirts, peeping at her from time to time as Clara gathered them together and led them into the chamber off this one for a nap.

This cottage was bigger than Coira's, having three rooms that Sorcha could see. Clara'd taken the bairns into one of those and Sorcha listened to the soft words of love and comfort between Clara and her children as they went off to sleep. Memories of her mother's voice, soothing and loving, echoed over her then. As her words did in that moment.

Honour. Loyalty. Courage.

Sorcha swallowed against the sense of loss and emptiness and searched for the courage she'd always sworn to her mother she would demonstrate. Sipping the fragrant brew, she let the warmth wash over and through her. She'd survived her father. She'd survived her mad flight into the night and the journey to this place. With several deep breaths in and released, Sorcha gained control over herself then and by the time Clara joined her there, she was ready to speak about her mother and her own future.

'When did she pass?' Clara asked. 'I have not seen her since I was a lass, when she lived at Cluny Castle.'

'She passed two months ago,' Sorcha said. 'She had been ill for some time.' Sorcha frowned then. 'So my mother was your mother's cousin? I thought she was yours.' Her mother had spoken of Clara in the last weeks of her life and Sorcha had thought their connection was closer.

'Aye, our mothers were cousins and your mother stood as godmother to me,' Clara explained. 'Though your mother often spoke of you in her letters to mine, we never had the chance to meet you.' Clara stood then and brought the pot of tea closer to fill her cup once more.

'And your mother? Does she yet live?' Sorcha asked. She had too little knowledge of her distant kin and needed to know it.

'Nay,' Clara said with a slight shake of her head. 'She passed some years ago. Just after I married James and moved here.' Clara smiled then. 'I came to visit my brother here and met James. I never left.'

'Ah, so your brother lives here as well?' Sorcha asked. She'd had so few kin in Knap, mostly her father's, and no siblings to call her own. How might it have been if she'd had brothers or sisters?

'There was trouble here—the clan split in two as Brodie battled his cousin,' Clara explained. 'Conall died in the fighting. But his widow still lives here.' Clara drank down the rest of her tea and put the cup down on the table. 'I could spend hours telling you the Mackintosh and MacPherson clan histories and lay out all our relatives on either side,' she began. 'But that would simply give you more time to avoid telling me the truth, lass. How did you come to be standing at my door, more than a hundred miles away from your home?'

Sorcha saw the strength of will in Clara's gaze. There was no way to avoid it any longer. Truth be told, the sooner she had things arranged, the better she would feel. On the last part of this journey, she had accepted that the convent on Skye would be the best place for her. Other than embroidery and prayer, she had few skills to offer as a man's wife. The jewellery and coins she carried would make the perfect offering to allow her entrance—no one would recognise them or her.

'I am journeying to a convent on Skye to seek refuge there.' It sounded reasonable when spoken calmly in spite of the pounding beat of her heart and the tightness in her throat. She clasped her hands together on her lap to keep them from trembling as she revealed the next bit. 'My father believes me dead, so he will not be an impediment.'

Her words met sheer and utter silence. Clara's gaze did not falter even then and Sorcha thought she might have stopped breathing. Then her cousin's lips moved but no sounds came forth.

''Twas my mother's plan, truly,' Sorcha added. 'To protect me from him.' She shrugged. 'And I have no skills or talents to offer for my keep anywhere else.' Just the few days spent with Coira and Darach proved how ill prepared she was for a life outside that of a noblewoman.

Clara shook herself free from the hold that the shocking news had caused and stood. After checking on the bairns in the other room and pulling the door closed, she crossed her arms over her chest and nodded. Her intense stare worried Sorcha.

'Tell me the rest of it, Sorcha. We must have our plan in place before the bairns wake and James comes home.' Now it was Sorcha's turn to be surprised. 'I think that Saraid fits you well as a name. Saraid MacPherson, my cousin whose betrothed died and who has come to visit with me for a wee while.'

Whatever she had expected, this was not it. Her cousin listened to her explanation and did not take long to come up with a story, a whole life in truth, and all before the three children woke. By the time James, the village blacksmith, arrived at the cottage, Sorcha allowed herself to hope that she was on the right path.

And she doubted not that if she needed guidance Clara would be the one giving it now.

Chapter Three

Alan noticed her first when he entered Brodie's hall.

She stood near to James and Clara, but not with them. It was almost as though she was trying to stay out of sight. She nodded if they spoke to her, came closer when they beckoned and then crept ever so slowly back away. She seemed to prefer the shadows over the light.

He strode past her and the others and climbed the steps up to the chieftain's table. Waiting for Brodie's nod, he glanced once more over to the corner and noticed she yet remained there.

'You know that is not necessary,' Brodie called out to him. 'Come. Sit. Eat.'

'I would not wish to abuse my welcome here,' he said, the sarcasm coming easily between him and the mighty Brodie Macintosh.

It was always good to have one of the most powerful men in the Highlands beholden to you twice over. No matter his uncle's demeanour or behaviour, Alan Cameron would be welcome here at Drumlui Keep and any place that Brodie controlled. He knew it and mayhap that was why this place felt more like home than Achnacarry or Tor did.

Servants served him from platters and filled his cup with a fine red wine. He nodded to several there in greeting, knowing he would speak with them later. The meal was pleasant, the company more so, but his gaze kept returning to…her.

It was not that she was a spectacular beauty that drew his eye. It was not that he recognised her, for indeed he did not. So, what did draw him to her?

'I see you have noticed our newest guest there,' his cousin Arabella whispered to him while Brodie's attention turned elsewhere. At first, he was tempted to deny it. Why bother when his cousin was right?

'Aye. Who is she?' he asked.

'Clara's cousin, recently widowed,' Arabella explained. 'Staying with James and Clara and helping her with the bairns.'

As Alan watched, the woman under discussion lifted her head and smiled. Though it was too far for it to be for him, he smiled as though remembering her. He could not help himself. He reached for his cup and drank deeply from it, swallowing the rest of the wine down. He could not see the colour of her eyes nor hear the tone of her voice, but the need to know both of those things and more about her nearly forced him to his feet. Only the soft chuckle from Arabella brought him under control.

'She is lovely, is she not?'

'Other than Clara's cousin, what do you know about her?' He tried to say the words calmly—hell, he even tried to convince himself it mattered not. The feeling in his gut and the way it was hard to take a breath said otherwise. What the hell was happening here?

'She is called Saraid MacPherson. That is all I know. Clara brought her here to make her known to Brodie and me a few days ago,' she said. 'Why do you not speak to her yourself, Cousin?' Arabella gave him a puzzling smile before nodding in the direction of the woman. 'She is, after all, a widow.'

His body understood what Arabella was saying even if he was tempted to scoff at the remark. A widow had certain freedoms that a married or unmarried woman did not. Good God, what had his expression been to give Arabella the idea that he wanted this woman? But then, Arabella never needed a reason to meddle in his life. For the last several years, she'd taken it upon herself to seek out a possible match for him.

Like Fia…

He cleared his throat and turned to face her then.

'There is no need for this, Bella,' he said softly. 'I know you wish me well, but there truly is no reason for you to be involved.' Tears glimmered there in her eyes and Alan felt her concern. 'Surely you understand that our uncle expects to dictate that choice and not allow me that choice by chance.'

The change in her demeanour was so quick and clear that it even drew Brodie's attention. The chieftain stiffened in his chair and slid his hand over to cover his wife's where it lay between them on the table. A quick frowning glance at Alan, then one filled with concern at Arabella was followed by a tense silence.

'All is well, Brodie,' she said quietly, stroking his hand until he nodded and turned back to the conversation he'd been having before he'd sensed her discomfort. Once more looking at Alan, she nodded. 'All will be well, Alan. I think things will work out, somehow, regardless of what Gilbert Cameron wants or how he acts.'

'Brave words, Cousin. Especially from someone who knows him as you do.'

They'd both grown up with the current clan chief, though Arabella's father had occupied the high chair before their uncle. In spite of the difference in their ages and their gender, each had witnessed many examples of Gilbert's true nature and temper.

'Well, I was not suggesting you marry the widowed Saraid,' she said then. 'I thought you might be interested in the company of a young woman.' She let out a breath then and shrugged, sadness and something uncomfortably close to pity entering her pale blue eyes then. 'I want you to find the happiness I have, Alan.'

It was not pity there, he realised. Arabella was more like an older sister to him than a cousin. She was having a care for him and it felt strange to him because no one else did. Here they sat, two Camerons amongst the Mackintoshes, welcomed more by this clan than their own.

'Is aught wrong, love?' Brodie leaned over and spoke to his wife. 'The two of you have the makings of some tragic story in your expressions.' Brodie's astute dark gaze met his own then. 'Something I should know?'

'Nay, Brodie,' he said, shaking his head. There was nothing about which he could or would speak to The Mackintosh, so he smiled. 'Arabella is simply...' He paused, searching for the best word to use, but Brodie beat him to it.

'Meddling? Overstepping? Controlling?' Brodie asked, moving his intent gaze now to his wife, who blinked several times at his words. Then, the chieftain lifted his wife's hand to his lips and kissed the back of it, softening what could have been insulting words. 'Bella likes everyone's lives to be orderly and has a way of trying to make that happen.'

'Brodie, I would never...' she began.

'Never meddle, my love?' Brodie kissed her hand again. 'Overstep?' Another kiss, this one on the inside of his wife's wrist. 'Control?' Alan watched, waiting as his cousin clearly did to see where the next kiss would be. Instead, Brodie laughed loudly, drawing the attention of everyone in the hall. 'Give over, Bella. You know you do all those things. It is part of you and you could not stop even if you tried.'

Arabella opened her mouth to argue with her husband and found herself being kissed, thoroughly by the looks of it, into silence. Alan sat back, giving them some bit of privacy and looked out at those yet eating and drinking in the hall of The Mackintosh.

With unerring and yet alarming accuracy, his gaze found that of the widow Saraid MacPherson. This time, she was staring back at him. Catching her, he nodded and smiled. Mayhap he should meet the widowed Saraid MacPherson after all?

'If you will excuse me,' Alan said as he rose from his chair. When Brodie waved him off without breaking the kiss he was giving Arabella, Alan considered himself free to leave.

He fought off the growing anticipation within him, now that he'd made the decision to meet the woman. He forced his feet to slow and greeted several people along the way to where she sat. When he realised he was counting the number of tables between him and her, he stopped and turned away. Reaching for an empty cup, he filled it from a pitcher and then drank half of it down in the first swallow.

Bloody hell, but what was happening to him?

He was not some untested, untried youth. He'd experienced first love and lost it and survived. He'd bedded a number of women. And yet, the way his gut threatened to heave, one would think he was a virgin. Alan forced a laugh at someone's words and tried not to glance over at her.

Three damned tables away, she spoke with Clara.

Standing next to each other, heads together, speaking together, they were a contrast in appearance. Clara stood tall and lush with dark auburn hair and a full smile that she used often and well while the cousin was shorter and dark-haired. As he'd watched, she smiled little and when she did, those seemed shy and tentative. But then one was kin and known to all in the hall and the other was a visitor and a stranger, which could account for the reticence in her demeanour.

Somehow, as he'd been watching and comparing the two women, his feet had led him right to them. Lucky for him, Clara's husband took note of him before they did.

'Alan,' James said, nodding to him. 'You're back from your travels then?' The blacksmith had been a friend for years now. They had both been close in age when they'd met during the struggle between the Mackintosh cousins that ended with Brodie's ascension to the clan's high chair.

'Aye,' Alan said, accepting more ale from the pitcher

that James lifted off the table. 'Done travelling for a while, I suspect.'

'Well, you ken I would gladly accept your help, if you are looking for something to fill your time,' James offered. Alan glanced over his shoulder as the man spoke. 'She is rather fetching, is she not?'

Alan could have ignored the question or tried to laugh it off. He decided to do neither.

'Aye.'

It was the only word he could utter as he took his first close look at the widow Saraid MacPherson. If he had thought her unremarkable, he'd been very, very wrong indeed. Alan blamed the distance that had separated them for the mistake. Now, as he walked with James towards Clara and her cousin, Alan could see that her eyes were an interesting blend of blue and gold.

Interesting? Hell, they were beautiful. As was the rest of her, from her heart-shaped face with full lips that begged to be kissed to the creamy skin of her graceful neck that led to... Hell! He was damned now! Worse, he'd been so entranced by the sight of her that James had continued speaking while he gawped and Alan had no idea what the man had said.

Yet Saraid had not even looked at him. Alan gathered his scattered wits and tried to follow James's words. The knowing sparkle in his friend's eyes told him that James was enjoying his discomfort. He would pay for that.

'My wife's cousin is visiting to help with the bairns,' James said, kicking Alan's foot to gain his attentions. 'Saraid, may I make you known to Lady Arabella's cousin, Alan?'

'My lord,' she said quietly, lowering her head respectfully and dipping into a curtsy.

'Nay, Mistress MacPherson, not a laird nor nobleman,' he said, shaking his head and watching a lovely blush creep up into her cheeks. 'Just Alan Cameron.'

While James laughed at his words and Clara smiled, the woman had a different reaction. The pink in her cheeks left abruptly and was replaced by a pallor that reminded him of…fear. What had caused that?

Sorcha fought the urge to clutch at Clara for support when the man spoke his name. She'd noticed him when he'd entered the hall and walked to the raised table in the front, joining those closest to the chieftain. What woman alive and breathing would not notice a man like him? Tall and muscular with his long, dark-brown hair gathered back behind his head, he strode through the place with the lethal grace of a natural predator and the confidence of one who knew his place and liked it.

She must have been too obvious in staring, for he'd looked in her direction several times through the meal. Sorcha tried to concentrate on Clara's words and introductions and to play along with the story of her that they'd created to cover her identity. In changing the detail of her betrothed dying to her husband dying, it had made some men here a bit bolder in their introductions. As she watched his approach, she wondered if it made a difference to him.

She'd seen men like this in her father's hall and noticed the way women watched them with hunger in their gazes. These same men never slept alone or wanted for companionship. As he came closer, it did not escape her that many women in this hall did not miss a move he made.

Now, as he stood before her, his blue gaze almost glowing as he stared at her, her mouth went dry, her palms sweaty and she lost her ability to think. Until she misspoke and he revealed his name—his full name.

Cameron.

Alan Cameron.

Cameron.

Her first instinct was to run. The urge came over her so quickly and strongly that she almost ran. But she'd not survived so far by acting on fear alone. No, she must control her fears once again to survive this situation. Sorcha coughed to make herself breathe and turned away to give herself a moment to gather her control. After smoothing her gown down, she faced James and Clara and…him.

'Your pardon,' she said, nodding to Clara first. If there was a small pause in the conversation, James had not noticed for he stepped right into the gap.

'Alan may be a Cameron, but we try not to let that colour our regard for him.' The smile that accompanied the mild insult told her that there was true affection between these two.

'My thanks, friend,' Alan said, aiming a mock punch at James's shoulder. 'And I try not to forget that you are a Mackintosh, Jamie.' Then, when a most mischievous and alluring smile lifted the corners of his mouth, he winked at her. 'But I am but one among many and must have a care.'

A wave of heat passed through her then, teasing and tickling its way through every bone and muscle in her. She did not know why he affected her so, but it could not go on. With his gaze on her and James and Clara glancing her way, they were waiting for her to speak. A question—she should ask a question. With no under-standing of his place here and worried over revealing too much of her own, she must tread carefully.

'Do you visit Glenlui often, then?'

'I do,' he said.

'He does,' James and Clara said together.

'That much, then?' she offered, catching the hu-mour in their tones.

'Since the truce has held between our clans, I split my time between here and Achnacarry, my uncle's seat.'

Gilbert Cameron was his uncle. Luck was on her side for now because she'd met or seen so few of The Cameron's men when he'd visited Sween Castle. And this one had not been one of those few. Alan did not react as though she was familiar to him, so she let out her breath and she nodded politely 'So are you from Cluny?' he asked.

For a fleeting moment, she thought on the story of her background they'd created and shook her head. With a shrug and then a nod, she sought to clarify it to him.

'Originally, aye, my mother's family lived in near Cluny. But my husband...' She paused and took a slow breath. 'My husband was kin to the MacNeills.'

'MacNeills are allies of the Mackintoshes,' he said, looking around the hall then. 'I am certainly outnum-bered here.' His laugh made her insides melt a little. Deep and full, it resonated through her. 'That was un-seemly, Mistress. My condolences on your husband's passing.'

She did not speak, but nodded at his kindness in spite of the false need for it. Clara's knowing gaze flashed a warning to her. Had she sensed the growing weakness in Sorcha at keeping up the pretence? She'd been introduced to so many people, both tonight in the hall during this gathering as well as in the village over the last weeks. And each one asked after her husband and her grief, expressing what felt like true concern and sympathy.

From what Clara had told her, all of them had dealt with death and loss over the last decades as war waged between their clan and the Camerons. Only the strength of will of their present chieftain and the powerful love of his Cameron wife brought it to an end with their marriage and a lasting truce. Which made it possible for this Cameron to be standing here in their midst without fear.

'I thank you for your kind words,' she said. Now it was James's turn to bat at his friend and laugh.

'Alan is many things, but kind is not usually his manner,' James jested.

She expected Alan to reply to his friend's jest, but another man approached just then and interrupted.

'Brodie wants to speak with you.'

This man was tall and very attractive. Were none of the Mackintosh men here plain of face? Though his tone of voice was mild, there was an undercurrent in his words and something more in the expression on his face. Sorcha had seen this man several times, in the village and here in the keep, but had not been introduced to him.

'Rob, have you met Clara's cousin yet?' Alan asked.

Rob. Rob Mackintosh. Commander of the Mackintosh warriors. A formidable fighter and most loyal man to his cousin Brodie. All those things Clara had mentioned now made sense on seeing the man. But not once had she spoken of his rugged attractiveness.

'Eva told me of you,' Rob said, nodding to her. 'Saraid?'

'Aye, Saraid MacPherson,' she repeated. Each time she spoke the name it felt easier. 'I met Lady Eva earlier,' she said, making the connection between this husband and his wife whom she'd met before. As she watched, Rob glanced over towards the lady at the mention of her name, his gaze filled with an expression of such complete and utter love that it made Sorcha's own heart pound.

'Alan,' Rob spoke his name and canted his head in the direction of his chieftain. 'Now, I think.' Walking off without another word, the man stopped and gathered a few others as he made his way to the front of the hall.

'I will see you in the village?' James said to his friend.

'Aye. In the morn if Brodie has no use for me,' Alan answered. Turning to face her, he smiled again. 'I hope to see you again, Mistress MacPherson.'

She said nothing, could say nothing to those words, but she did smile and nod. Then he walked in that same predatory gait away from her. Sorcha could not move her gaze from him and part of her hoped he would turn back once more.

Clara spoke to her and yet the words mattered not. James's voice entered the conversation with his wife and still Sorcha heard nothing and saw only Alan as he moved in purposeful strides away from her. Then as he reached the steps and climbed up them, he stopped and did turn, meeting her stare with one of his own. A smile followed and Sorcha could not stop herself from returning it.

With a word from Brodie, he was gone, off to some chamber behind the table with the others and she was left with what must be a silly smile on her face. She faced Clara then, finding her cousin and her husband gawping at her, open-mouthed and slack-jawed in astonishment.

'I thought you said she was going to a convent on Skye,' James whispered loud enough for them both to hear.

Clara grasped her arm and pulled her close. 'I think we need to talk, Sor… Saraid.' As they took a few steps towards the doorway, Clara whispered again, 'About that convent.'

James burst out in laughter as they walked away, not even trying to be subtle about it. The Mackintosh's hall was a rather boisterous place so it did not seem awkward. Clara glanced over her shoulder, gifting her husband with a threatening look that quelled him a bit.

Sorcha could not explain her reaction to Alan Cameron. Of all the men here, he was the most dangerous to her. God forbid his uncle come here and recognise her. God forbid she slip up and err in front of him. What had James said about him? Ah, aye, he liked to find things. He found and sorted clues to find missing things and people.

He'd found Lady Arabella when she'd been kidnapped by Brodie. He'd tracked another of their kin when outlaws had attacked the village and taken her. He found people…

All the enjoyment she'd felt during the last few hours soured as she realised he was the worst possible man or person at that for her to spend too much time around. Her inexperience with men while under her father's protection left her with little knowledge of how to protect herself from him. She would need to rely on Clara for guidance in this. When she let out a sigh, Clara held on to her tighter and walked faster away from the keep and back to the village.

Sorcha understood the danger of him. Of his appeal. Of his smile. Of the way he met her gaze and stared back. But, for tonight, she would allow herself the weakness of savouring those few special moments in which he'd been with her. The cold light of day and the reality of her situation would be forced on her soon enough.

Worse, in the dark of that night, Sorcha dreamed of the one man she could never claim as hers.

Chapter Four

$\begin{matrix}\end{matrix}$

Alan followed Brodie and the others closest to him in loyalty and kinship out through a doorway to a chamber off the kitchens where they would have a measure of privacy. Though he did not ken the subject to be discussed, Alan suspected that word of his uncle's actions had gotten back to Brodie through a means other than himself.

And Brodie would ask for his opinion on the matter.

He exhaled as he considered what his words might be and what they must be. No matter how much he liked and admired Brodie or disliked his uncle, he was first a Cameron. Entering the surprisingly large chamber, he walked across and stood, back against the wall, waiting for Brodie to begin.

Rob, as always, stood at his side. A few of the elders were here as well. Alan recognised Grigor, the man Brodie thought would lead the clan after the infighting that nearly destroyed them. Magnus, a warrior married to Rob's sister, now served on the council of elders. He smiled then, remembering Magnus's reaction to being called an 'elder'—no one did that after the first time. Fergus, Brodie's steward here at Drum-lui Keep, was the last man to enter and one he had not expected to be present. He closed the door and stood in front of it, waiting on his lord's words.

'I have received word that Gilbert met with Hugh MacMillan near Ballachulish recently,' Brodie began. The chieftain's dark gaze did not leave Alan's face as he spoke. 'They met for the purpose of a betrothal.'

Though the others were surprised by this news, Alan did not, by word or look, feign ignorance of the event. He owed Brodie his honesty even if he could not disclose what he knew of the matter.

'Who was to marry whom?' Rob asked. Since both The Cameron and The MacMillan were widowed, either could have been seeking a bride. Alan almost smiled at the astute question from Brodie's friend.

'Apparently The Cameron went seeking a bride,' Brodie answered.

'Who is he to marry?' Grigor asked, crossing his arms over his massive chest. 'How many daughters does The MacMillan have?'

Though older than any of them, the man seemed to grow in robustness as he added years to his age. Having taken Arabella's aunt to wife recently, he was both strong and content and Brodie always counted on him for his support and knowledge. Alan waited to see exactly how much Brodie knew about The MacMillan's only daughter.

'He had one,' Brodie said, again staring at Alan as he spoke. Alan gave a slight nod, confirming his knowledge.

'Had?' Rob asked. 'What the bloody hell happened to her?'

Alan wanted to laugh at the way Rob managed to curse in almost every sentence he uttered, but this was not the time for levity. The lass's demise bothered him still. Brodie watched him, waiting, so Alan stepped away from the wall and crossed to stand before the chieftain.

'The MacMillan's only daughter apparently fell into the rain-swollen river in the middle of the night and drowned.' Silence lay heavy over those present for a few moments and Alan added nothing more.

'Better a quick death in the river than a slow one married to Gilbert.'

Alan whirled around to see who had spoken those words, both shocked and intrigued that someone else had come to the same realisation that he had. But, of course, he had never said it aloud. Magnus met his stare and nodded.

'Is there anything else you can tell us, Alan?' Brodie asked, drawing Alan's attention back. Not 'want to tell us'. Brodie understood his predicament, for he was a man caught between honour and loyalty.

'Nay, my lord,' he said, bowing then to the powerful man.

'Then I pray you to seek out your cousin and escort her to our chambers.'

Without another word, Alan accepted the dismissal and walked to the door. Fergus stepped aside and opened it for him. It closed behind him and he'd taken only two paces when the uproar within the chamber erupted. Between the deep distrust that yet ran deep between their clans and that which they held for Gilbert, the shouting and arguing did not surprise him. Knowing Brodie, he would allow each man a say before coming to any conclusions. And before coming back to Alan.

He walked back to the hall and found Arabella deep in conversation with Rob's wife and sister. When they all looked up at him at the very same moment with their gazes narrowed, a strange fear shot through him. Oh, he'd faced death and dismemberment in his life already, but the thought of being in the aim of these three women terrified him…as it would any sensible man who had even a bit of self-preservation in his blood.

'Is the discussion finished then?' Arabella asked first.

'Nay, it continues without me.'

'If it involves the Camerons, why are you not there?' she asked, probing into uncomfortable matters as she always did—with a remarkable sense of what would be best left untouched. He did not question how she knew Brodie discussed the Camerons, for she had as many sources of knowledge and gossip as her husband did, possibly more.

'The Mackintosh dismissed me.'

The three let out gasps as one and leaned back in their chairs, surprised by this news.

'And you know not why?' Eva asked.

Rob's wife was no stranger to the machinations and manipulations of clan chiefs. Her own father had forced her into marriage with Brodie's closest friend for his own benefit. For them, though, the marriage had turned out for the best.

'I am not privy to Brodie's reasons,' he said. Not exactly the truth, but close enough for now. 'Mayhap Arabella can discover it when he returns to their chambers?' Alan held out his hand to his cousin. 'Which is where he's asked me to take you.'

The women looked one to the other before looking back at him. He continued to wait for Arabella to take his hand. Arabella took pity on him and rose from her chair then, accepting his arm and nodding to Eva and Margaret. From the expressions on those two faces, Alan understood that they expected that she would reveal the reason he was expelled from Brodie's gathering and what was truly happening.

She remained silent as they walked through the hall, up the stairway that led to their chambers. But he knew that restraint would not last long once they reached the privacy promised in her room. Tempted to leave the door ajar, he waited for her to enter before standing before it.

'Oh, do close the door, Alan. You know that will not stop me from having my say or asking my questions of you.'

He did as she ordered and watched as she crossed the room and poured wine into two waiting cups. She carried them to the small table in the corner and sat, arching a brow to give him another order without words. Alan sat and accepted one of the cups.

'So, Brodie truly dismissed you? What were his words?' she asked, taking a sip from her cup.

'He simply bade me to bring you here.'

Her foot tapped impatiently on the floor between them. Arabella would think on this until she was ready to pounce. Or until her husband arrived.

'You will not reveal to me the purpose of calling you all together?'

'I will say it involves the Camerons and the Mackin-toshes.'

Alan waited for the explosion of temper from his cousin, but none came. Instead, she pursed her lips and looked over his shoulder towards the door. He turned and saw Brodie standing there.

'Come now, Bella,' Brodie said, walking to where they sat. 'Abusing your cousin will not loosen his lips. You should know that by now.' Alan tried to stand, as he should in the presence of the chieftain, but Brodie's hand on his shoulder kept him sitting. 'He has been in this same situation before and he is now and always be loyal to his clan first.'

Somehow, when Brodie spoke those words, ones that echoed his own thoughts and vow, guilt washed over him. And he had no reason to feel that at all. He'd helped the Mackintoshes a dozen times over and would again if he could. He would not, however, betray his own clan or disobey a direct order from his own chieftain. He did stand then, pushing free of Brodie's hand to look him in the eye.

'Aye. I am loyal to the Camerons, Brodie.' Anger built in his gut then and he wanted to rage. The strange thing was that he was not certain who his target should be.

'Hold,' Brodie said, putting his hand up between them. 'I meant nothing more by my words. And I ken that your uncle's actions will cause strife between us.'

'My uncle's actions?' Arabella rose now and approached her husband. 'What has he done now?'

'Gilbert has been negotiating with Hugh MacMillan of Knap for his daughter's hand in marriage.' Brodie's gaze never left his own.

'Another marriage?' Arabella gasped at this news. 'How old is she?' she whispered. The words lashed out at him and Alan could not help but flinch. *How old?*

They'd never spoken of Gilbert's penchant for young women openly and it should have surprised Alan to hear it from her, but somehow it did not. Arabella missed little, whether here in Drumlui Keep and village or at the home of her childhood Achnacarry. She'd learned early in life that she would be the wife of a powerful man with many under her control and supervision and had learned the skills needed to live that life. Breaking from Brodie's stare, Alan looked at his cousin.

'It matters not for The MacMillan's daughter drowned on her way to the betrothal.'

Arabella began to say something, but she pressed her lips together and swallowed. He could guess that her words would be close to those uttered by Magnus just a short time ago in a different chamber.

'God rest her soul,' she whispered, lifting her hand to her head, chest and shoulders in the gesture that usually accompanied such prayers. A few moments passed before she reached out to touch her husband's arm. 'There must be more to this if you are so concerned. Tell me the rest of it, Brodie.'

'I suspect there is more to this than a simple betrothal, Bella,' Brodie said. 'There have been whispers for months about dissatisfaction with the treaty between our clans. But nothing more. Nothing substantial. Nothing I can prove.'

'Alan, do you know of this?' she asked him next.

'In all candour, Arabella,' he said, glancing first at

Brodie, then back to her, 'I know nothing of plans to undermine or weaken the treaty.' He took a breath in and let it out. 'As to the other, I know only what Brodie told you.' He looked at Brodie once more. 'In either of these, though, my uncle does not keep my counsel or invite me to share in his, Brodie.'

'I wanted to tell you that you have a place here, Alan,' The Mackintosh said. 'No matter what actions your uncle carries out or treachery afoot, you are one Cameron that will always be welcomed here and in the Chattan Confederation.'

Tears had begun trickling down Arabella's cheeks at her husband's words. A sick feeling flooded him for, by those words, Brodie had confirmed one thing and, at the same time, hinted at so much more.

'What do you know? What treachery do you speak of?'

'Brodie. Alan. Can we three not speak plainly here together? We have given ourselves into this treaty and have seen too many die before it was in place to want it weakened. We are more than allies here,' she pleaded. Her eyes bright with tears, she touched both his and Brodie's hands. 'We are kin. We are family. We are friends who have protected each other and even saved each other's lives when we needed saving.'

Her soft words crushed his pride and the tension in Brodie eased as well. He stepped back and nodded at his wife.

'You are right in this, my love.'

Brodie walked to the pitcher and brought it to the table with another cup. Pouring a generous amount in each of the three there now, he drank deeply and Alan wondered if the news Brodie would share was so bad he needed the fortification of strong wine.

'First, word came to me that The Cameron has sent and received many messages to Alastair MacDonald of Lochaber in recent months.'

Feeling somehow responsible to defend Cameron honour, Alan was tempted to offer some sort of explanation. Instead he waited to learn more about Brodie's suspicions and whether they were groundless. Alastair MacDonald had been behind attacks on Mackintosh holdings, and villagers, a few years back. He'd deflected his guilt on to the Camerons until Alan had discovered the truth of it. Would his uncle truly be contemplating some sort of alliance with the MacDonalds of Lochaber now?

'More recently I received reports about this betrothal with The MacMillan's daughter. His claim on Castle Sween is tenuous at best now that his wife is dead. But if his daughter married the Cameron chieftain, he might be amenable to defending her father's claim.'

'How is that trouble for the Mackintoshes or the treaty? The MacMillans are long-time allies to the Chattan Confederation. Would that not bind the Camerons more closely to your side?' he asked Brodie.

Brodie's smile then was stark and devoid of mirth. Alan tried to think of all the ramifications of the match that had almost happened. There were so many bonds and feuds between this clan and that one all over Scotland that he found it impossible to see all the strands in the spider web of connections. Clearly, Brodie had been thinking about this for some time.

'Hugh MacMillan is an upstart who claimed Castle Sween from the MacNeills. He would change allegiances if it benefitted him.' Brodie crossed his arms over his chest. 'I will be watching to see their next moves.'

'If I learn anything that I can tell you, I will,' Alan said. 'You ken that I will, do you not?'

He would. He could not let this honourable man face destruction or mayhem without warning, if he knew about it. There were ways to walk that narrow path between friendship and betrayal and Alan had been learning that well these last years since he first met Brodie Mackintosh.

Alan drank down the last of his wine, realising how late it was, and bade them both farewell. As he reached the door, he needed to ask something of Brodie.

''Tis clear that your spies are effective, my Lord Mackintosh,' he began, bowing his head in a mock salute. 'I would ask the same of you. That you inform me of anything you believe I should know.'

Arabella smiled then, for the first time since their earlier discussion at supper about the attractive widow Saraid MacPherson. She wanted peace between all of them, all her kith and kin, and trouble and discord tore at her heart.

'And you as well, my Lady Mackintosh,' Alan said, nodding at his cousin. He rarely used a title when addressing her. 'I ken that some of your sp…inform… sources ken as much as your husband's and would appreciate being told what you discover.'

Thinking that was the end of their discussion, he lifted the latch and pulled it open. As he tugged it to close behind him, Arabella called out to him. He slowed to hear her words.

'My informants have told me that the widow Saraid MacPherson plans to enter a convent on Skye when she leaves here.'

The door was closed with some force so Alan knew there was no chance of saying anything back to her. Or asking her any questions. He walked away, listening to the laughter coming from inside the chamber—his cousin's and Brodie's, too. He thought about his experience with women and let out some words that would rival even Rob Mackintosh's best, or rather worst, efforts.

He'd searched for his cousin and found her, but got captured, too.

He'd fallen in love with Agneis, but lost her to Gilbert.

He'd searched for, found and lost Fia Mackintosh, who then turned down his offer of marriage.

He'd searched for the MacMillan girl and found that she'd died.

Alan shook his head and let out an exasperated breath then as he realised that even showing interest in a woman seemed to move them out of his reach. As Saraid MacPherson would be when she left Glenlui and travelled on to Skye.

A nun.

A bl—

Alan stopped at the blasphemous words he almost thought and laughed at the irony of his situation instead.

The man known throughout the Highlands as the best tracker of all manner of things seemed to lose the women he wanted to find and find the ones he could only lose.

As he made his way to the chamber he used here, he could almost hear the Fates laughing at him.

Chapter Five

Sorcha followed the two older children out of the cottage, carrying Robbie on her hip in the way she'd watched her cousin do. The bairn was a happy one, content to gurgle and drool and smile most of the day. This morn, while the weather was clear and brisk, Clara announced it was a good day to walk to the baker's and miller's cottages and see to some other errands.

So, while Clara finished up inside, the four of them followed the path from Clara's cottage back towards the road leading to the village's centre and then the keep in the distance. Wee Jamie and Wee Clara chattered and called out to children along the way. Sorcha had met many of those who lived here over the last weeks.

With Clara's introduction, no one thought she was anyone but the widowed MacPherson cousin. Even James had not been told the truth and, for that, Sorcha felt guilty for asking her cousin to keep it from him. But, until she left, she wanted no one else privy to her true identity. If they knew not her true name or what she'd done, they could not be punished or be held responsible. Clara assured her it would all work out, though Sorcha was not so certain. She'd almost reached the first place on her list when Clara caught up with her.

'I finished sooner than I thought,' her cousin said, holding out her hands for the bairn. 'Was he fussing?'

'Nay,' she said. As it turned out, there was little demand in their household for the fine embroidery skills of which she could boast. Of all the tasks she'd tried to help Clara with, seeing to the babe was the most pleasant and one which she could claim she could do. Or at least until he was hungry.

That happened the moment he saw his mother. As though the sight of her reminded him that he had not eaten for several hours, Robbie scrunched up his little face and cried out his displeasure. Clara just smiled and shrugged since this happened several times each day.

'If you will see to getting the flour from the miller and collect my loaves from the baker, I will take him home,' Clara said. 'And bring the other two along with you, if you would?'

Sorcha smiled and nodded, trying to exude confidence when she really wanted to beg Clara not to leave her alone in the village with the children. The bairn was easier in that he did not yet walk on his own. The others, well, they had a habit of scampering off so quickly she could hardly keep up with them.

That had been the latest in her series of discoveries of her lack of experience and knowledge on the simple matters of living. She'd been brought up in a cocoon, surrounded by servants instead of friends and kept apart by her father's orders and mandates. In her early years, she'd run playing with some of the servants' children, but her father stopped that.

And with just that moment's inattention, Wee Jamie and Wee Clara ran off. Sorcha chased them towards the miller's and caught up with them, taking the little lass's hand in hers to keep her near. The miller handed her the sack of flour and she walked over to another path and down it, the smell of baking bread leading the way. No sooner had the man offered them each a piece from a fresh and hot loaf then the children both took off running. By the time she gathered up Clara's bread and the flour and stepped outside, they were gone.

Turning this way and that, she listened for the sound of their laughter. Nothing. The area was silent but for the sound of winds flowing through the trees around her. Glancing in as many directions as she could, she could not see them. A noise caught her attention and she ran off in that direction, calling out their names. Another noise took her down another path and then another until she realised two things—she was well and truly lost and the children were nowhere to be found.

Her chest tightened with fear and worry and it became hard to breathe. The weight of the flour and the loaves made her arms shake and her legs felt wobbly and weak. She put the bundles down on the ground and shook out her arms to make them stop trembling as she tried to come up with a plan. The sound of a horse's approach made her turn and run towards the road there. Mayhap whoever was coming could help her?

A dark horse trotted closer as she ran out into the road and threw up her hands. Its rider cursed and pulled up hard, bringing them to a stop before her and scaring whatever breath she still had right out of her.

'What kind of fool…?' he yelled first. 'Saraid MacPherson?' She sucked in a breath and met the angry gaze of Alan Cameron.

'The children,' she gasped.

He jumped from the horse, landing so close to her she could feel the heat of his body. Clutching her shoulders, he pulled her up and searched her face.

'What children?' he asked. Looking past her and into the distance, he shook his head.

'Clara's wee ones,' she forced out, her lungs finally able to take in air. 'I've lost them.'

A myriad of expressions moved quickly over his face, from surprise to confusion to disbelief. 'How did you lose them?'

'I was running errands for Clara,' she said. She remembered the dropped bundles off the road and ran to retrieve them, calling back to him. 'I turned my attention from them for but a moment and they ran.' Grabbing up the sacks, she ran back to where he stood watching her. 'I just pray that nothing has happened to them. I could never forgive myself…' He took the items from her as though they weighed nothing and checked inside the sacks before shaking his head.

'The miller's is on the other side of the village. How did you get here?' he asked.

'I did not pay heed to where I was running. I only followed the sounds I thought were the children.' Then, she whispered her most embarrassing admission. 'And, as you can see, I am lost.'

He walked back to his horse and climbed up on the

massive animal. Leaning over, he held out his hand to her.

'Come. I will take you to Clara's,' he offered. 'The children know their way and are probably there already.'

Sorcha looked up into his eyes and saw compassion and not pity or mocking. In the light of the sun, those eyes were a blend of blues and greens and greys and not the pale blue she'd thought. Much as some described the mixed colour of hers, too. Taking his hand, he guided her to step on his foot as he lifted her up and guided her behind him. He gave her a moment to settle and then touched his legs to the horse's sides. Unused to riding this way, she grabbed at his plaid to keep from swaying too much and unbalancing both of them.

Still, this close, she was overwhelmed by him. His size. His nearness. His scent. Him.

'You made only one bad turn,' he said over his shoulder. 'If not for going in the wrong direction right there…' he pointed off to his left '…you would have circled right back around.' When she leaned over to look past him, she began to slide off the horse. 'Hold tight now.' Without thinking, she reached around his waist and held on.

Because of his size, her hands barely made it around him. And the action forced her to rest her face against his back. His muscles rippled under her cheek as he controlled the horse. His long hair, pulled back and tied with a strip of leather, tickled her nose as she rested there. When she realised what she was doing, she eased her grip on him, sliding her hands back to rest on his hips.

'I am sorry to take you from your own tasks,' she said.

'Since my destination is yours, you are not.'

Sorcha remembered his offer of help last night to James. What was the nephew of the Cameron chieftain doing working with the Mackintosh's village blacksmith?

'Have you known James a long time?' she asked, trying to understand his connections to this place and these people.

From his place at the chieftain's table and the call for him to speak with those closest to Brodie—a call delivered by the man known for his loyalty to the laird—he was well known and well regarded here. Was he to the Lady Arabella as Padruig was to her mother? One of her kin who stayed on for years as a faithful friend?

'Aye, for years.'

Uncertain if his curt reply was due to the riding or not, she held any other questions she would have asked back. But her curiosity got the better of her as they rode through the centre of the village and many called out greetings to him. Especially the women.

'Are you a blacksmith then?' she asked when they slowed and he would be able to hear her words. The question she truly wanted answered involved personal details she would ask of Clara and not dare to speak to the man directly.

'Och, nay!' He laughed and it made her blood heat. The deep tones of his voice echoed through her. Again. 'I am a tracker.'

'Tracker?' Her blood, heated just a moment before, ran cold then at the reminder of his skills. 'What do you seek?' How could she have forgotten such a critical part of him? His answer chilled her even more.

'Whoever or whatever is lost.'

They arrived at Clara's cottage and, just as he'd predicted, Wee Jamie and Wee Clara were there waiting. Relief poured through her as they discovered the children were well and not lost.

'Your bairns gave Mistress MacPherson quite a scare, Clara,' he called out as he reached back to help her down. With a strong grip on her arm, she slid over the side of the horse and stood as Clara came out, carrying the youngest one. Sorcha noticed the loss of the warmth of his body as soon as her feet landed on the ground there. 'I found her over near the stream on the other side of the village.'

'I lost them and feared they would find harm,' she said. 'One moment we were all enjoying a bit of warm bread and then next, they were gone.'

Clara laughed as she approached Sorcha. Throwing her arm around her shoulders, her cousin pulled her close. Alan climbed from his horse then and stood watching.

'They are fast ones,' Clara agreed. The woman released her when her husband came around the side of the cottage from the building where he worked. 'Jamie, the wee uns gave Saraid quite a scare.'

James smiled at her and nodded. 'You are not the first one to find them gone.' He walked over and extended his arm to Alan in greeting. 'But I see the Cameron tracker found you right quick. He is skilled at finding things and people, too.'

A wave of warning unlike anything she'd ever felt passed through her at those words. Another reminder that she could not let this attraction to him go any further than it had since she doubted she could stop the physical reaction of her body to his strength and his heat. But she needed to be circumspect and not give someone like Alan Cameron a reason to look more closely at her. She swallowed the ever-present fear and nodded at James.

'Aye, I was lucky that he was travelling past when I found myself running in circles with no idea of how to get here.' Sorcha smiled then as the others chuckled at her words. 'Better for me was that he knew the children well enough to assure me that they would be safe.'

Alan took the sacks from where he'd tied them and held them out to her. Retrieving them, she walked to the cottage doorway. Clara guided the children to her and, as they went inside, Sorcha fought the urge to stand and gawp as he followed James back to the smithy. She did take one last look and was startled when that blue-green-grey gaze stared back at her.

Alan could not help staring back at Saraid.

He'd known he'd see her here, for she was living with Jamie and his wife now and he would be spending time here working with his friend. Seeing the panic and fear in her gaze when she ran out on the road tore him apart. Then, the hope in her voice when he spoke of the bairns' habit of doing this gave him ease. He'd met her once and yet found himself with some sort of connection or affinity to her. Strange that.

The feel of her body leaning against him during

the ride here had been a pleasurable torment. Her soft curves pressed against his back and her hands around his waist made him wish she would move just a bit closer. Tempted to grab her hands and guide them down, he fought the need and allowed her to find purchase by grabbing his plaid instead.

The purely physical reaction surprised him because he knew about her plans.

A convent. A nun. She was so full of life that he could not imagine her shut away from the world to face a future of sacrifice and prayer. He hoped the Almighty was not offended by his thought that the religious life would be a terrible waste. Or that the way his body reacted to her nearness and innocent touches counted as a sin against his soul.

Following Jamie past the cottage and to the smithy, Alan hoped that some hard work would drive this unusual fascination and fleshly need from him. And take his mind off the concerns over his uncle's possible machinations.

When her laughter first drifted from the cottage's open windows across to where they plied the fire and iron tools, he lost the battle. He forced his attention on the tasks he carried out once, then twice and then again before Jamie laughed aloud.

'A bit distracted, are you then, Alan?' Jamie said. He put down the plough blade he was cleaning and sharpening and wiped the sweat from his brow with the back of his arm. 'She is a fair one.' Alan put down the large hammer he was using to pound out a new horseshoe and nodded.

'Aye. What do you know of her, Jamie?' he asked. 'How long will she be visiting?'

'Are you planning to be here more often or avoid us depending on the answer to that question?'

Alan answered with a rude gesture and shook his head.

'Nay, neither. I am just curious.' He wiped his own brow and shrugged. 'There is something different about her. Something...interesting.'

'You mean other than her beauty and her kindness to my wife and bairns?' Jamie offered. 'And that I never knew my wife had a widowed cousin?'

'You did not know?' At Jamie's shake of his head, Alan continued, 'When did you know she was coming to stay?'

'When I returned to the cottage from working up at the keep with Dougal and found her here. But, she's kin, aye? So she's welcome here as long as she needs to be.'

'That's what kin does,' he agreed as he picked up the hammer and turned back to his work.

They worked in silence for some time, but one thing yet bothered him. If it did not bother Jamie that his wife's kin showed up, unknown and unannounced, at their door and planned to stay for some uncertain amount of time, then it was not for him to be bothered either. Yet, one thing did. It ate at him though he had no rights by kinship or claim to be concerned for a moment over it. Finally, it pushed its way out and he said it aloud.

'Is she truly going to Skye to be a nun?'

'So you heard? Did Clara tell you?' Jamie laughed.

'Nay. Arabella told me.' Alan faced him and crossed his arms over his chest, now bare due to the heat of the fire pit. 'She just does not seem to be the type of woman who would give up m…life and seek prayer and silence.'

Jamie looked as though he would argue or add to his assessment, but instead his friend just watched him through narrowed eyes for a few seconds before going back to work. It was just as well, since he had no standing about any of this. If anyone did, it would be the lass's father or brothers or even her dead husband's family.

By the time they finished for the day, Alan had come to some conclusions.

First, he knew he would not seek out problems that were not already his.

Then, he would make it a point to visit Achnacarry more often and keep watch for anything out of the ordinary for his uncle.

Finally and in spite of his body telling him otherwise, Alan accepted that he could not and would not interfere with Saraid MacPherson and her plans for her own life. He knew nothing about the young woman and had no right to think she could not choose her own path.

Returning to the keep that night, he was proud of his decisions and knew they would make the next months go much more smoothly for him. At least that was what he thought until he caught sight of Arabella and her women watching his every move. What forced him to worry was not words, but the lady's expression as he bade her and her husband a good night later after the meal.

A smirk lay on her lips and a twinkle of mischief

sparkled in her eyes—two things to be wary of and two things he'd learned, as had Brodie, to worry over. He'd always had sympathy for Brodie when he'd been the target of it, but now, now it seemed that Brodie had deserted him.

No matter that. He had his plan and had made his decisions.

Chapter Six

In the first few minutes each morning when she awoke, Sorcha wondered what new challenges she would face that day. So far, in the weeks since her disappearance into the night, she'd faced many of them.

She'd never had to prepare her own food.

She'd never had to ride for hours and days.

She'd never truly feared for her life. Oh, her father would make it miserable, but she served a purpose until she married.

But, and this was an alarming and enlightening revelation to her, she'd never been amongst people who cared.

These Mackintoshes cared about each other and that extended to their chieftain, too. For they did not seem to fear him as her kith and kin feared her father, rather they respected him and even liked him. Stranger still was that here in Glenlui village and in Drumlui Keep asking questions was not forbidden nor even discouraged. If anyone raised a voice or question to her father or his orders, their life and limbs were in peril.

Oh, she'd seen The Mackintosh stand his ground

over a few things and, when he did that, everyone supported him. When she considered to whom he listened, she was confused even more.

The only other person of noble blood living here was Lady Eva. She was the daughter of a powerful nobleman in the north. Everyone else, all those who counselled this laird, were family and friends who had proven their loyalty and worth in the fight that nearly destroyed this clan.

And here she was, in the midst of people who took her as she was. Clara and James opened their home to her and, in doing that, the rest here welcomed her. The biggest challenge she faced was these people.

So many times each day, she was tempted to tell her story to one or another of them. Margaret, Clara's sister by marriage, was the worst. The woman had a way of drawing Sorcha in and then asking her insightful questions. Sometimes, Sorcha wondered if she had a bit of the Sight and knew all her secrets already.

'You are awake?'

Sorcha glanced over at the door to her cousin's bedchamber and nodded. After stretching slowly, she pushed back the blankets and stood. The morning chill, even in late summer, made her wrap one of the woollen blankets around her shoulders.

'I am.' Glancing past her cousin, who carried the youngest on her hip, Sorcha saw no movement to indicate anyone else was awake. Yet.

'I could almost hear you thinking,' Clara said, walking to the bucket of water and dipping a cup for herself. She offered a few sips to the bairn before she held it out to Sorcha. 'Are you still thinking about the porridge?'

Sorcha laughed and shook her head as she accepted

the cup of water. Each day Clara had taught her, or tried to teach her, a new skill or task. Yesterday's morn it had been to make porridge, something she'd eaten enough to know how to make it.

Porridge, good porridge, was harder to make than it seemed it should be. There were still burned bits on the bottom of the iron pot that she'd used to make it! Just as the children took advantage of a moment's hesitation or inattention, so did the porridge for it burned, thick and black, when she'd turned away from stirring it.

'Nay,' she lied. 'I have let the disaster of the porridge go now, Clara. On to other tasks!'

'Worry not,' Clara said, holding out Robbie to her so she could see to her personal needs. 'We will find something for you today.'

Sorcha held the bairn close, rubbing his head as he grabbed as much of her hair as he could and shoved it in his ever-open mouth. Until the fire in the hearth was lit, the chill would remain so she lifted one end of the blanket and wrapped it around him. He leaned against her and she closed her eyes, enjoying the warmth of him.

This was another thing she would give up by entering the convent.

The blessing of children.

Sorcha would not think on that right now. For the next weeks or month, she would allow Clara to teach her some basic tasks and help her cousin as she could. There was no way to adequately repay all that she'd done already, but Sorcha knew that some of the gold coins would help them.

Clara returned then, hair covered and dressed for the day, and held out her arms for her bairn. But her cousin studied Sorcha as she lifted Robbie away.

'I have seen this expression in your eyes many times now,' Clara said. Reaching up, she touched Sorcha's cheek. 'You have lost so much in such a short time. And you have faced some impossible choices. Worry not, Sorcha, it will all be for the best.'

'Sorcha?' James said, walking into the common room. He rubbed his face and pushed his hair back. He glanced at them, one at a time, then back to Sorcha. 'Is her name not Saraid?'

Silence met his words and Sorcha wondered if it was time to tell him the truth. Clara had other ideas.

'Her mother's name is Sorcha, Jamie. She looks so much like her, may her soul rest in peace, that I called her it by mistake.'

'Ah,' he said, kissing Clara as he did each morning. 'Just as I call the bairns by most any name I can think of when they jump on me.' His acquiescence seemed too easy a thing given.

As though it was an invitation, Wee Jamie and Clara ran out of their bedchamber and jumped on their father. It would seem to be their morning ritual, for he would stumble around the cottage, with one grabbing each leg, until he fell to the floor and they climbed on top of him.

Such innocent fun. Somehow the tears had gathered without her realising it. Only when Clara used the corner of her apron to dab at them did Sorcha feel them. Clara mouthed some words to James, who nodded and met Sorcha's stare with a sympathetic expression.

'I will get water,' she declared. Clearing her throat and wiping away the tears, she knew she must get out of here before the self-pity overwhelmed her. 'And, aye, I know the way.'

She grabbed an empty bucket and left, even while trying to ignore the whispering behind her. Why the scene had bothered her, she knew not. She suspected that having seen the warmth that could be between father and bairns, it reminded her of the gaping lack of it in her own upbringing.

Sorcha's upbringing had been like that of many noble women and based on the value she held. For her father, she was linked to the castle that they held for the MacDonalds. Her mother's family were castellans and controlled the headlands, or had until her marriage to Hugh MacMillan. Now, an heir was the only way for him to retain control. So, either she had to marry someone strong enough to fight the Lord of the Isles or her father needed to get another heir.

Her mother's death had given him an opportunity to seek another legitimate heir, the son he did not have yet. Her value as a female was tentative and only based on what it would bring him. Whether or not her father would have affection for a male heir, she knew not. Yet, watching these people, she knew it would never be like this for anyone born to Hugh MacMillan.

Sorcha reached the well and nodded to the others already there. Located in the centre of the village, it was a meeting place during the day. Even now, just past sunrise, there were villagers filling their buckets for their daily tasks. She nodded to the baker's lad and the cooper and his helpers. A few of Clara's neighbours stood whispering, as was their custom, sharing the latest bits of news and gossip. She knew from her time here that those bits of gossip would make their way all around the village and back by nightfall, enhanced and changed by each person who shared it.

With the help of a tall, strong young man, she'd just filled the bucket and turned towards the path when she saw James standing there studying her with a dark expression. Sorcha tried to smile but could not. From that gaze, she suspected he knew the truth…her truth.

'Here,' he said, approaching with an outstretched hand. 'Let me take that.' With his height and strength, his hands were double the size of hers and he took the full bucket as though it weighed nothing more than a bird's feather. 'Clara worried over you so I said I would fetch you back.'

'I did not mean to worry her, James,' she said, following him down the path. It was not the one she would have chosen if left on her own. 'I just…I…'

He stopped then and motioned for her to come off the path and into the shadows there. When she saw the fierceness in his expression as he put the bucket down at his feet, she feared his words. James lifted a hand and ran it through his reddish-brown hair, pushing it out of his face. Then, stepping closer, she saw not ferocity but compassion in his forest-coloured gaze.

'First, my name is Jamie,' he said. 'My father was James and so was my granda. So, call me Jamie as everyone does.'

He crossed his arms over his chest and waited for her to agree. Although familiarity such as this had always been discouraged by her father, it warmed her that her cousin's husband attempted to put her at ease. Sorcha nodded. 'Jamie it is, then.'

'I know who you are.' He said it in a calm voice but it struck terror into the deepest part of her. 'Clara and I have no secrets from each other, so I have known since you arrived on my door that there was more to you than you let on.'

'But she said…' Clara had promised her. She'd promised not to share her truth.

'She did not want you to worry,' he said, shrugging. 'She did not break any confidence or word given to you.' He stepped closer and lowered his voice though they seemed alone. 'I did not press her for the details that would have done that. I trust her and her judgement. She said you are her cousin and you need a refuge while you sort out things. That was and is enough for me to ken.'

His kindness overwhelmed her and the trust he placed in his wife awed her. Sorcha did not know whether to smile or cry or fall to her knees and thank him. So she offered him the only thing she had.

'My name is Sorcha,' she whispered.

'I suspected that much,' he said. 'I have reminded Clara to have a care around the wee ones. They repeat all sorts of things that they shouldna when you least expect it.' From the mischievous glint in his eyes, she had no doubt that they had repeated the worst things at the worst possible time. 'So, shall we return home before Clara sends out Wee Jamie to find us?'

Her heart lighter, she nodded and walked beside him the rest of the way back to the cottage. This path brought them in from a different direction, to the smithy first and then around to their croft. She took the bucket from him when he stopped there.

'Are you serious about seeking a life in the convent?'

Of all the things he could have said or asked, she'd never thought he would ask about that.

'Aye,' she said. 'If I must remain hidden, 'tis the perfect place.'

'I go to the keep this morn,' Jamie said. 'If you wish to go to the chapel and speak to our priest, I can take you there.'

She'd heard about their priest, Father Diarmid, from Clara and Lady Arabella, but had not met him yet. Though he lived at Drumlui Keep, he travelled to other villages to minister to the spiritual needs of the Mackintoshes. He'd been away for several weeks when Sorcha had arrived. 'He is returned?'

'Aye. If you wish to seek his guidance, I have always found him a fair man, one who will listen and not judge too harshly.'

'I would like that, Jamie. Tell me when you are ready and I will go with you.'

He walked away, glancing past her for a moment before he made his way to his work. Sorcha heard the footsteps and knew Clara had been watching and waiting for her. Facing her, Sorcha recognised the guilt in her cousin's eyes and understood the reason for it. She walked to Clara, put the bucket down on the ground there and took Clara's hand in hers.

'With only my mother and father to judge marriages by, I had no idea of the faith and trust that could exist,' she said softly.

'Puir lass,' Clara whispered back.

'I am glad I have witnessed what marriage could be at its best.' She patted Clara's hand. 'Jamie has offered to take me up to the chapel when he goes to the keep. To meet Father Diarmid.'

'So, if you have courage to do that, do you have enough to learn to make bread this morn?'

'Is it as hard as making porridge?' she asked. Her heart felt lighter after seeing the love and trust between Clara and Jamie. Now, she would meet the priest and begin the journey forward. Surely she could conquer a bit of flour and water?

'Nay, not harder. It just takes some strength and patience.'

Which was exactly how Clara described each and every chore and task she'd taught Sorcha since her arrival there.

'I thought it might.'

Together, they went back inside and spent the next several hours trying to mix the perfect loaf of bread. Lucky for her, Clara had both the strength and the patience to dominate the unruly mixture of flour and water and yeast. By the time Jamie sought her out, she wore enough of all the ingredients to make another loaf. But Jamie, being the wonderful husband whom Clara praised, knew better than to point that out to either of them.

Soon they were riding up to the keep in a small wagon with Jamie's tools that were too heavy to carry. The chilly morning fog had burned off and the sun looked as though it had gained control of the day. Sorcha loosened her cloak and pushed it back from her shoulders.

'That cloak is quite heavy,' Jamie said. She thought he commented on the changeable summer weather here in the Highlands, but when he continued, she understood it was not the weather of which he spoke. 'I have a strongbox with a stout lock in my workroom where your valuables would be safe.'

The jewels and coins were still sewn into the hem

and the pockets of her cloak. Jamie knew it. Sorcha did not say anything, but nodded.

'You might want to keep one or two in place. If you have to leave quickly or have need of such a thing.' She looked at him then. 'I know you sought refuge, so you must be running from something or someone. If the time comes when you must flee, at least you will have something to help you on your way.'

'Very practical,' she said, glancing down at the cloak. 'Something that my mother would have said.'

Sorcha smiled then, remembering several times her mother had offered such advice, even before she'd explained about the need to run. It would seem that her mother had been planning this for much longer than Sorcha had known and she'd had faith that Sorcha would be able to do this.

The rest of the way up the road to the keep and through its open gates was accomplished in silence, but for greetings called out to Jamie. By the time they reached the small stone chapel, the yard was busy with those going about their duties. Most attention seemed to be on the training yard where Robbie Mackintosh worked with his men. On previous visits here, she'd witnessed part of the tough regimen he put his warriors through, in sun or rain, to keep them well prepared.

From her place on the wagon, she could see the two men fighting within the larger circle. One was Robbie and the other one was Alan Cameron. Her gasp drew Jamie's attention and then he looked over to see what had caught her eye.

'I wondered when he would challenge Rob,' Jamie said. 'Do you want to watch?' He climbed down and held his hands up to help her to the ground. 'Though I suspect prayers might better serve him in this.'

'Why?' she asked, following him without thought towards the fence encircling a large clearing there.

'Because Rob is one of the best fighters,' Jamie said over his shoulder as he cleared a path for them to the front. 'And Alan has not trained with him for a while.'

When they reached the fence, Jamie called out a bit of advice to his friend. Even though she wanted to watch, it was unseemly to do so. She stood back behind Jamie, letting his size block most of her view until the two fighters moved towards them. Bared to the waist, with their hair pulled back and out of their faces, Sorcha saw the blood already flowing from Alan's mouth and one eye. Rob looked untouched but out of breath.

But Alan's chest glistened in the sun's light as they turned and spun and stepped this way and that. Muscles she'd felt when she'd held on to him on the horse were now visible and she watched as they flexed and tightened with each movement. He smiled at Rob, but it was a grim one, promising pain and defeat. Sorcha could not breathe as they circled each other, delivering blows when they discovered a weakness or opportunity.

The two did not use swords due to their deadly nature. Instead they used wooden poles which, as much as she could tell, could still inflict a goodly amount of pain and damage. At least those weapons would not kill the one receiving the blows.

They feinted. They struck. They circled. All the time others cheered or booed, calling out insults and advice. Rob and Alan appeared impervious to all the interference and Sorcha found herself staring at his every move. At some point, she moved to Jamie's side to better see them.

Then, Alan managed to back Rob up against the fence in front of where she and Jamie stood and she gasped aloud as he hit the wood with enough force to shake it.

Which drew Alan's attention to her, his eyes widening a scant second as he recognised her there.

Which was enough to give Rob a chance to take control once more.

Which he did.

Horrified, she watched as Rob rolled to his side and swiped Alan's legs out with the pole. Alan fell hard, his breath knocked from him as he landed in the dirt. As Rob made a final move to complete his win, Sorcha stumbled back and ran to the chapel, hoping no one had noticed her there.

But Alan had. His gaze at that moment told her so. A flash of recognition in those stormy eyes, followed by a second of something else, unidentifiable and yet something that sent a thrill through her at the same time.

She grabbed the cloak she'd heedlessly left on the wagon and made her way into the cool, dark chapel. Tossing it around her shoulders, she sought refuge in the shadows of the silent building.

Chapter Seven

Alan spat out the dirt from his mouth and wiped the blood off his face as Rob reached out his hand to help him to his feet. Waving him off, Alan pushed up and brushed more soil from his skin.

'Not quite ready,' Rob boasted with a wink. The man comprehended how close he'd come to defeat in front of his own warriors but would never admit it now. 'A little more work with the quarterstaff should help.'

Tempted to wipe the smirk off the commander's face with his fist, Alan nodded and clenched his teeth together to avoid saying what he knew to be the truth. The lass had done it—distracted him and given Rob the victory in their skirmish. One moment Alan was winning, about to take Rob down, and in the next, he stared into those amber-and-blue eyes of hers, recognised her concern for him and lost his concentration. It was all it took for him to falter and for Rob to take advantage.

He walked over to a large barrel of water at the side of the training area and splashed himself to wash off the worst of it. His eye would swell a bit, but the cut was more bluster than substance. His lip was split and not for the first or worst time. Overall, his pride took more damage because he'd been trying to beat Rob Mackintosh for years and this had been the closest he'd come to accomplishing it.

Until he saw her face. She might have gasped— that might have been what drew his attention. Either the sound or the sight of her witnessing the brawl—it mattered not what had drawn it. Now, with the fighting done, the crowd drifted off as he washed and retrieved his shirt and plaid from the fence. When Rob came over, Alan shook his head.

'You were lucky, old man,' he said, glaring at the man. Rob had been the one who'd gotten him drunk for the first time in his life when he'd been two and ten and a prisoner of the outlaws of Clan Mackintosh. Though he was older in years and experience, Rob Mackintosh was still the strongest and fittest warrior outside of their chieftain.

'Aye, I ken the truth of it though I would never admit to it.' Rob reached out and smacked Alan on the shoulder. 'If not for the lass stepping up just then, I would have had to break into a sweat to take you down, lad.' They both laughed at the blatant lie even though it revealed a truth.

For some reason, the lass affected him in a way that other women had not, did not. The rush of interest and attraction that filled him in the hall when he'd first seen her rose even now as he wanted to glance around the yard to find her. He resisted because he neither wanted to give Rob another reason to taunt him nor expose this strange weakness in his concentration.

Just then, Rob's wife walked out of the keep, carrying their newest bairn in her arms. Rob stopped breathing, stopped talking, stopped everything as he gazed across the distance at her.

'Damn women,' Rob whispered a few moments later, his voice full of awe and worship and yet frustration, too. 'They grab you by your bollocks and you cannot do anything but follow them around.'

As Rob climbed up and over the fence, shirt in hand, and gazed on the lovely woman holding his child, he shook his head at the last moment and smiled at Alan.

'At least you know that lass is headed for the convent,' he said. 'No need to get yours in a vice when you know you cannot have her.' And with those words, Rob was gone, off at a fast trot to reach the woman who held his b—though to be candid, Alan was certain it was Rob's heart that Eva held.

Looking around, Alan did not see the woman who had been the cause of his defeat. Jamie's cart stood nearby and Alan knew he was working at the stables this day. On the morrow, he would be at the miller's house. Alan had purposely not gone to the village this morn because she, Saraid, had rattled his control with the instantaneous attraction to her. He'd known she was someone to avoid, someone who would avoid entanglements. But when he had noticed her there watching, it had been even worse for him than he'd expected. He spit into the dirt again, his mouth yet carrying the reminder of his defeat because of her.

Alan did glance around then and wondered if she had sought out the chapel. Was that why she was there? Surely not to watch him fight with Rob, for that was an unplanned opportunity he'd seized, both to defeat the strong Mackintosh commander and to work out some of the tension that yet hummed in his blood and his muscles. Instead of the relief he'd hoped for, her presence made it worse.

Now somewhat clean, he pulled on his shirt and wrapped the plaid over his trews and around his waist, tossing its length over his shoulder as he walked up to the stone building. Father Diarmid lived in a small annexe added to the back of it some years ago when Brodie convinced the priest to remain here. There were enough souls needing tending that the priest was kept busy most days. He'd returned just yesterday from a journey across Mackintosh lands. A young woman considering entry into the religious life would wish to speak to him, so that was her most likely reason for being here in the keep.

Alan stood in front of the door with his hand on the latch and unexpectedly hesitated to open it. Mayhap he should not invade her privacy at prayer? Mayhap she was speaking to Diarmid and should not be disturbed? He'd not been this unsure of himself or his actions ever before, so he stood there, stunned at that realisation.

She was not for him and could not be, as Rob had reminded him. A simple concept, but he had to tell himself that a few more times as he waited there. So this could only be simple curiosity or a gesture of friendship towards Clara's cousin who was both new and alone here in Glenlui—something he had been and understood how it felt to be so. Convinced now, he lifted the latch, tugged the door open a bit and slipped inside.

Two small windows on either side of the low-ceilinged chamber let in light. Candles burned on the unadorned altar there all hours of the day and night whether the priest was present or not. It was something he'd insisted on when he agreed to serve the people here and something that Brodie agreed to—the chapel was open to everyone no matter the time or day. Benches sat around the outer perimeter of the chapel and would be moved into rows during Mass or other services. So, Alan glanced along them until he saw her.

She sat, head bowed, lips moving silently in some prayer as he watched her. Though her hands were empty, her fingers moved as if she clutched prayer beads in them. Alan smiled at the sight of it, remembering his mother's hands as they moved in the same way. Not wishing to disturb her devotions, Alan slid on to the nearest bench and leaned against the stone wall at his back.

The silence between them was soothing in a way. He'd always found it to be so here in this place of God, though he would not consider himself an overly prayerful man. He sought the peace it brought during difficult times in his life as most did—begging for forgiveness after trespassing or thanking the Almighty for favour or mercy shown. When kith or kin passed. When word of Agneis's death reached him.

A few minutes passed and Alan wondered if he should indeed say something or simply leave when she broke the silence and spoke.

'I pray you will forgive me,' she said. Her soft voice echoed across the chamber to him. 'I did not mean to…' The words drifted off as she clearly searched for the correct one. 'Draw your attention from your opponent.'

'I think you gave me the excuse I needed for losing,' he replied, laughing softly. 'I have never been able to best the man in battle.' It was the truth he offered her.

'Though I have tried many, many times with a variety of weapons and even with none.'

'He was impressive,' she admitted. It stung his pride for a moment, but it was the truth so he agreed.

'You should see him fight with Brodie. Now that is a battle worth watching.' He stood and walked to where she sat. Pausing for a few seconds so that she could object if she so wished, he sat down near her. 'And when Magnus makes it a battle of three, it is a sight to behold. The whole of the keep and village turn out to watch.' He slid a little closer then, stopping when his knee almost touched her skirts.

'Magnus is…?' she asked, turning towards him then.

'Margaret's husband. He sits on Brodie's council.' He faced her. 'You have met Margaret, have you not?' he asked.

'Aye, she has been quite kind to me. She's taught me about many things.' A frown wrinkled her brow for a moment and her narrowed gaze lit on him. 'Margaret's first husband was Clara's brother.' Though a statement, the tone of her words turned it into a question.

'It must be intimidating, meeting them all at once and trying to sort out who belongs with whom?' He laughed again. 'At least I met them all over some time.'

'How long have you lived amongst them?' Saraid asked him, sitting up and shifting a bit closer to him. They both kept their voices low out of respect for the place.

'Ten or so years,' he said. 'I came here first with my uncle when the truce was being negotiated.' Something changed in her at the mention of his uncle. ''Twas my Uncle Euan who was chieftain at that time. Arabella's father.'

'Is that not unusual? A Cameron living among the Mackintoshes?' Her manner became somehow colder then, a distance opening between them at this topic.

'Aye, well, with the truce holding as it has, 'tis not so unusual.' Had she heard about him from Clara or Jamie? About what had brought him here and why he was more welcome here than at Achnacarry?

'I did not mean to pry,' she said. 'My curiosity must be unseemly for a stranger.'

'Nay,' he said. 'Not a stranger but kin of my kin.'

The silence gathered once more around them.

'Did you have a reason for coming in here?' she asked. 'Do you seek Father Diarmid, too?'

Why had he come in here? Because he needed to see her. But he could not admit that, for he had no right to want such a thing as her company or her attentions. Trying to remember which need drove him in here, he remembered—she had gasped so loudly during the fight that he and most around them had heard it.

'Nay, not the good priest,' he said. 'You looked alarmed during the fight. Then you disappeared. I wanted to make certain you were well,' he admitted that much to her. 'Now that I see you are, I will leave you to your contemplations.'

If he admitted the truth here in God's house, he really wanted to lean over, pull her closer to him and taste her mouth. Instead, he began to stand to put some space between them before he did what he'd been thinking about and did it in a holy place such as this.

She placed her hand on his, stopping him. Alan noticed the way the porcelain-white colour and softness of her skin contrasted with his as she touched him. His control diminishing, he needed to leave, now, but her words gave him pause.

'Can you tell me of this priest? Jamie spoke of him but I worry, for the one who served my...who lived in our village was a harsh man and stern priest.'

'Fear not, our priest is neither of those things. He will give you good counsel in whatever matter you place in his hands.'

Alan did stand then. Too much time in her presence, alone with her, could give rise to gossip, even if that time was in a chapel. And give rise to things he could not allow.

'His practice is to go to the hall to break his fast after morning Mass. He should return soon. Or you can find him there?'

'I will wait here,' she said. She smiled then and he lost the ability to breathe. He wanted...

But the door opened then, startling them both, and she jumped to stand next to him as the light and wind seemed to bring in the portly priest. She barely reached his chest when she stood this close. Alan stepped back a pace and nodded to Diarmid as they waited for him to close the door behind him.

'Father, this is Saraid MacPherson,' he began to introduce her.

'I thought it must be her,' Father Diarmid said, holding out his hand in greeting. 'Lady Arabella spoke of you and your admirable desire to seek entry into a religious community.' Diarmid paused then and looked directly at Alan.

Knowing he was not needed or desired here and

now, Alan nodded to both of them and took his leave of them.

'Come, mistress, let us pray first for God's guidance along the path He has chosen for you.'

She walked with unexpected grace, like that of a lady, to the priest's side. Diarmid led her towards the altar and, as Alan glanced back from the doorway, helped her to kneel before it.

As he closed the door quietly, he found himself praying words he suspected were the complete opposite of the ones both the priest and Clara's cousin were offering.

Alan went about his tasks for the day and decided that it might be a good time to make a visit back to Achnacarry. Some distance from the fair widow might ease his growing desire for her and, with Brodie's concerns over Gilbert's possible treachery, matters needed his attention away from here. And it was time to re-establish some connections to his own family.

He would speak to Brodie about it later. Mayhap Brodie would come up with some message or other task that would give Alan a good enough reason to be there without suspicion. Alan shook his head over the fact that he, a Cameron, needed a reason other than kinship to return to his home.

Father Diarmid was much nicer than the priest who served the people of Castle Sween. He did not call down the damning power of God to smite her once during their prayers or discussion. Indeed, he should have considering how much lying she did when explaining her circumstances to the priest...without actually explaining *her* situation and history. He was patient and answered her questions and even shared the story of his own time in the monastery learning to be a priest.

Father Laurence had no pity or mercy within him, God-given or otherwise, and Sorcha had feared confessing anything to him. The penance he required were as harsh as he was and did not inspire one to believe in a merciful God. Father Diarmid's approach made her want to beg his forgiveness for lying to him. As in the example of marriage learned mostly from her parents, this stark difference between priests surprised her as well.

Sorcha left the chapel some time later with a lighter heart. The priest, having learned that she could both read and write in Latin and the native tongue, invited her to use his prayer book during her visits. Father Diarmid recommended daily prayers, in the chapel if possible, and contemplation of the path she wanted to follow. He even offered to contact her cousin at the convent on Skye to let her know she was coming, but she found a way to decline that kindness…with another lie. If she did not take heed, Sorcha would find herself facing a tall pile of penances if held accountable for every lie or omission she spoke here to these people.

Jamie had not finished his work in the stables, so she left the keep to go back to the village by herself. Although he laughed when she told him she could find her way, he nodded and went back to his task. Walking back around the training yard, she noticed that few watched the men practising there now. No spectators calling out cheers and jabs. No raucous yelling. Just Rob and another man, guiding those practising through their paces. Sorcha nodded when Rob waved at her as she passed on the way to the gates.

The weather had remained fair, so she carried her cloak rather than wearing it. The weight of it was noticeable and Sorcha decided she would remove most of the jewels and coins hidden within it and store them in Jamie's strongbox when she arrived back at the cottage. Soon though, she ended up at the miller's cottage next to the stream instead of Clara's and realised she'd missed a turn or several along the way.

'Good day, Mistress MacPherson,' a voice said from within the millhouse. A man stepped into the daylight and nodded to her. 'Are ye lost once more?' It was the miller's son, Dougal, and she nodded with a laugh.

'Aye,' she admitted. 'I cannot seem to follow the same path twice.'

'Come then,' he offered, pointing off to the right of the building and across the stream. 'Let me show you.' They walked in silence along the stream until they came to a small bridge over the water.

'I do not remember this bridge,' she said, stopping before crossing it.

'You may not because Clara and Jamie's croft is over the other side of the village from here,' he explained.

She met his dark-brown eyes and saw merriment in them. He could not be much older than she was, but had the height and strength common to the men here. He wore his hair cut shorter than most, shorter than Alan did. Sorcha looked away for a moment, aghast that she would compare Dougal, or anyone, to Alan.

'Coming?' he asked. When she nodded, he led her across the bridge to the third road they crossed.

'If you follow this straight to its end, you will find Jamie's smithy.'

'My thanks, Dougal,' she said. 'I will try not to get lost again.' He laughed at her promise and watched as she walked away from him.

'To its end, Mistress MacPherson,' he reminded her. 'Look for me if you find yourself lost again.'

She smiled once again at his kindness and paid heed to the path before her. How she'd made it halfway across Scotland without getting lost, she did not ken. Somehow she could not go from one end of this village to the other without it happening. When she turned back, Dougal was standing there, watching her make her way. She waved once more and did as he bade her do, walking without making a turn or deviating from the pathway. Soon, he was out of sight as the path curved and ended before Jamie's smithy.

She walked past the building, knowing Jamie had not yet returned, and found Clara in the cottage, the quiet cottage, mending some clothing while the bairns napped.

'Come. Sit,' Clara invited her. 'You have been gone for a while.'

'My apologies, Clara.' She put her cloak over a stool and walked to her cousin's side. 'I should have returned sooner.'

Sorcha reached down and took some of the torn garments from the pile. Accepting a needle and a spool of thread, she sat and began working. Sewing and embroidery put her at ease. Embroidery of the kind at which she excelled had no place amongst the villagers, but sewing was always needed.

'You helping with the bairns was part of our story,

but I do appreciate your efforts with them,' Clara said as Sorcha settled and began working. 'Did you speak with Father?'

'Aye.' Sorcha smiled, remembering the priest's advice and guidance. 'He is so very different from the priest who served our clan.'

'And what did he tell you?' Her cousin shook her head then. 'Or more importantly, what did you tell him?'

''Twas difficult not telling him the truth of it. I explained it as you told me—my husband had died, his family was not welcoming,' she said, listing the important details of her story. 'No family left of my own. My devotion to God.' She paused for a moment, praying that God would forgive her trespass. 'He urged me to pray and think on it for a while. He offered to contact my cousin there, but I declined.'

'Are you not ready to go then?' Clara asked her.

'I…' Sorcha put the mending down on her lap and looked at Clara. 'I did not want him contacting her and mentioning someone who does not exist, Clara. She may remember Sorcha, Erca's daughter, but Saraid MacPherson would mean nothing to her and yet would begin to raise questions. Questions that would be dangerous to me if asked of the wrong people in the wrong places.'

'That makes sense,' Clara agreed.

'I cannot remain here for very long though. Not with the ties that are between the Mackintoshes and the Camerons. Someone may recognise me at some time. Nay,' she said as she placed the garment in her hands on her lap. 'The convent is my choice.'

'I am not trying to rush you or make you leave here,'

Clara said. 'Once made, it is not a vow that can be undone or denied.'

'I understand. I have made the decision.' She let out a breath. 'It would be safer for me and you and Jamie if I left soon.'

Silence met her declaration. Clara had not withheld her opinion on any matter since Sorcha had arrived at her door those weeks ago. So, this absence of a comment or advice was startling. She waited, for she knew her cousin well enough now to know it was simply a pause and not something that would not happen. Sorcha smiled when Clara opened her mouth.

'I think you should stay here a bit longer,' she said. 'Truly, Sorcha, you are too young to lock yourself away for the rest of your life. Whether for the good purpose of devotion to God or to protect others, do not do that yet.'

When Sorcha would have spoken, Clara gestured with her finger on her lips to stop her.

'Besides, you do not even ken how to make a decent porridge yet.'

'Or a loaf of bread,' Sorcha added.

'Or a savoury stew.'

'Or wash a tubful of laundry,' she said. 'There is so much I have never had to do before, Clara. And though I have failed, there is much I would like to learn.'

'You have not failed,' Clara assured her. 'Your life has been a privileged one as befits one of your birth. That your mother taught you to want to do the simple things is a credit to her and to you.' Sorcha felt tears burning in her eyes and a tightness in her throat. 'Your mother would be proud.'

Honour. Loyalty. Courage.

Her mother *had* taught her so much. An appreciation of the service others give you. A sense of curiosity and wonderment. A need for joy.

So, would it be a bad thing that, before she entered the convent and gave her life over to God, she would live it a bit first? As Saraid MacPherson, widowed cousin, staying on to help Clara and Jamie. And she would learn to do the things that people like her cousin took for granted.

In that moment, the image of a tall, strong warrior with long brown hair and eyes of blue and green and grey came to mind. Was he part of the reason she wished to stay here now? Sorcha decided not to examine *that* too closely right this moment.

Sorcha stood and retrieved her cloak and the small sharp knife that Clara used to cut fabric and threads. Sitting down under her cousin's watchful gaze, she cut along the hem and took out the treasures she had carried with her from Castle Sween…and from her mother. When a small pile sat on her lap and only a few remained in place, Sorcha gathered them into a small sack and held them out to her cousin. Clara did not speak, could not speak, Sorcha would guess. The sight of so many jewels of such value rendered her speechless and surprised beyond words.

'Jamie suggested these might be safer in his strongbox. Since I am staying, I think it's best if they are put away.'

'You are?'

'Aye. I am. There is much I would like to ken and to learn before facing the convent and its walls.'

'How long will you stay?' Clara asked, as the bairns began to wake and whisper in the next room.

'For the rest of the summer. Unless I am found out sooner.'

As the children woke and the next set of chores and tasks began, Sorcha smiled. The strange thing was that amidst the dread of cooking a meal and washing clothes, a sense of anticipation grew over next seeing Alan Cameron.

But he did not visit and she did not see him at the keep or in the village for several days.

Chapter Eight

Lucky for Alan, Brodie had given him a task, a message to take to his uncle, or he would have turned and left Achnacarry as soon as he'd arrived. As it was, his visit was cut short after only two days, for his uncle played host to Hugh MacMillan. And the chieftain from the south showed no sign of grief over the recent loss of his daughter just after the loss of his wife.

His disregard for his daughter's death irked Alan for some ill-defined reason. Surely even a daughter deserved a proper mourning? A brief but poignant pause to mark her life and her passing? Comparing this man's reaction to the loss of a daughter to what he'd witnessed when Brodie had lost a child not yet born just made Hugh seem that much more heartless. Still, this attitude was not so different from many high-born men. His uncle would be the same as Hugh, seeking only sons on his new wife. Any daughters would be a disappointment to him.

The feast in progress on Alan's arrival just made it clearer to him, especially as the presence of two marriageable Cameron cousins sitting on either side of

Hugh at table told of his uncle's decision that Hugh should marry a Cameron. The two women were as different as could be. Margaret was a young widow with several young sons. Hannah was unmarried and untried at bearing children. Alan huffed out a short breath as he made his way through the hall to a table closer to the front. This feast was a marriage mart as his uncle gave The MacMillan a choice of women knowing either one would tie him to The Cameron.

As Brodie had said, Hugh MacMillan's claim on Castle Sween was tentative at best now that there was no heir from Erca MacNeill. Her family could rightfully claim the castle back from the Lord of the Isles, The MacDonald.

A marriage linking him to the powerful Camerons would give pause to the weaker MacNeills about making that claim and facing the wrath of the Camerons. If they knew that the Camerons would answer the call to defend their kinswoman's home and family, they would hesitate to attack. But would it benefit the Camerons and especially his uncle? What did MacMillan offer to balance the bargain?

So, Alan took a place and watched the interactions of those three and his uncle's scrutiny of the whole scene. There was such a self-serving smirk of satisfaction in his uncle's dark gaze that it made Alan uneasy. Brodie suspected something more was going on between these two and now, after watching, Alan had no doubt of it.

But what? To anyone watching, it was the simplest and most common of all alliances—a marriage between clans. The tingling that crept up and down his spine as the feast continued confirmed to Alan that it was so much more. Who would know what was going on and if it would be trouble for the rest of the clan?

Alan's father might.

He waited a respectable two days after watching The MacMillan choose the well-proven but still young widow as his bride before he left and rode south to Tor Castle. His father served as castellan for the clan in a castle that they had taken from the Mackintoshes more than a century before during the years before their feud grew so deadly that a truce was sought. Alan offered to carry any messages his uncle had to his father or back to The Mackintosh in taking his leave. A cold blank stare was his uncle's reply.

Travelling along the lochs and rivers, he could make the journey to Tor in one day, so he set out in the morning. By the time he crossed the River Lochy and as the sun set, he reached the gates of the castle and was greeted by his cousin Culloch who stood guard. Entering this keep was easier than Achnacarry, for his parents made him welcome. When he reached the hall inside, they were waiting for him. Though the evening meal was done, servants stood at the table ready to fetch food and drink for him.

'Mother,' he said, as she wrapped her arms around him. 'Father.' He nodded in greeting at his father as his mother continued to hold him tightly to her. It had been too long.

'It has been too long a while since you were here, Alan,' she whispered, echoing his thoughts aloud.

'Come now, Elizabeth,' his father said as he gently pulled her from Alan. 'You know Gilbert keeps him busy.'

'Or away rather,' his mother muttered. She stepped back and examined him from the top of his head to his boots. 'You are not eating well,' she declared. Pointing to the table that had been empty, but was now filled with all sorts of platters and bowls and cups, she waved him to it. 'Come. Eat.'

He had learned long ago not to refuse his mother's orders and so he sat and let her force him to eat. After the bowl of well-cooked, well-seasoned venison stew and half a loaf of bread eased the worst of his hunger, he slowed down and leaned back on the chair. His mother, as always, watched him take, chew and swallow every bite and mouthful of food. Only when she relaxed her close vigil did he stop eating.

'What brings you here now, Alan?' his father asked. 'I did not expect you.'

Everyone said that Robert Cameron was a vision of Alan in a score of years. The same brown hair and blue eyes. The same muscular, tall build. Some of the same temperament, too, apparently, if kith and kin were to be believed. To know how he would age, he had but to look at his father to ken it, they said. But Alan never did see the resemblance that everyone spoke about.

'Can I not simply wish to see my parents?' His father glanced at his mother and then back to him. Then, as one, they both shook their heads. 'I have been at Achnacarry,' he began.

'Has the MacMillan chieftain chosen a bride yet?' his mother asked.

Elizabeth MacSorley looked much as she did every time Alan saw her. Other than a few grey hairs mixed in with the brown and one or two new wrinkles at the edges of her green eyes, she had not changed in the years since he began noticing such things.

'Then you know about it? You know that Uncle Gilbert's betrothed died? And that now he seeks to bind the MacMillans to us by marrying Margaret to him?'

He had not meant to blurt it out like that, but once the words escaped it was too late to withdraw them. His father stood then and held his hand out to his mother. The servants here were loyal to Gilbert and would report back to him if they thought it needed to be done.

'Come, join us in our chamber and we can continue this.'

Alan nodded thanks to the servants and followed his parents up the stairs in the round tower to their chambers. Instead of separate rooms for each of them, they continued to share one room and one bed even after many years of marriage. Once the maid poured wine for them and closed the door, Alan waited for his mother to sit before facing his father, who stood a few paces from him.

'Did you know? Of either of his plans?' he asked. Was his father complicit in whatever Gilbert was manoeuvring into place around them?

'I knew of his seeking a betrothal to the MacMillan chief's daughter,' his father admitted. 'I saw nothing amiss in it, other than the usual things for Gilbert.'

'Robert!' his mother whispered.

'Alan understands what I mean, Elizabeth,' his father said. 'As chieftain, he has the right and the duty to seek a wife and heirs. He holds title to lands that must stay in the clan.' His father let out a breath and shook his head. 'I do not approve of his treatment once he marries, fear not.'

His mother's mutinous expression did not soften even with his admission. She had known how Alan had felt about Agneis and his plans that were crushed by her marriage. And how his spirit was crushed by her death.

Worse for Alan was the powerlessness that proved total when it came to dealing with Gilbert. Once he ascended to the high seat of the clan, no one could touch him. Questioning his actions was tantamount to betrayal. And after having watched the Mackintoshes almost tear themselves to pieces, no Cameron would risk that within their clan.

'Well, he seems to have put off marriage for the time being,' Alan said. 'I suspect he will commence his efforts once The MacMillan is married and whatever pact they have agreed to is in place.'

'What do you think is the benefit?' his father asked. 'They are not especially wealthy or powerful. So what will Gilbert gain by tying us to them?'

'What would happen if our truce, our treaty, with the Mackintoshes was broken?'

His mother's gasp did not surprise him. The deaths and destruction caused by the feuding was not so long ago that his parents did not recall the cost. She began wringing her hands and shaking her head.

'I pray nightly that it never comes to that,' she said. He realised then that she was not wringing her hands, but moving them as though praying. An image of Saraid doing the same thing crossed his thoughts.

'As do I,' his father agreed. 'What made you even think on something like that, Alan? What have you heard?'

Instead of answering or revealing anything he might know, he asked another question of his parents.

'Does Gilbert have the support of the Camerons? Or do they fear him?' Taking in and letting out a deep breath, Alan asked the question that worried him the most. 'If Gilbert breaks the treaty, will the clan follow him down that path?'

For a long minute, neither of his parents spoke a word. His mother sat back down and his father drank down his wine in two swallows before placing his cup on a table there. Crossing his arms over his chest, his father met his stare.

'I think many will,' he said. 'Many will not want to, but are called by honour and clan loyalty to follow their chieftain.'

'That is what I feared,' Alan admitted. 'Is he planning to do that, Father? Do you ken?'

'I have proof of nothing,' Robert Cameron said quietly. 'But I think that your loyalty and mine will be tested in the coming months.'

'My loyalty?' Alan asked. 'My loyalty is to the Clan Cameron as it always has been.'

'As is mine,' his father said.

His mother stood silently by, watching this exchange. She would be caught in the middle no matter what happened. As most women were in any conflict. As would Arabella and Eva and all those on both sides. Nodding at both of them, he knew his father would say nothing more.

What Alan wanted was an explanation of why his father had not pursued the high seat or a place on the council when Euan Cameron passed. As an able-bodied male kin of the chieftain, he was eligible. He had the skills and experience needed to lead the clan and yet he had allowed Gilbert to take it without a challenge. Others had wondered the same thing, but Robert Cameron never spoke of his reasons for his actions, or lack of actions. Even when his uncle tried to shame him and put him aside, his father said nothing.

Now, he was tanist and that chafed at Gilbert every moment he ruled without a male heir of his body. That was what drove Gilbert to marry and marry again, to relentlessly pursue a childbearing wife who would give him a son. A son would sustain his claim, would strengthen his rule and would reward him for all his actions.

'I bid you a goodnight,' Alan finally said. 'Mother. Father.'

'Alan,' his mother began, taking a step towards him.

'Worry not,' he said, taking her by the shoulders and kissing each cheek. 'I will be here in the morn and we can speak more.'

'How long will you stay?' his father asked.

Alan wondered if it mattered. Would staying two days get him more answers than staying a sennight? If it would, he would stay as long as need be. But, in the end, his father had already given him the knowledge he needed.

Robert Cameron would not rise against his younger brother and claim the seat that belonged to him.

'A few days, I think.'

'Good,' his mother said as he lifted the latch on the door to let himself out. 'We should speak on the matter of marriage.'

He wanted, he wished he could, to misunderstand her words, but Alan understood she spoke of his marriage now and not his uncle's. But, as he and Arabella had already realised, Gilbert would not allow him his own choice in it. For he was too close in kinship and could also be used to forge alliances where the chieftain wanted.

'I am certain that my uncle will decide that once he has settled the question of his own next marriage.'

He had not meant to be harsh and he regretted the way he'd spoken when he saw the colour drain from his mother's cheeks. There was nothing he could say to ease the fear or worry for he'd spoken the truth. A truth both of them understood. A truth that confirmed his father's choice those years ago that gave up his right to speak for his son.

Alan left without another word, pulling the door closed quietly though there was a need within him to slam it until it fell from its frame and hinges. A rage burned deep inside of him, one aimed at the impotency he felt when it came to his uncle. As he made his way down to the chamber he used when here, he realised that he was also angry with his father. He'd thought he would grow to accept what he could not change. Instead, it festered within him, made worse every time he faced his uncle or his father.

No wonder he felt more at ease at Drumlui among the Mackintoshes.

The next two days were filled with an awkward dance of avoidance by both him and his parents. They pretended that he'd said and asked nothing during their discussion and he pretended not to notice. He allowed his mother to fawn over him and it seemed to make her happy and less tense around him. His father studied him silently and would look away when Alan faced him rather than meet his gaze.

So, even with the possibility of a growing threat to the peace in these lands and between the clans, his father would not act. That fact kept him awake for the three nights he stayed at Tor Castle. And it haunted his journey back to Glenlui.

At times, he wondered if his uncle was right. Mayhap his father was the coward Gilbert accused him of being? Mayhap Robert Cameron was not strong enough to rule over the clan? And every time he even allowed those doubts in, he knew that his father would be a better chieftain than his uncle had been.

As he travelled back with no reason to rush, he also discovered that all the thinking in the world could not solve the puzzle that was his father. Mayhap Brodie knew more of it? It was something he had never brought up to The Mackintosh before, but now, with the threat of war between their families, it might be the best time to do so.

He arrived at Drumlui Keep just as the news of Hugh MacMillan's marriage did. Alan knew that pieces were being put into place and readied for a match that would pit old enemies and new allies against each other. Aye, the pieces were moving in a game that his uncle was playing. God help them all.

The strange thing was that with each mile closer to Glenlui, his thoughts strayed from the concerns of his family and turned instead to the young woman who stayed with her cousin in the village. Was she already on her way to the convent? Would she be at Clara's side when he visited? Would she smile at him in the way that made her eyes sparkle? Cursing himself a fool for hungering for a woman who had chosen God over men, he rode through Drumlui Keep's gates and sought out the chieftain.

Chapter Nine

'Would you stay for supper, Dougal?' Clara asked as Sorcha and Dougal arrived at the cottage after her visit to the keep.

'I…' Dougal hesitated in his reply.

'I made the stew, Dougal,' Sorcha said proudly. Had this been even five days ago, she would not have offered, but she'd learned so much these last few days.

'Aye,' Dougal said. 'I would be glad of it.'

It was the least she could do for his acts of kindness to her. He had not again mentioned her habit of getting lost on her way through the village. He just appeared at her side when she walked on her way to or from the keep each day and wordlessly guided her steps along the right path.

They spoke of the village and all sorts of topics she experienced living here. His questions never strayed to personal matters, so she never truly had to lie to him. And they spoke of his father's plans for the mill now that his two uncles had arrived to help with the expansion and repairs for it. And, sometimes, they just walked in companionable silence through the village.

This was the first time Clara had invited him to stay and she watched Clara for some sign of her intentions. Helping to bring the bowls and spoons and bread to the table, she sensed nothing amiss. Jamie arrived and continued discussing some repairs of the mill with Dougal as she and Clara herded the wee ones to their places for the meal.

The meal was filling and plain but pleasant. Several times, Sorcha looked up to see Dougal staring across the table at her, but he did not say anything when she glanced back at him. Inexperienced at such conversations and experiences with men, Sorcha waited for the same reaction to happen as it did when Alan stared at her so.

Yet, it did not happen. No heat. No spark of excitement that moved along her skin when their hands touched while passing a plate across the table. Clara kept a conversation going with bits of news and gossip and questions, so that, by the time they finished eating, Sorcha knew much more about Dougal than she had before.

He was the middle of three brothers and the only one who worked the mill with their father. He had a younger sister. He enjoyed his work. He respected his parents and wished to visit the other Mackintosh lands soon. And Dougal never gazed at her with the intensity she saw in Alan's scrutiny.

She startled at that and Clara cleared her throat, for she'd missed something that Dougal had said as she'd been remembering Alan's way of staring at her.

'Dougal asked if you were going to the keep on the morrow, Saraid.' Clara repeated his question.

'Oh, your pardon, Dougal,' she said. 'I was thinking about something Father Diarmid said to me.' And now praying for forgiveness for *another* lie told. 'Aye, Lady Arabella asked me to speak to her on the morrow. After the noon meal.'

'I will be there with Jamie in the morn,' Dougal said, nodding to Jamie to confirm it. 'Seek me when you finish if you wish to walk back together.'

Clara wore a strange expression when Dougal finished speaking and she exchanged some glances with Jamie before standing and taking some of the plates from the table. She did the same, putting the bowls and spoons into the large bucket they used for washing them. In a few minutes, the table was empty and the children sleepy and ready for their beds.

'See Dougal out, Saraid,' Clara directed. 'I will get the bairns to sleep.'

Sorcha followed Dougal as he thanked Clara and Jamie for supper. Night had fallen while they ate and the village had quieted. He stepped away from the door and she watched as he turned back to her.

'The stew was as good as my ma's,' he said with a smile. Though she had never tasted his mother's cooking, she took it as a supreme compliment. For a son to say such a thing as that surely was one.

'I am glad you enjoyed it, Dougal,' she said. 'Mayhap you can join us again? I am learning to make a new dish each day.' She'd never explained why she was so late in learning to cook and he did not ask or look askance at her admission.

'I would like that, Saraid.'

He had finally stopped calling her Mistress the fourth time she'd given him permission to do so. Of all the things that were different, not being called 'lady' was one she'd noticed. And by using a different name, she sometimes would not realise someone was speaking to her until they repeated it twice or even thrice. The people in Glenlui were going to think her hard of hearing if she did not pay heed. Dougal took a half-step closer and began to lean in slowly.

Puzzled, Sorcha watched as he neared and then stepped back away. Surely he had not been about to kiss her? She met his stare then and he seemed surprised by the action, too.

'Good night to you,' he said softly before calling it out a bit louder. 'Clara. Jamie. Good night.'

Jamie came to the doorway now and Sorcha knew that whatever impulse had caused Dougal to even consider such a thing was done and gone. They watched as he made his way from the cottage towards the centre of the village. When he faded into the shadows, Sorcha walked inside with Jamie only a pace or two behind her. Clara stood waiting for them just inside. As the door closed, Clara untied her apron and tossed it on the table.

'What do you think, Jamie?' she asked. Sorcha looked over her shoulder, sidestepping to get out of their way.

'Aye, love,' he said, nodding at Sorcha. 'He is wooing her.'

Of any words she could have heard, these were astounding and unbelievable. She was a stranger here. Worse, she was a deceitful stranger, telling everyone in this place a concocted story that had so little truth to it, it counted for nothing. Sorcha shook her head at both of them.

'You are mistaken,' she said forcefully. 'He is being

nice to me. As you have been. As Alan…as everyone here has been. Nothing more.' Her words must have been strong for both Clara and Jamie blinked several times before responding.

'Lady,' Jamie began, using a courtesy that so few knew applied to her, 'I have seen men woo women and that boy, that young man, is wooing you.'

'Sorcha,' Clara whispered as she reached out and took her hand, 'I fear you have little experience in this. Your father had chosen a man to wed you and that man knew you would be his. Or he would have shown up at Castle Sween and made some overtures to you. As a man who wishes to marry a woman does.'

'As Dougal is doing,' Jamie repeated. 'Watching and waiting for you to arrive or to walk past. Escorting you where you need to go. Talking about all manner of nonsense and things. Coming to supper with your family. 'Tis how it is done in most places by most people.'

Her mouth dropped lower with each of Jamie's examples. She had not noticed or realised the implications of Dougal's acts, but now, it was quite apparent—he was wooing her. Even while acknowledging this as a fact, something within her wanted it to be Alan who pursued her. Alan who…wooed her.

'But I am going to the convent.' She shrugged and shook her head. 'He knows that. Everyone knows that.'

'Aye. Everyone knows. But you are not at the convent yet, are you?' Clara asked. 'His actions are respectful. Well, they were until just now.'

'Just now?' she asked. She touched her fingers to her lips and understood that Clara had witnessed his attempt at a kiss. ''Twas nothing. A misstep.'

'He almost kissed you.'

From her tone and the glint in her eyes, Sorcha could not tell if Clara was happy or shocked by Dougal's attempt. No man had ever even considered such an act with her. For the first time in her life, she was exposed to men who were not kin and not approved by her father. Yet, in a way, she was complimented by his action. Or, rather, his almost-action. For he did it based only on what he knew of her during her time here.

'I am certain that he did not mean such a thing,' she assured Clara while not quite believing her own words. 'He does not know me enough to want to kiss me.'

Jamie burst out laughing and Clara shushed him, but Sorcha saw the smile on her cousin's face. She believed it.

'You have no idea of your appeal, Lady,' Jamie said. He walked closer and moved a stool for her to sit as he did. Clara stood at his back, her hands caressing his broad shoulders. 'Part of it is that you are new here. Part of it is your beauty.' Sorcha could feel the heat of a blush rise in her cheeks at his words. 'And part of it is your plan to enter the convent.'

'But why would that appeal to anyone? I am going to serve God.'

'Aye, but to most men, that is a challenge they cannot resist. Oh, a God-fearing man will give pause, but he will still take it as a challenge to turn you to more earthly pursuits.'

Sorcha gasped then, comprehending how that could be.

'Then there are your manners, Lady. Nothing about you makes a man think you are a common villager. Though you can hide your name, you cannot hide the way you walk and talk and even the way you eat,' Jamie explained. 'Your hands. Your hair. Your complexion. They all give away that you have not spent your life working as we have.'

He gentled and lowered his voice then. 'I ken you have been trying your best. 'Tis clear to me that you cannot hide what you truly are for very long. And Dougal, or most unmarried men here, would have no chance of attracting Lady Sorcha's attention. They would not even attempt such a thing.' Jamie motioned to her. 'But as Mistress Saraid MacPherson, widow, with intentions of leaving the world behind, well, they have a chance with her. And more than Dougal have enquired with me about your situation.'

Sorcha felt as if someone had knocked the very breath from her body with those words. She sank on the stool, absorbing his words and trying to understand what she could do.

'So, I should leave now for the convent.' She shook her head, pushing her kerchief off her hair. 'I did not mean to...mislead anyone or lead anyone to false hopes or conclusions. I just wanted to hide until I could make my way to Skye.' It was not the best way to begin a life of service to God.

'Sor... Saraid,' Clara said, glancing at the door leading to the bairns' room. 'You could not come here and announce who you were. I agreed to hide you and thought that hiding in plain sight would be easiest. I still do.'

'As do I,' Jamie added, covering Clara's hands with his own. 'Other than hiding in a barn or a cave, this is the best way.'

'And rushing into a decision that could just make things worse for you is not the thing either,' Clara added. 'You were and still are grieving, Cousin. I just wanted to give you a place to rest and get strong enough to make your choice.'

'And I have.' She stood then. 'But I must be doing something wrong if Dougal thought...'

'Men will think what they want,' Jamie said. 'I just did not want you misunderstanding, or worse, missing the signs he or any other might be giving you. With no experience in such matters, it would be easy enough to misunderstand.'

'I thank you for your concern and your help.' Feeling overwhelmed by all of these new concerns, Sorcha needed to be alone. 'I am just going outside for a few minutes,' she said as she grabbed up her cloak and threw it around her shoulders.

They did not speak or try to stop her as she left. Though the moon was bright enough, she would not dare wander too far down any road away from the cottage. She did not have the surefootedness that Dougal and the others who'd lived here their whole lives did. As she walked away, she heard whisperings within the cottage and knew that Clara and Jamie now argued over her.

Sorcha found a bench next to a tree near Jamie's smithy and sat there, listening to the sounds of night around her. During the day, Jamie would sit here cool from the unrelenting heat of the forge. Clara and the bairns sat here to watch Jamie work. Sitting here now, Sorcha realised how significantly different it was for her.

She'd never been permitted to simply sit outside by herself when she was still at home. There was always a servant or maid or guard or relative to accompany her every venture from the safety of the castle. Here, she could sit by herself in the quiet for as long as she wanted. Or as long as she needed, in this case.

Leaning against the tree, she loosened her braids and ran her hands through her hair to release it. Undone, it flowed over her shoulders and down to her hips in waves of brown so dark a shade that it sometimes looked black. Disguised as a widow, she wore it covered, but at home it would be loose like this, wearing only a circlet to hold a small veil in place.

She would be the first to admit that letting it loose would be dangerous as she worked alongside Clara cooking or caring for the bairns. Now though, with the cooler breezes rustling through it, she enjoyed the freedom for this short respite. Since no one could see her, there would no harm done.

Not like the harm that could be done if she were not more careful during her stay here. Sorcha closed her eyes and tried to remember back to a time when she lived her own life—an orderly, comfortable life.

To the time before her mother warned her.

To a time when she knew who she was and what she would do. She could see her mother's taut and pain-filled expression as she explained her plan to free Sorcha from the bonds that her father would inflict on her. Before her mother died.

Before Padruig died helping her carry out her mother's plan.

Was this God's punishment for rebelling against the role she should have played? The one of dutiful daughter, obedient to her father's will. The one of the nobleman's heir who would marry to cement alliances. The woman who did and said what a woman was supposed to. Was she so foolish as to think that she could thwart those who were in power over her?

Her mother told her she was strong. That she could take care of herself. That she could live a life of honour and loyalty and courage. At this moment, she'd never felt so weak and frightened. And lonely. When the tears came, she could not stop them. Gathering her legs up under her gown, Sorcha wrapped her arms around her knees, leaned her head down and let them flow.

The soft sobbing echoed across the clearing and brought him to a halt. He thought his sight had adjusted to the moonlight and yet he could not see the source of the sound. Alan was close to Jamie's cottage and remembered the wooden bench that his friend positioned under the large tree across from the smithy. They'd drank many cups of cold water or cool ale under that tree after working close to the powerful fires in the forge.

Now though, it was the place where someone, where Mistress MacPherson, sat crying.

He was reluctant to invade her private moments, but she seemed in true distress. He walked several paces closer, not caring about the noisy steps he took, waiting for her to hear him and raise her head. When she did not, Alan knew he must break the silence and seek to aid her.

'Mistress?' he said softly. 'Mistress MacPherson? Are you well?'

The crying ceased then and he thanked the Almighty for he could not bear to see a woman crying. She slowly lifted her head from where she'd rested it and rubbed her arm across her face, first in one direction and then the other. Then her voice whispered in reply, carried like mist on the wind to him where he waited.

'Nay.'

So many choices ran through his mind in the moment after that one word. Alan's first reaction was to go to her, pull her into his arms and soothe whatever fears or ailments afflicted her. His next reaction was the opposite to that—he should bid her a good night and walk all the way back to the keep without seeking out Jamie as he'd planned. Rather than the one extreme or the other, he chose the middle path.

'Is there anything I can do? Should I fetch Clara for you?'

An offer of help without forcing his way into her private matters. He thought that was what she would want him to do. Her next word ruined his chance of being successful and of walking away before he acted on the growing desire he felt for her.

'Nay.' And then nothing else.

She was sitting there in the dark, in the night, under a tree. He could not tell whether she was looking at him or not, for the shadows under the tree's branches were too deep for the moonlight above them to illuminate her.

'So, you are not well, you do not wish me to aid you and you do not want your cousin either?' he clarified her answers with his questions.

'I just want to be alone,' she said after a long sigh. Her voice gave every sign that she was not being truthful.

Now that she knew of his presence, he walked closer and could finally see her better. She did not appear to be ill or harmed. Then he noticed that her hair fell around her like a fine, silken curtain, covering her form all the way down to the bench's surface. Alan's hands wanted to touch it and he began to reach out just before gaining control over himself and those wayward hands.

'Then, I will leave you,' he said. It was the smartest thing to do—leave a woman alone when she told you to do so. But her voice had trembled and was filled with uncertainty and sadness when she'd spoken. Surprising even himself, Alan walked to the bench and sat next to her. 'If that is what you want?'

A sigh that told him of a world's weight bearing down on her was her reply. He turned to her and waited for words. When none came, he spoke.

'Has something happened? Have you received ill tidings mayhap?'

She shook her head and it created wondrous little waves that moved through her curls as she did. After a moment, she slid her legs down and let her feet rest on the ground. The urge to reach out and touch her grew stronger.

'I fear I am allowing self-pity to overtake me,' she explained. Then she reached up and gathered her hair back over her shoulders. 'It will pass.'

Although drawn to the way her hair moved around her as she did, Alan knew she was lying. Somehow he knew she was avoiding whatever had caused her upset. She did not have to reveal anything to him, but he found that he wanted to know what had brought on this upset.

'Did someone say something unkind?' he asked. He slid his hand across the bench to where her hair pooled and touched it, hoping the darkness covered his movement. It was as silky as it appeared.

'Nothing like that. Everyone has been kind and helpful. Nay,' she said, as she stood. He stood as well, releasing her hair from his grasp. She was much shorter than him, shorter even than Clara. She smiled then, a watery, weak one that faded quickly. 'Actually I should feel complimented, but considering my status and my plans, it does not feel like that.'

Now, he was intrigued as well as concerned. 'And this compliment was…?'

'Dougal, the miller's son,' she began.

'Aye. A good fellow.'

'Dougal has decided to woo me.'

Chapter Ten

Of all the things she could have said, of all the things he'd considered that could have happened to make her so miserable, being wooed was not one of them. But at least her misery seemed to be tied to Dougal. Not that he himself was wooing her.

'He kens you seek the convent's walls, does he not?'

She nodded.

He'd never thought Dougal a stupid or stubborn man, yet wooing a woman promised to God was one or the other of those. But here he was, doing something that had not even crossed Alan's mind. Not that he had not been attracted to her, for he had. Even knowing his uncle would make arrangements for his marriage had not made her unappealing or convinced him not to admire her.

'Yet, he is wooing you?'

'Aye. Even Jamie and Clara said so.'

'And you did not know it?' he asked.

'Well, I have not been thinking on that possibility lately,' she snapped at him. 'Your pardon, I pray you. I was taken by surprise for a number of reasons.'

'And his wooing made you cry?'

Alan swore he would never, ever comprehend the workings of the feminine mind. He thought women liked to be fawned over and complimented. He thought they liked soft words and gestures. She shook her head at him.

'Nay, his kind attentions brought up other considerations and memories and I ended up out here trying to sort things out.'

'You ended up out here crying.'

'Aye. Sometimes, 'tis the only way to make sense of things.'

He reached out and took her hand, smiling when she did not refuse him the gesture. As he stroked her with his thumb, Alan tugged her a little closer. He suspected she did not even realise how close she was to him now.

'Have you reconsidered entering the convent then? Do you wish to accept his attentions?'

He'd hesitated to ask that question, but he truly needed to know. Had she changed her mind about seeking the religious life? Had Dougal won her while Alan had been travelling hither and yon to his uncle and his father? Part of him did not like that possibility at all. Part of him wanted to take her and claim her and push any memories of Dougal's wooing out of her thoughts. Another part of him…

Alan entwined their fingers and he leaned down. He would kiss her. He would taste her mouth and—

'Alan, is that you?' Jamie's voice called out, interrupting before she could answer. Sadly, she pulled out of his grasp and moved too far away for him to kiss.

'Aye,' he called back. 'Come,' he said to Saraid, 'let me walk you back inside.' She looked at his outstretched arm for a moment. 'If you are ready to return?'

She placed her hand on his arm with the grace of a lady allowing a laird to assist her. Something niggled at him as he watched her walk at his side. She walked liked someone noble-born. As a woman trained to the gentle manners and bearing of a lady. One born and raised in the keep and not the village.

She stumbled then and Alan reached out to steady her once more with his other hand on hers, forgetting about the strange impressions he was having about her. Jamie stood by the door, holding a lantern to light their way now. When they reached him, Jamie studied Clara's cousin closely.

'Are you well, Saraid?' he asked.

'I am well, now, Jamie.' She lifted her hand from Alan's arm and nodded at him. 'My thanks for coming to my aid.'

Alan did not reply, but instead watched her enter the cottage. Clara waited there for her. When the door closed, Alan turned to his friend and spoke before Jamie could say anything about what he must have seen there in the moonlight. 'Dougal?' he asked.

''Twas quite a surprise to me, as well,' Jamie said. 'The boy has more courage than I suspected.'

'He has not taken notice of anyone since Fia left, has he?'

Strange that. Both Dougal and he had offered marriage to Fia Mackintosh for different reasons and both had been turned down. Dougal had been taken with the lass and had offered out of true love. Alan had been responsible, in part, for Fia's loss of honour and had offered in an attempt to help her. After all, they'd been friends since meeting in the camp of exiled Mackintoshes during the schism in the clan.

Sent by Brodie to track her when she'd been kidnapped during an attack on their village, Alan had failed her—finding her, but not freeing her soon enough. Her ruination had been caused and redeemed by her current husband, Lord Niall Corbett, the man who had claimed her heart when neither he nor Dougal could.

Now, a few years later and both Alan and Dougal found themselves circling another woman…again. Dougal, though, had already expressed his interest openly, while Alan had been trying to convince himself there was nothing there. In spite of it being the worst time to be distracted by a woman he could not have, he was.

No matter how enticing and tempting the widow MacPherson was, it did not mean he would act on that attraction. He would not. Too many things were happening around him, in his clan and in the Mackintoshes, to allow an attachment to interfere with his concentration on the rising danger.

'Nay, he has not, but I suspect he realises it's time to seek a wife and make his own life. Though, I doubt he will get far with Saraid,' Jamie admitted. 'She is allowing herself time to grieve her loss before travelling on.'

Somehow that news, the part about Dougal not getting anywhere with the widow MacPherson, cheered Alan.

'So what brings you here at this time of night?' Jamie asked.

'I was restless after my journey and thought to share

a cup of ale with you,' he said. Jamie was a good friend. He truly needed no excuse to come to see him.

'I can have one cup before Clara puts you on your way back to the keep,' he said, laughing. 'Are you sure you did not come for a glimpse of Clara's cousin?'

Alan would deny it, even if it were the truth.

Because, if it were true, it held the promise of trouble. If he was interested in her, nothing could come of it.

'Nay, I think I will leave the wooing to Dougal,' Alan said, deciding that was the best he could say. Jamie answered with an incredulous frown. Alan would need to divert his friend's attention to this growing fascination. 'Well, let us have our one cup before your wife chases me away.'

Jamie went inside and brought out two cups of ale. They walked back around to the bench, keeping their voices down now that most of the village had settled for the night.

'So, if not to see Saraid, then what brings you here... this night, when we could speak on the morrow?' Jamie asked.

'My father.'

'Ah.' Alan looked at Jamie when he spoke that one word. One word that carried so much within it when pronounced as Jamie had.

'When Uncle Euan died and the high seat was open, do you remember any talk here about why my father did not make his claim?'

'It troubles you now, does it?'

'Aye. More and more with each encounter and each conversation.'

'And with each of Gilbert's marriages.'

Very, very few people could bring that topic up without Alan taking action, but Jamie could and did so now.

'Observant, are you now?' he said. 'Aye. 'twould seem that does cause me to think on those matters. About what Clan Cameron would be like if my father was chief.'

'But your father is not. Is it wise to worry over it?'

Jamie was asking if it was worth the risks Alan was taking by speaking of it at all. Gilbert would see such things as treachery. Ironic when treachery was exactly what Alan thought Gilbert might be planning.

'It may not be, my friend, but wondering, I am, and worrying, I am near to.' They both drank deeply from their cups before he spoke again. 'So, what was the talk when Gilbert made the claim instead of his older brother?'

Jamie did not answer directly, he seemed to think about it as though sorting through the words he would parse in reply. But his pause told Alan that there had indeed been talk about it.

'What you would have expected—your father being the elder, in possession of his mind and able-bodied, would have made the claim. That the elders and clan would have supported him. Surprise when it went the way it did.'

Exactly what he'd expect would have been said.

'Once it was said and done and Gilbert laid claim, Brodie gave his backing and no one spoke much about it at all.' Jamie narrowed his gaze at Alan. 'The better question would be—did you expect your father to claim the chieftain's seat?'

'Aye.'

He'd never admitted that to anyone. But these days, all manner of things ignored or unspoken seemed to be examined and heard.

'And you realise that to do that openly would question your own motives? You might be seen as second-guessing both your father and your uncle.' Jamie shifted to turn towards him. 'As though you might be craving it for yourself in the years to come.'

Alan had not considered this before. Truly.

Well, when his friend spoke it aloud, it did have the ring of authenticity. So mayhap the idea, the desire, for such a thing was somewhere deep within him. Had he tamped it down just as he'd tamped down the rage and the desires that seemed to be making themselves known these last weeks? Had he reached the point when he could no longer ignore these needs and this anger?

'There comes a time when a man must make his stand. For better or worse. In spite of the risks. No matter the outcome. So, my friend,' Jamie asked as he stood, 'is this that moment for you? Is this the matter that will force your hand?'

Jamie began walking back towards the cottage, not waiting for his reply. And those words were all Alan could think about the rest of the night. During the long, dark walk back to the keep and throughout the rest of the hours of the night.

By morning he understood that, nay, this was not his moment. He also knew to the marrow in his bones that the time was coming. With each new piece put into play by his uncle, something stirred within him.

With each regret exposed and each desire awakened, he grew closer to that moment.

What it would mean, who would stand by him and who would oppose him, he knew not. But he knew as surely as the sun rose on the next morning that it was growing closer.

'Did you know she can read and write?' Arabella said to him as they ate the noon meal together. 'Latin as well as Gaelic. I suspect French as well.' Brodie was not here so the meal was informal.

'Who can read and write?' he asked back. Their discussion so far had been about horses and the weather and his parents. Did she refer to his mother's skills?

'Mistress MacPherson,' Arabella said, nodding to the back of the hall where the woman stood.

'I did not know.' That was quite an accomplishment for any woman.

'It does give her some choices that another woman without those skills might not have,' his cousin informed him. 'I have asked her to come speak to me.'

'She told me she is determined to enter the convent, so I am not certain it will make a difference.'

He'd taken a bite of roasted mutton and only noticed the silence when he swallowed it and drank some ale. Turning, he found Bella staring at him with a look of complete and utter astonishment on her lovely face. He reached up and closed her mouth since it hung open now.

'When did *she* tell *you* that?' she asked, sputtering out the words.

'Cease, Bella,' he said, reaching for a chunk of bread to sop up the juices on his plate. 'I went to speak to

Jamie when I returned last night and found Mistress MacPherson there. We spoke,' he said, pausing for a moment to remember the way she looked in the moonlight and how much he'd wanted to kiss her then and there. 'She told me she was planning to enter the convent…'

Had she ever confirmed her intentions? Alan interrupted them before she could say so. But she had not denied it.

'That is a strange conversation to have with a stranger,' she insisted.

'Well, I am kin of a sort of her kin,' he said. 'Not complete strangers.'

Remembering it now, she truly had not confirmed her intentions during their encounter in the dark of the night. Alan would have discussed it more, but Jamie arrived and Saraid seemed reticent to continue. Glancing at Bella, he knew she would be able to offer counsel. Mayhap she already planned to do exactly that, hence Mistress MacPherson's presence?

'Is she waiting for you to finish?' he asked.

'I suppose so,' Bella said. The lady of the keep looked to the back of the hall and then at him. 'I wonder if she has eaten yet.'

'I have a boon to ask of you, Cousin,' he said, putting his hand on hers before she could have the woman brought forward. Bella stopped and watched him with some suspicion in her gaze. 'I think she needs the counsel of someone like you.'

'Me?'

'Aye. You are educated. Can read and write. You are married as she was. You have faced your own collection of difficult if not impossible situations. I think your advice and opinions would matter to her and help her in this time of loss and grief.'

He stopped short of voicing the growing suspicion of his own that Mistress MacPherson was either more than or different from what she presented herself to be. It was just a feeling on his part for now, so he did not wish to give Arabella something that was more whimsy than substance. Or give her a reason to fear the woman.

The other thing he relied on was Arabella's excellent talent at meddling in the lives of others. It was worse if you were kin or if she liked you. But anyone who walked through her gates was a possibility to her and she flourished truly when she was meddling here or there. He saw the flush rise in her cheeks and the glimmer in her gaze as Bella studied the widow MacPherson. With the slightest movement of her hand, Lady Mackintosh sent a servant to bring the woman forward.

Alan watched as Mistress MacPherson made her way behind the servant. He was trying to decide if his opinion about her manners was correct or not. From here, her genteel movements were even more obvious to him as she moved along through those gathered for the meal. Though her gown was clean and her hair covered in the way of married women here, Alan could imagine her in the finest fabrics and jewels. Without even thinking, he stood when she reached the table and arrived behind Arabella.

'My lady, 'tis good of you to speak to me,' she said. 'Sir.' She nodded politely at him. 'But I did not wish to interrupt your meal.'

Her eyes were clear and bright as she looked at him. Clearly she had recovered from whatever worries or concerns had afflicted her last night.

'Join us,' Arabella invited. 'Bring a chair for Mistress MacPherson.'

Her servants being very competent, only a minute or two at most passed before the lovely widow was seated between them with a platter of food and a filled cup in front of her. Alan took his seat as she had.

'So, did you spend the morn with Father Diarmid?' Arabella asked her.

'Aye,' the widow replied. 'I went with him as he called on those in need of his guidance and prayers.'

'Is that something you have done before?' Bella asked.

'I visited the sick…' For a moment that he might have missed if he'd been looking away, Alan saw the stricken expression in her eyes as though she'd made a terrible error. 'I visited the sick in our village.'

'Was that in Cluny?' Alan asked.

'Nay,' she said, shaking her head and putting down the cup she'd only just lifted to her mouth. 'We lived in the south, near my husband's kin.'

He was about to ask which branch of the MacNeills her husband called his when Arabella glared at him.

'Alan, Mistress MacPherson and I would speak of womanly matters, if you would excuse us?'

He had no choice really then to retreat strategically for the moment. Arabella had taken up his challenge, his invitation, and wanted to accomplish it her way. Having seen her methods in the past, he had no doubt that she would discover all the possible secrets that the widow MacPherson brought with her to Mackintosh lands.

'I should find your husband, Lady,' he said, standing and bowing to his cousin.

'He is training with Rob,' she replied. 'You should find them in the yard for the next few hours.'

Much as he did not wish a repeat of his last battle in the yard, he would gladly watch Brodie and Rob fight it out there. As he walked out, he glanced back to see the two women talking quite seriously and Alan was not certain if he felt anticipation over discovering more about the enticing Widow MacPherson or fear over her being left alone with his cousin.

Only time would tell.

Chapter Eleven

Courage.
 Courage.
 Courage.
The word repeated over and over in her thoughts as they finished the meal at table and as she followed Lady Mackintosh out of the hall and up to her solar above-stairs. With a discreet motion of her hand, she dismissed anyone who thought to follow or enter the room when they arrived. With the grace of an angel and the appearance of one, too, the lady crossed the chamber to a table and some chairs before stopping.

This woman did not have the reputation of being the most beautiful woman in the Highlands, if not all of Scotland, erroneously. Though that reputation was born out of her lovely looks at an earlier age many years ago, neither ageing nor strife nor a marriage to one of the most powerful men in the land had diminished that appearance. Not one grey hair showed on her head and her skin and eyes carried the brightness of a much younger woman. The lady sat in one chair and, as befitted her new identity, Sorcha remained standing opposite her.

'Father tells me that you have excellent skills in reading and writing, Mistress MacPherson.'

'Aye, my lady.'

'Those could be of benefit in some convents,' the lady added.

'Some convents, my lady?' she asked. Sorcha's mother had spoken of how few women, even noblewomen, had those abilities and how even fewer used them well. The convent would be the place where she could.

'Some convents welcome women with skills and put them to use for the good of the Almighty and those whom the convent serves,' Lady Arabella said. Sorcha nodded for that was exactly what her mother had told her.

'But some convents, some orders of holy sisters, ignore any and all talents and spend their waking hours on their knees in prayer only.'

That was not what Sorcha had intended to do for the rest of her life. She'd imagined herself spending time in prayer, aye, but also at other tasks as well. Possibly teaching others to read. Or…

'Truly, it depends on the convent or monastery and the order that they serve. Clara said your kin—a cousin?—serves a convent on Skye?'

'Aye, my lady.'

'Do you know which order she serves?'

'Nay, my lady.'

Sorcha had not bothered to ask. She had only focused on following her mother's plan and going to Skye. The rest had seemed so far away in both time and place that there was no need to worry over those details. She'd never thought on such things. Sorcha noticed that the lady was watching her closely now.

'I confess, my lady, my only thought was to go to my cousin and handle the rest of the matter there and then.'

Arabella stood then and walked to one of the open windows that looked out over the training yard from the sounds below. The lady leaned up on her toes and watched out at whoever was fighting. Without turning away from that scene, she spoke.

'Did you ken that my husband's uncle is The MacPherson?'

Sorcha clenched her teeth together to prevent the terrible words she wanted to utter just then from escaping. Brodie Mackintosh was related to the MacPhersons. Could her luck be any worse? When the lady turned and smiled, Sorcha thought it probably could and it could right now.

'If you would like, he could intervene with his uncle to make other arrangements for you? If you have somehow become estranged from your kin, would it help if he mediated the issue? I could ask him to do so.'

Courage. Courage. Courage.

Though her link to the MacPhersons was real and true, Sorcha could not have The Mackintosh or his wife contacting them and asking questions about their treatment, and seeming abandonment, of their widowed kin. That would take her one step closer to having Sorcha MacMillan rise from the dead. If Clara remarked on her resemblance to her own mother, others among the MacPhersons would do the same. Others who had seen her mother, and possibly her, more recently.

Nay, she must keep Lady Arabella from doing this.

'I beg your pardon, lady, if I have given the impression that The MacPherson or his clan have, in some way, shirked or resisted their duty to their kin. 'Tis not the truth.' She inhaled and released the breath slowly, trying to calm her racing heart that pounded within her chest. 'Entering the convent was my desire.'

'And you would not consider other choices?'

'Other choices?' she asked. She could not help that her hands crept together. She clutched them tightly to keep them from shaking.

'As kin to both Clara and my husband, you are welcome here. I could certainly use someone with your skills to assist me in my duties as Brodie's wife in overseeing the Mackintoshes.' The lady smiled then. 'The children take more and more of my attention and, God willing, there will be more of them soon. To have someone I could rely on to carry out some of the tasks I do now would be more than just helpful, Saraid. 'Twould be a godsend, truly.'

And that would be as close to living her own life as was possible without proclaiming her identity. For a moment, Sorcha allowed herself to dream of that impossible thing. Worse, in that weakness, she began to think that she could marry and have children of her own.

But, none of that was meant to be. To honour her mother's efforts and plans and Padruig's sacrifice in getting her away, she must keep on the path she'd chosen. And she had chosen it when she left with Padruig into that dark, stormy night. And again when she chose to come here rather than returning to her father. She could have concocted a story of kidnap on her return and married the chieftain of the Camerons as her father wished her to do.

A chill passed through her then, making her shiver from inside out. She tried to control it, to hide it, from the lady, but she doubted she'd been successful. Lady Arabella missed little even if she did not deign to comment on it. As she did not now, choosing to turn and peer out the window instead.

'I am honoured at your invitation, my lady. Truly, anyone would be. But, I am decided on this matter.' Sorcha tried to make her words calm but forceful enough to convince The Mackintosh's wife. A true Christian would not presume to decide where God would wish her to serve or in which capacity. 'I will offer myself to the Almighty's service at the convent of my kin and I will allow Him to decide where my skills should be used.'

Sorcha tried not to smile as she watched the lady try to figure out how to circumvent the rationale she'd just used. It was true—an applicant to holy orders or the religious life did not choose their service. That choice was left to those in charge…and to God. Even Arabella Cameron, Lady Mackintosh, would not argue against God's right in this.

Or would she?

A smile lit the lady's face then, but it did not reach her eyes. Sorcha understood then that she would agree with Sorcha's words even while still questioning Sorcha's motives and actions. It was there in the way her mouth curved while her eyes remained unmoved.

Had she just made an enemy of Lady Mackintosh?

'Worry not,' the lady said as though hearing Sorcha's thought. 'You must do as your faith and honour demand.' The lady walked to the door and lifted the latch, dismissing Sorcha by her action. 'If I can be of service to you in your path forward, you have but to ask.'

'My thanks, my lady,' Sorcha said as she curtsied and then walked past her. 'I am grateful for your interest and your concern.'

As the door shut behind her, Sorcha understood her time here was limited. A few more weeks, a month, at best. If the lady chose to intervene or interfere and contact The MacPherson, it could be even less time than that. As she retrieved her cloak from where she'd left it in the keep, Sorcha decided to put a few of the coins back in the garment. Better to send back for the rest when she arrived at the convent than to need coins to travel quickly away from Glenlui and not have them at hand.

Arabella closed the door behind the enigmatic young woman.

This Saraid MacPherson was hiding something. Oh, Arabella could feel it, hear it and almost smell it when she answered the questions put to her. But, at the same time Arabella sensed intelligence and something deeply honourable about her. A loss and pain lived within this young woman as well.

Was she a danger to the Clan Mackintosh? Arabella did not think so.

Was she lying about her connection to the MacPhersons? Arabella thought not.

That clan, like most of the largest and powerful families in Scotland, had many branches with even more septs and connections. Saraid could very well be a cousin of a distant or smaller branch who had no contact at all with the chieftain or his closer relations. When Fia served Arabella before her marriage to Niall, she used to jest about counting the number of Mackintosh cousins when bored. She'd once reached seventy before stopping.

So, even if Arabella were to contact Brodie's uncle, there was a good chance he might not know of this Saraid. Though part of her wanted to do that—reach out to the chieftain—another stronger part warned her from taking that action. Going back to the window, she watched Brodie and Rob fighting below. Saraid walked out of the keep and faced the yard, standing separate and alone there.

This woman had faced not only sorrow, but also danger and loss. Something in her demeanour told Arabella that the danger yet existed. If Arabella meddled, as her husband would call it, it could bring irreparable harm to Saraid and possibly her cousin Clara. As she watched the scene below, wincing when Rob landed a particularly strong punch on Brodie's jaw, Arabella observed what she needed to see to make her decision.

Alan noticed the young widow as though he'd been watching and waiting for her to come outside. He walked to her side and, after a few words were exchanged, led her to a place by the fence where she could see the battle rage. They continued to speak, with Alan pointing out various moves and steps and Saraid nodding and engaging with him.

There was something between them that she had suspected when they were at table and that she could see now even more so from this distance. Alan's request for her to help the widow spoke of an interest that he'd not shown in a woman in a very long time, since he was more boy than man and in love with the young woman who would eventually marry his uncle.

Though Saraid had plans to enter the convent, Arabella saw the cracks in the edges of her resolve in the matter. There was some very crucial reason for the widow's decision to do it, but the way she looked at Alan and now stood closer to him spoke of another kind of desire on her part. So, what was forcing the young woman to a life behind the walls of the convent? What would make her give up on kith and kin, and a possible marriage and family of her own?

The cheering of the crowd below drew her attention back to her own husband who, it appeared, had not fared as well against his cousin as he had in previous fights. Those watching began to drift back to their tasks and Brodie and Rob returned to work with the warriors there in the practice yard.

Alan and Saraid yet stood talking quietly there, as though they had not noticed the others had gone and the fight was over. Because they had not.

Arabella did not need to see more to understand what was happening between the two. As she went off to seek out her husband and soothe his wounded pride and his jaw, she wondered how long it would take Alan and Saraid to realise it.

One moment he'd been pointing out the best moves of the two extraordinary warriors as they fought inside the fence before a large and raucous crowd and the next they stood alone. The fighting was done and the crowd gone. Alan glanced around and saw no one taking note of them. Brodie and Rob were now working with the men on the other side of the yard. Most of the others who'd watched were now back at their chores or duties.

As soon as he'd seen Saraid come out of the keep, he'd known it had not gone well with Arabella. He could not say what had happened, but the guarded expression, the way her usually bright eyes were hard somehow, spoke of something gone awry. And he wanted to fix it.

'What did you think?' he asked, nodding towards the two men across the yard. 'Impressive, are they not?'

'They are,' she agreed. 'I cannot believe they were both on their feet as long as they were.' Whatever had agitated her dissipated as she watched the scene before them.

'They push each other to be better and better. I would hate to face either of them across a field of battle.'

'Yet you fight them here,' she said, glancing at the yard.

'Aye, but we are not trying to kill each other here.'

They observed the two for some time before Mistress MacPherson began her questions. If she thought they were too personal or prying, she gave no sign of it.

'How old were you when the feud was settled?' she asked.

'The feud has not been settled,' he explained. 'There is a truce in place. Brodie's uncle and mine forged the agreement to stop the destruction of both of our families.'

'I thought that ended it?' She winced as Rob punched Brodie in the face and he stumbled before landing on his knees in the dirt. Another wince when those around them cheered loudly. 'How long has it been going on?'

'Two score years—nay, three, I think,' he replied, trying to sort out the details of how and when. 'A fight over land claimed by both clans generations ago was the start of it. Most of Lochaber is Cameron lands, but somehow the Mackintoshes ended up here in Glenlui. A marriage settlement, I think. Then my family decided to take it back. The Mackintoshes did not care for that.'

'I would think not,' she said. 'Was there still fighting going on when you were young?'

'Oh, aye,' he replied. 'Though Uncle Euan took the first steps towards a peace when I was young. The last raid that spilled blood between us happened before I was born.' He shrugged when she glanced at him. 'The last deaths were in the fight between the Mackintosh cousins. But, as kin to them, you might ken that already?'

All of her attention, her body even, turned back to the demonstration happening before them as though it was of the utmost importance just then. After a pause or hesitation of a few moments, she nodded.

'I ken some of it,' she said. 'But my family is but a minor branch of the clan and none have claims that rise to the right to be on the council of elders or serve as tanist. So we have little contact with The MacPherson.'

It was the way of it amongst the larger clans. So much land was held across the width and length of the Highlands that many offshoots of families lived in ignorance of the rest. Until or unless hostilities broke out and they needed to call on kin to come to their defence.

For a short while, they talked and he lost awareness

of anything but the sound of her voice and the way she smiled or frowned. He lost himself in the way she gestured while speaking, her slender hands moving with so much grace that they seemed to dance before him. When he next looked around, everyone was gone. He and Saraid stood before an empty practice yard.

Alan was about to ask a question until he noticed Dougal heading in their direction. He knew what the man wanted—to escort Saraid to Clara's. But right now, Alan wanted no interruptions. So, he held out his arm to her.

'If you have finished speaking to Arabella and are ready to return to the village, I can take you there, Mistress MacPherson.'

Those enticing eyes made of the palest of blue and shards of gold met his and widened ever so slightly before she nodded. Then she touched him, only a passing touch of her hand on his arm, but he could feel the heat of her through the layers of clothing there. Or he imagined he could. As he watched her hand slide down his sleeve towards the skin of his hand, Alan held his breath waiting for her skin on his. She lifted her hand away just before it could happen.

'I pray you, do not call me Mistress MacPherson,' she said. 'Mistress MacPherson makes me feel older than I am.'

'What would you have me call you?' he asked.

'As most here do, you could call me Saraid.' She placed her hand once more on his arm and he began walking with her at his side. 'In the midst of kith and kin, it somehow feels strange for you to call me something other than that.'

'Very well then, Saraid,' he said. 'What did Arabella want of you?'

Bold, but he wanted to know how Bella had approached her conversation with their guest. When she stumbled at his words, he reached out and steadied her…and continued to keep his hand on hers now.

'Have a care there,' he warned. 'The ground is uneven until we reached the bridge.' An excuse, but it also gave him one to keep hold of her hand.

Her skin was as soft as it appeared and no roughness or cracked skin marred it. It was almost as though she'd never toiled at chores or other household tasks. Tempted to turn it over to study it more carefully, Alan decided to simply hold her hand.

'The lady kindly offered me a place in her household,' Saraid said as they walked. 'I am, certainly, most honoured by such an invitation.'

'And? Will you accept her offer?' he asked.

One breath in and released and one pace taken. A second breath in and out and a second step. Then a third and a fourth until Alan realised he was counting her breaths and her paces at his side. Why should it matter? Why did it matter? He kenned only that it did. He wanted to stop and pull her into his arms and convince her that she should stay here.

'Nay.' With one softly spoken word, some strange hope within him paused. 'I am committed to my path.'

Damn it!

Had he so misread her hesitation or had she truly been considering Bella's offer seriously in those moments before she'd declared it otherwise? With each stride he took, he became more convinced that he could change her mind on this matter. If others like Dougal, and more if Jamie was to be believed, were attempting to dissuade her from the convent and taking of vows to that life, then why was he standing by the side and watching it happen?

Why was he letting it happen without him?

One thing stood in his way and it was not the woman there. It was Gilbert Cameron. His uncle be damned! Alan would choose his own path and his own wife, if it was time for that.

As the road turned on to the pathway that would lead to Jamie and Clara's, he'd talked himself into and out of doing what he wanted to do several times. As they slowed in front of the smithy and she began to lift her hand away from his arm, Alan decided his own path.

In spite of the knowledge that his uncle thought he would decide the rest of Alan's life, in spite of knowing that it would cause a battle that would drag his father and mother into taking his side or his uncle's, Alan knew that he must take a chance and try to make her his. As he let her go, Alan grabbed hold of her hand and lifted it to his mouth, kissing the soft skin that he had touched all the way here.

It was only a kiss and not even one on that lovely mouth that beckoned him forward. A kiss on a soft hand. He met her startled gaze and placed another nearer her wrist where her heartbeat could be felt. Her soft gasp revealed that he'd both surprised and affected her with the touch of his lips there.

It was only a kiss, but it was the beginning of something much, much more, if he had his way in this.

Chapter Twelve

A<small>NY</small> attempts to maintain a balance between her curiosity and her chosen path deteriorated in the next days. After that intimacy, Sorcha questioned every decision she'd made and her own integrity. She'd tried to walk away without shaking in reaction to the searing touch of his mouth on her wrist and thought she'd succeeded. Yet, she could not help but turn back to see if he'd been affected as well.

His dark gaze rested on her in spite of the growing distance between them and each time they met or passed one another in the next days, that same intensity filled his. Regardless of what Jamie had said about her not being prey to his hunter, her skin tingled and heat pooled in her belly when he looked at her so.

Even when it happened during innocent encounters.

Sorcha was walking with the boys back from the well when Alan rode through the village and called out to them. With the bairn on her hip and Wee Jamie running circles around her, she held her hand over her eyes to block the sun and nodded to him, keeping her distance even while taking in his appearance. But the boys both reached out for him and Wee Jamie took off running in his direction.

Something in his gaze and reaction to the child eased her immediate fear and she watched as he controlled his horse while leaning over and scooping the boy up in his arms. Wee Jamie's happy chortling mixed with the deeper, more masculine laughter of the man and her heart beat faster at the sound.

Then Robbie began crying out and fussing in her arms until Alan walked the horse closer and held out his hand to take him. With the deft movement of past experience, soon both the bairn and the boy sat happily in Alan's lap, babbling and chattering at him in their obvious joy.

Her own heart filled with a hunger she'd not felt before. A need so deep it took her breath again as she watched this man with these young boys. He needed bairns. He needed family. He needed… His gaze met hers and the hunger for such things intensified until she thought she would burn from it. Wee Jamie's near escape broke the moment and Alan nodded to her.

'I will take them to Clara and return for you,' he said.

Sorcha feared being too close to him right then. If he touched her now, if she sat behind him and wrapped her arms around him, she might never let him go.

'I will walk.' It took a long, noticeable pause before she could utter the words, but she did…finally. He nodded and rode off with the wee ones in his arms and Sorcha wanted to weep.

With sadness at what could never be.

With regret over how they'd met.

With emptiness at the needs that swelled now within her for family and a future.

Lucky for her the next time she encountered Alan she witnessed a different side of him, or she swore she'd break down and cry each time she did.

The next day, Sorcha found herself in the lady's solar with the other women, when Brodie came to seek out Arabella's opinion over some matter or another. Alan followed Brodie into the chamber and greeted each of them. From the brief words exchanges between Alan and Eva, Arabella, Margaret and the others serving there, Sorcha saw the genuine esteem which he had for them. And, the honest regard they each had for him.

She was blinking away tears when Alan walked to Brodie and offered some comments to whatever the topic of their discussion was. It was not the words, but the way in which he spoke to Brodie and Arabella and offered not only his opinion but his help in the matter that drew her attention. Try as she might to force her attentions away from the conversation, she could not. Though she did not watch them, she listened to his reasoned tone of voice during the back and forth between the three of them.

'Saraid?' She blinked and glanced up to find Alan standing before her now. 'Are you going back to the village soon? I must speak to Jamie and could take you.'

Her resolve not to be alone with him nearly melted away in that moment and she was only saved from foolishness by the lady.

'I need Saraid's help with a task here, Alan,' the lady said. 'If you would?' Her words turned an order into a request and Sorcha nodded to her.

'Certainly, my lady,' she said softly.

Alan nodded at her then, an expression of candid disappointment in his eyes as he followed Brodie out of the solar. At the last moment, he turned and glanced back at her and she expected to see the heat there once more. Instead, he smiled at her and it warmed her heart. No man in her life had ever considered her in that way.

Not in the way her father watched her, nor in the way his allies and friends did. Not in the way her servants or the villagers at her home did. Alan looked at her as though she was someone worth seeing. A woman worthy of his time and attention. As the door closed behind him, Sorcha understood that it was something she would never forget no matter what happened to her.

The next few days turned dreary and wet and she did not spend much time outside or far from Clara's cottage. The rains matched her mood this third morn since that kiss.

Standing in the doorway of the cottage, Sorcha watched as the rains did not so much fall as they instead flowed around the houses and down the paths and roads of Glenlui village. These were not the torrents of rain that had covered her escape from their camp next to the river that night. No, this was more like all around them than pouring down on them.

Like walking inside a cloud must feel, as Clara described it.

The clouds were low in the sky above them and thick. Shades of grey almost alive and swirling over their heads as the storm tried to decide if it would be a thorough drenching or just a quickly moving mist.

But, by midday, it was much the same as it had been all morning.

Several days had passed since Alan had kissed her hand and yet she found herself lost in reverie over it even now. Oh, her hand had been kissed before, out of respect and in greeting when various nobles and important men visited her father and were introduced to her. A few times the polite gesture turned into something else, something...*possessive*. Ill at ease over such presumptuous intimacies, she'd look to her father for guidance and he'd ignored her and the action. So she did.

But when Alan had touched his lips on her skin, it had sent waves of pleasure through her. His gesture had been intimate and possessive and yet not threatening. A sense of anticipation grew within her and the sinful part of her wanted him to continue. To move his mouth over her skin, to kiss her mouth and more. Even now, remembering it brought a trembling heat to the deepest place in her body.

Which was wrong. So wrong for so many reasons.

To be honest, she felt unsure of how to act after his gesture. Sorcha made certain she went to the keep earlier rather than later on that first day. Though they'd not spoken in private since that kiss, she'd watched him more than she wished to admit.

No matter that she yearned for more. No matter what she wanted. Even if she decided not to enter the convent, this could never be the place she remained. If her identity was discovered, too many would pay for her deception.

As The Cameron's nephew, Alan was absolutely the worst man to pay her heed or for her to get close to. And his tracking skills made it more dangerous. If anything should prick his curiosity about her, she had no doubt he would seek her truth and discover it. So, instead of thinking on him, she should be planning ways to avoid his company and his scrutiny.

And not about that kiss at all.

Once the bairns were down to sleep after their noon meal, Sorcha knew she needed to get out of the cottage. She had not planned to visit Father Diarmid until the next day, so she had no excuse to walk to the keep. If she walked around the village, she would, no doubt, get lost even while meeting Dougal or one of the other men who seemed to appear on the road when she did. Sorcha would not have believed they were there for her but for Jamie's explanation.

If they knew her true identity, none would be worthy of her. If they knew how unprepared and ill suited she was for marriage, none would want her. She could not cook or clean or care for a household or bairns—skills these men would need in a wife. Clara had tried and Sorcha had given it her best effort and yet she still burned the food, left soap in the clothing and lost at least one of the bairns every time they set foot out of the cottage.

No one seemed worse for it though. The children kenned their way home or were helped by villagers back to the right place. Clara managed to save most of the meals Sorcha attempted and to remove the soap before anyone itched or scratched because of it.

She was about to tell Clara of her plan to walk when the deep masculine voices drifted through the misting rain to her. As she followed the sound to the back of the cottage, she recognised both voices. Jamie and Alan Cameron. Staying in the shadows of the corner of the croft, Sorcha watched as they worked there. It was a failing, for certain, but she found the sight of him to be alluring. As long as she kept in mind the dangers he presented to her and her plan, Sorcha was sure it would all work out well.

Glancing over, she caught sight of the two men who were oblivious to her gawping there. Both men were tall and fit and strong. They matched each other in ability and rhythm as they hammered the iron horse-shoes to the shapes and size they needed. This was a usual practice of theirs, she could tell, and she took advantage of it now.

They worked in silence and occasionally they would pause and laugh at some jest or comment from the other. Sorcha could not turn away or keep herself from staring. Both men laboured bare-chested, as though they did not feel or pay heed to the rain and the cool-ness of breezes carried by the storm. When Alan turned away, she stared at his body, enjoying the view of his powerful back and shoulders as he toiled at the de-manding work.

Why did he do this? He was cousin to the lady and nephew to the chieftain of the mighty Camerons. He did not have to work as a common villager. And yet he did. In good spirit and in willingness. This was a strange way of living and so different from the way her father ruled over his kin.

'Well,' Jamie called out a short while after she began observing them work, 'have you had enough yet?'

Jamie put down the hammer he held and wiped his hands on the plaid that hung around his waist. Alan stopped then, breathing hard, and shrugged. Walking to the bucket, Jamie dipped the battered cup into it and drank it down. Dipping again, he held it out to Alan.

'I can tell how upset you are by how many days you show up here willing to work with me,' Jamie said, once Alan had taken the cup. 'Three days in a row means you are very upset.' Jamie laughed and Alan replied with the darkest frown she'd seen in a long time. The crude movement of his hand just made Jamie laughed louder. 'You told me a bit, but I would guess there is more to tell?'

Alan tossed the cup into the bucket and used his hands to smooth his hair back away from his face. With his arms raised like that, it made his chest seem even larger than she'd thought it. The muscles of his stomach rippled and tightened as he replaced the leather strip holding his long hair back. Sorcha could not breathe as she watched the display of muscles and masculinity continue.

Heat unlike anything she'd ever felt poured over her. Not even sitting close to the huge hearth in her father's hall had made her anxious and restless. She struggled against the urge to walk to him and to reach out and touch him. To slide her fingers over the defined pattern in the muscles of his stomach and to feel the rippling as he moved under her touch.

Instead of giving in to the compelling need that flooded her, Sorcha stepped back and leaned against the cool surface of the cottage. Her breathing was shallow and quick, she tried to slow it down and understand the torrent of sensations that were now attempting to control her body.

This was desire!

She'd felt stirrings of it before—when he held her

hand, when he stared in that intense way at her and when he pressed his mouth to her hand and her wrist. Her body had responded when she'd sat behind him on his horse, somehow heating and loosening and aching all at the same time. Sorcha closed her eyes and waited for it to ease. His words brought it to an abrupt halt.

'My uncle and The MacMillan reached an agreement.' She sucked in a breath as she heard his reference to her father.

'Your uncle was to marry that one's daughter. The one you searched for and found dead?' Jamie asked.

Ice now froze her in place. As though the rain had changed to sleet and coated her, Sorcha could not move. Alan had searched for *her*? He'd been there? Worse, Jamie knew of his involvement?

'Aye, that one,' Alan said. 'And I searched for her but never found the body. The river was so swollen and the storms so intense, she could not, she did not, survive her fall into it that night. God rest her soul.'

There was a mix of profound sadness and pity in his voice that it made her chest tighten. For a young woman he'd not met, well, not truly met. Yet something else swirled around that pity in his voice. A pain that was very personal. As though the thought of Sorcha Mac-Millan's death was tied to something else. Otherwise, how could he feel so much for a complete stranger?

'So, who is your uncle marrying now?' Jamie asked, moving their topic off the dead heiress. So, the Cameron's penchant for marrying and marrying again was known. Did they also know of the rumours of his implication in his previous wives' deaths?

'Not my uncle this time.'

'Truly?' Jamie laughed then. 'So then, who is The MacMillan to marry?'

Her thoughts scattered at those words and she fought to pay heed and listen. As her stomach threatened to heave, Sorcha forced herself to remain silent there in the shadows. Oh, she'd known of her father's desire for a son. And of his need to hold his claim to Castle Sween. Worse, she knew that his planned alliance with The Cameron was for a reason bigger than even that.

'Another Cameron cousin. One who has proven herself fertile and able to bear sons.'

The loathing in his voice surprised and puzzled her. To whom did he direct such disgust—her father, his uncle or this cousin who was, no doubt, a pawn in the machinations of the other two?

'Well, the only good thing is that she is old enough to have been married and had bairns.' Jamie's tone had changed and his voice had grown softer as he spoke. 'When does this marriage happen?'

'They are to be wed within a fortnight and to return to Castle Sween then.'

Pain pierced her at that revelation. Why she was so shocked or horrified, she knew not, for her father had made no secret of his desires for a son. But, to do so within months of her mother's passing and within weeks of her own was an expediency that bordered on indecent.

Jamie asked another question, but Sorcha could not listen to more. The fear of Jamie revealing her true identity to Alan, the reality of her father's disregard and the irreparable loss of everything she once was struck her in that moment. Without care for the rain or being seen, she walked from the shadows of the cottage and away.

Just away.

The rains that had been more like a mist now turned to angry downpour and she saw others scattering off the road ahead of her, seeking refuge from it. But she welcomed it.

Her every tie to her own life was now gone. Her father had not even paused in his own plans to mourn her loss or her mother's. She'd known the fact of it, but she had not believed he would so simply and quickly move on so clearly with such a clean break.

Her mother's plan to protect her had worked. With his attentions elsewhere now and his intentions on a bigger plan with The Cameron, he would not even seek her.

Somehow, her own part in this made it worse. With few choices and none of those acceptable to her, she'd chosen to flee. Chosen to leave behind everyone and everything she'd known. But only now was the true understanding of that choice becoming real to her.

She began to run then, with the rains slashing across her as she splashed through growing puddles along the road. Sorcha ran and ran and ran until she could no more. She stumbled off the road and fell to her knees there, wondering if the rains would wash away whatever was left of the once Lady Sorcha MacMillan.

Alan only noticed her when he saw her run from next to Jamie's cottage. The rains, which had been mild until now, turned fierce and would drive them inside until the worst passed. They put the tools away and sought the dryness of the croft. Clara was waiting for them.

'What happened?' she asked.

The way she placed her hands on her hips told of a coming storm of a different kind than the one that began to rage outside. They both shrugged and shook their heads.

'We were working and talking as we usually do,' Jamie said. 'Where did Saraid go just now?'

'That was my question of you both. She's been out of sorts all morn and I saw her go outside. When I went to get her, she was running down the lane there.' Her hands were still on her hips which told Alan she was not done. He did not have to be married to her to understand that much. 'What were you speaking about?'

Jamie shrugged, but the guilty expression in his eyes as he looked at his wife spoke of a shared knowledge of something to which Alan was not privy.

'Do you think she is ill?' Alan asked, looking down the road and not seeing Saraid. 'Does she need aid?'

He left before waiting for her reply, grabbing his shirt and pulling the plaid at his waist up to cover him.

Alan considered getting his horse, but decided to follow on foot instead. The road was growing worse by the second and would be covered in puddles and holes quickly during a storm like this. He had a better chance of seeking her on the ground.

He did not bother to call out her name. The winds and the heavy sheets of rain pouring down would be too loud to yell over. Alan trotted along the side of the road, searching for her. About a mile from the cottage and far enough along to be outside the village, he spotted her, kneeling just off the road.

'Saraid?' he said as he approached. 'Saraid.'

From her drenched condition and the rain that yet poured down on both of them, he could not tell if she was crying. Pale and silent, Saraid did not object when he lifted her to her feet and guided her under a stand of thick trees that could block some of the storm. Once they were out of the worst, he turned her to face him.

She'd lost the kerchief she usually wore and her hair was now matted down by the rain. Her eyes were vacant and she did not answer him. He needed to get her out of this storm. Alan glanced around and noticed a shelter in the field, one where hay was kept to feed the horses that were used to work the fields. With little help from her, he half-dragged and half-walked Saraid towards the shelter, whispering to her the whole way.

Her whole body quaked with shivers by the time they entered the small place, a tarp pulled over a simple frame of wood to keep the bales of hay covered. But it kept the rain off them and Alan suspected that was exactly what she needed at this moment. The only good thing was that it was a summer storm rather than a winter one and it might blow over quickly. The winds that rose just then belied his hope.

'Saraid,' he said as he tugged more of his plaid free from his belt and threw it around her shoulders. Gathering her in close, he used his crumpled shirt to dry her face and sop up some of the water from her hair. 'What happened, lass?'

She tried to speak, but the strong shivering stopped her efforts to do so. When her teeth began to chatter, Alan put his arms around her and rubbed briskly up and down on her back, trying to share his warmth and encourage her body to make some of its own. After a short time, he felt the tremors lessen but did not release her.

Saraid still not speak or explain what had happened. Thinking back on what he and Jamie had been talking about, the realisation struck him—every time he mentioned his uncle, she reacted in fear. What connection could there be between this widow and his uncle? Before he could ask another question, he felt her chilled fingers move across the bare skin of his chest and on to his stomach. The caress happened so quickly and was done that he questioned whether or not she had truly touched him.

'I am lost,' she whispered. 'Lost.'

Did she refer to her inexplicable ability to get lost any place in the village? Her tone was one of desolation and sadness, so he thought not. This went deeper.

'Do not worry then for I am good at finding things,' he said, trying to ease her despair. 'Or so I am told by my kith and kin.' Alan could not resist holding her a wee bit tighter then. 'I will find you.'

Whatever response he expected, the one that happened was not it. She slumped against him then and when he lifted her chin, he realised she'd fainted. Alan shifted his hold on her and eased her up on his lap so he could get a closer look at her. Or to be ready to carry her back to Jamie's if need be. She was rousing even as he moved her.

'Are you well, Saraid?' he asked. She was a slight thing in his arms. 'Or did I frighten you in some way? 'Tis not my usual manner in dealing with women.'

He felt the moment when she realised she was in his arms for she stiffened the tiniest amount before holding still. It was not a bad thing, holding her like this.

'I…' she began, but stopped several times without actually saying anything. He gently squeezed her and nodded. 'I fear I have been dwelling much on the loss of my mother in the last days,' she whispered. 'I am alone now.'

'She passed recently then?' he asked.

'Aye. Only a few months ago. The sadness just over-whelmed me and I could not breathe. I needed to get… away. Out.'

He understood that feeling, for it was one that happened to him often. When the newly risen rage within him began to push free, he did the same thing—he walked or rode or worked the iron with Jamie.

'Well, you did not pick the best weather in which to leave,' he said, softening his tone so she would ken he was jesting.

'Nay, I did not.'

In that moment, they both seemed to become aware of how he held her. How she sat on his lap. In his arms wrapped in his plaid. Alan loathed giving up this close-ness. He stared at her mouth, wanting to kiss her. His body responded to this sudden awareness of her close-ness in its own way. He had to move his legs or she would feel his arousal, which only forced her to grab hold of his shoulders to balance.

Now her mouth was even closer. All he had to do was lean his head down a scant inch or so and he could claim her lips. When the tip of her tongue slipped out and moistened those enticing, pink lips, he did just that.

The best part came before he touched his mouth to hers, for she lifted her head and touched his lips first.

Chapter Thirteen

It was not what she had planned to do at all.

And certainly not with the one man who could discover her secrets. The one whose word had declared her dead. The worst man in the entire world for her and the secrets she held.

When she woke from her faint, on his legs, in his arms, Sorcha had planned to stand up and move away from him. To return to Clara's and avoid him now that she knew his part in her charade. It was too dangerous to be around him.

That was what she would tell herself later. But now, when he shifted beneath her and she held on to his strong shoulders, she wanted him to kiss her. She wanted to forget the woman she'd been and be a different woman with him.

He wanted it, too. She could tell by the way he eased closer and bent his head down. He stared at her mouth as though hungry for a last meal. Though she'd never been this close to a man before, she kenned what she felt as he moved his legs underneath her. He wanted her in the way a man wants a woman.

Her breasts swelled and the tips became hard inside her gown. Whatever chill she'd felt from the cool, damp rain disappeared as that strange heat filled her. When Alan tilted his head a bit closer, she lifted hers and took the kiss she'd been wanting.

That momentary delay was the last bit of control she had over the situation, for that kiss quickly grew into something she had not planned and did not ken how to stop. Not that she wanted it to stop. Nay, she did not want to stop once she touched his lips with hers.

His hands moved down to encircle her waist and pull her closer even as his mouth took possession of hers. His tongue teased her lips and when she parted them, he swept inside, tasting her and allowing her a taste of him. Startled at this intimate caress, she opened her eyes and found him staring at her.

'Open your mouth, lass,' he whispered against her. 'Let me in.'

A thrill rushed through her body, making places she'd not noticed ache and throb as she followed his instruction. When she relaxed her lips, he pressed closer and began to suckle her tongue. Drawing on it, he pulled it into his mouth and swirled his against hers until she did the same thing. Every pull of his mouth sent shivers of pleasure to those deep places until her whole body felt alive and awake. She heard a noise and did not realise she'd made it until he spoke against her mouth again.

'Sigh for me, Saraid,' he whispered before he dipped his tongue in and tasted her again.

He slid one hand up and tangled it in her wet hair, cupping the back of her head. She relaxed into his hold and he brought her even closer. Sorcha melted against him—his hand, his mouth, his body. And rather than fighting it, she gave him what he'd asked for. The breathy sigh she released turned into something deeper and more needful when his other hand slid up and covered her breast. Her body arched into his hand, aching and wanting more. When his thumb rubbed across the tip of it, she was lost in the unexpected and absolute pleasure from such a caress.

Sorcha covered his hand with hers, both urging him on and trying to stop such a thing. As heat gathered within her belly and lower, she knew this could not continue. She must stop him and stop him now. But, pulling away from his mouth and his touch were not within her power just then. He laughed against her lips as though sensing her struggle.

'Easy, sweetling,' he whispered, as he moved both hands into her hair and plundered her mouth, deeper and hotter than before.

Her own fingers clutched once more at his shoulders as she resisted the urge to slide them down over his bared skin again. Over and over, he slanted his lips over hers and plunged his tongue within her. Breathless and overwhelmed, Sorcha finally pulled back and stared into his now stormy eyes.

Did her own eyes reveal the astonishment she felt at the way her body responded to his kisses? Did her innocence and inexperience show in the way her chest struggled and shuddered to draw in breaths? Did he realise she'd never been kissed by anyone before? And especially in this intimate manner?

He searched her face for something, puzzlement clear now in his gaze, before lifting her off his legs and holding her steady. Neither spoke a word then—

she knew not what to say and he did not seem inclined to speak. The shiver that raced through her then had little to do with the cold and more to do with the heat pouring off his body.

'I should get you back to Clara's, so you can get out of these wet garments and not catch a chill,' he said, softly.

He did not move or release her from his hold for several long moments. She took a step back as he stood, bringing them into closer contact than they had been for that moment. Forced to look up at him, she was unprepared when he leaned down and kissed her once more. It was a quick touch of their lips and done before she could do anything. She mourned the loss of him as soon as he moved away from her, tugging his plaid loose from around her shoulders and tossing it over his.

'The rain has eased,' he said. Sorcha looked out and noticed it had faded in intensity, back to a thick mist from its recent deluge. She nodded.

'Clara will worry,' she said. Sorcha gathered her hair back and tried to braid it quickly. A married woman, even a widow, should have her hair covered, but her kerchief was long gone in her haste to get away. The braid would have to do for now. She wondered how long it would take for Clara to realise that something had happened between her and Alan. She let out a sigh and glanced at the road that led back to the village.

'Aye, she will. She does.'

Alan picked up his own damp shirt and tugged it over his head. Then, he held out his hand to her and she took it, allowing his strong fingers to close around hers and give her support as she took those first few shaky steps. A tenseness and heat yet coursed through her blood, one that she feared would be hard to extinguish. At least as long as he was near and looked at her with that hunger in his gaze that she saw there now.

'She sent me to follow you, Saraid.' Alan watched as her eyes widened a tiny bit at that disclosure. 'Come, let us return there and ease her fears.'

Still holding her hand, he tugged a bit and drew her next to him as they walked from under the shelter, across the edge of the field and back to the road. He tried not to notice her kiss-swollen lips and the way her breasts rose and fell with each breath she took. He laboured to forget the feel of her nipple tightening under his thumb and the taste of innocence on her lips. But, mostly, he really needed his flesh to relent from its state of hard arousal so he could regain control over himself.

Innocence. Innocence? How could she taste as though untouched and new to kissing? Married and widowed, she surely had been kissed and tupped by her husband. If she had been his wife, he would have taken her to bed for days to bury himself deep within her body and show her every pleasure that could be between them. To claim her and mark her with his own scent and seed. If she were his...

He shook himself free of such a path, for she had not been his nor would she be. Her choice was in another direction completely. Alan glanced over and saw the troubled expression on her face and the way her brow tightened. Had she not welcomed his actions then? Was he guilty of trespassing in a grievous way?

So how could she retain the taste and manners of a woman untouched? Her artless kisses, no less arousing for their obvious inexperience, spoke of a woman unfamiliar with the action. But how could that be?

They walked in silence back towards the village. He glanced out the corner of his eye to make certain he was not walking too quickly for her much shorter stride. And to make certain she was well. And to watch how she touched her fingers to her lips when she thought him not looking.

Astonishment. Wonderment. Surprise. All words to describe the expression in her eyes as she'd lifted her mouth from his. Not what he would have expected from a married and widowed woman.

Even more surprising to him was that, when he questioned her about her grief, she'd never mentioned her husband's passing. Only her mother's.

Strange bits of insight into the enticing Saraid MacPherson that made him hunger for more. After taking the first steps across the barrier between them, Alan was determined to convince her that she had another choice in her life. That entering the convent was not her only path.

Alan kenned he should feel guilty about turning her intentions away from the service of the Almighty and to something much more human, but he did not. The only thing that would stop him would be the woman herself.

They soon reached Clara and Jamie's cottage. Alan felt the loss of her touch when she slipped her hand from his as they followed the last curve of the road around and her cousin's home was revealed. He could feel her warmth grow distant with each step and Alan knew he could not allow it. Not now. He took her hand once more and pulled her to stop and face him.

That was his first mistake, for the sight of her tousled, wet hair and swollen lips brought back his cockstand within moments. He would not have made his second error if she'd not stared at his mouth and touched the tip of her tongue to her upper lip just then. Did she ken that he was at the limit of his control? Deciding that distance between them would lead to more measured actions, he stepped back a pace, yet still held her hand.

'Part of me thinks I owe you an apology for my forwardness,' he said softly. He lifted her hand to his mouth and turned it, placing several kisses along the sensitive skin there on her wrist. The whispered sigh made him smile. 'But I cannot apologise for what I did. What we did, Saraid. And, if I have anything to do with it, those will not be the last kisses we share.'

Alan had never been a vain man and had never taken the affections of a woman for granted. And he'd certainly never considered himself a rogue who took advantage of a woman's favours. But, when Saraid gifted him with a soft smile and slight nod to his declaration, he thought he had won the hardest-fought battle. Tempted to do more than simply kiss her, only Clara's voice stopped him.

'You found her!' Clara said, rushing to them. She stopped as she reached them and stared at her cousin first before frowning at him. Clara touched Saraid's shoulder and then gathered her in close. 'You are soaked and cold, Saraid. Come with me.' If she'd noticed their joined hands, she did not comment on it as she tugged Saraid along to the cottage.

Jamie watched from the door and Alan could read nothing from his stance or his stare. From the shuttered expression earlier, his friend knew something more than he was sharing about Clara's cousin. The question was whether or not the man would reveal it to him if it meant taking sides across the divide of kith and kin. As Jamie opened the door wider to allow the women to enter, he shrugged and shook his head. Alan was on his own in his pursuit of Saraid.

It was neither a new thing for him nor one he feared. Indeed, his spirits rose as he considered his next move in his strategy to claim the Widow MacPherson. Should he discuss the matter with Brodie? If he did succeed, Alan had no doubt that his uncle would make his life miserable and seek to ruin any chance at happiness he had. Arabella's husband had always promised Alan a place here or anywhere on his lands where Alan wished to live and now, it would seem, Alan might need exactly that.

Her mother had taught her to sew in wonderfully small and accurate stitches. And how to add and subtract numbers and keep records. And how to speak and read in their language and that of the court and church. With patience and guidance and by example, her mother had taught her about the virtues and about loyalty and honour and courage. If Sorcha could demonstrate even half of what her mother had taught her, it would be a fitting tribute to the woman that Erca MacPherson MacNeill was.

As Sorcha unlaced her gown with chilled and trembling fingers, she realised that the dangerous gap in her education was not one her mother would have or could have foreseen or prepared her to face. It involved men.

Actually, it involved one man—Alan Cameron.

Her mother's plan had been clean and clear, for she would go from her father's house to God's and therefore men were not a matter for consternation. But the situation just now had shown Sorcha just how unprepared she was to face life outside her protected existence as Sorcha MacMillan. And it had made it clear to her that she would find life in a convent difficult at best.

Lady Arabella's words about her lack of choice once she entered the convent had unnerved her. Alan Cameron's touch and kisses made her question her resolve very quickly and with a thoroughness that would have made her mother blush. Had that kind of passion and excitement ever existed for Erca MacNeill? Sorcha found it impossible to believe that her father would be so gentle towards any woman, especially not his wife.

Was that why her mother had never spoken of matters of the flesh between a man and woman? Because her own experience had been a poor and failing one and she'd never dreamt her daughter would be tempted by such a thing? Surely, Sorcha never had.

Oh, she'd heard and seen things, private things between men and women at her father's keep. A glimpse here, a word or expression there. The harlot who lived in the village made no secret of her profession or her lures. But not once had Sorcha ever felt a moment of attraction or arousal as she had when Alan touched her hand. Or kissed her. Or, even more so, when his hand slid up and covered her breast.

A sigh escaped her as she remembered the pleasure of his caress and her body reacted, too, heating and throbbing in memory.

'You do not look chilled to the bone,' Clara said quietly from the doorway of the smaller chamber. With the bairns being seen to by their father, Sorcha had use of the room to change out of her wet garments. 'That blush speaks of heat and more.'

Sorcha touched her cheeks then and found them hot. She turned to face Clara, still fumbling with the laces.

'Here, let me see to those,' Clara said.

With sure and steady actions, the laces were loosened and untied and with a little more assistance, Sorcha found herself in a clean and blessedly dry shift and gown. A thick blanket tossed over her shoulders drove the cold from her bones and skin. From Clara's lingering, Sorcha knew she has something to say.

'Is he what has distracted you all day?'

'Aye,' she answered truthfully. 'Him and more.'

'The bairns are at Margaret's and Jamie waits without. Come, we should speak plainly about this.'

There was no condemnation in her tone of voice in the invitation to talk about what had happened. What *was* happening. And Sorcha would welcome plain counsel over the final steps she must plan and take. Desire had caused some change within her as it woke. Desire for him brought with it a myriad of problems and impossibilities.

'And Alan?' she asked for the first time. Speaking his name aloud made her voice tremble and her body react once more. 'Is he working with Jamie?' Sorcha both wanted to see him and feared her ever-weakening will when he was close.

'Nay. He left when you returned. Headed to the keep from his direction.' Clara walked past her to find the comb on the table. 'Let me comb out your hair while you warm up. Then we can speak with Jamie and sort out the rest.'

With her experienced hands, it took Clara no time at

all to untangle the wet strands of her hair into a proper braid. The blanket tucked around her shoulders now, Sorcha walked into the main chamber of the cottage and sat at the table where Jamie waited. She took in and released several slow breaths before speaking.

'I think it's time to leave Glenlui.' Silence but several speculative glances between husband and wife met her words. She looked at one then the other. 'It is too dangerous for me here.'

'Well, if you speak of Alan, that might be true,' Clara admitted as Sorcha nodded. 'He is relentless when he fixes his sights on a task. By the looks of it, that task is you.'

Jamie did not laugh as much as smother a laugh that threatened escape. The sound was that of someone choking. Clara's sharp and narrowing gaze prevented him from adding more sounds.

'And his attention is too dangerous,' Sorcha said. 'He will discover my truth and then…'

'Hell will break loose on earth?' Jamie asked. He shook his head at both of them. 'You do not ken him as I do. He is not looking for your secrets, Sorcha, he is looking for your…looking at you. As a man looks at a woman, not a hunter at its prey.'

'I heard you two speaking of it as you worked. He was the one who declared me dead!'

'Aye. Dead and gone now. He has relegated the Lady Sorcha MacMillan to another of those lost in his uncle's machinations.'

Startled by those words, Sorcha wondered if she should share the rest of what she knew about his uncle's plans with Clara and Jamie. Deciding to keep it to herself for now, she nodded.

'What he sees is a lovely, widowed, young woman with fine manners and a gentle heart who is helping out her kin while recovering from her losses. And that, Clara's cousin, would call to most every man.'

'Do you not understand? He is the worst possible man to pay heed to me. He is the one who could put all the pieces together. He is the one who could expose me and make matters far worse than any of you can imagine. Alan Cameron is the one man I should stay away from. He is…' She paused then, surprised at the vehemence of her own words. Worse, surprised by what she wanted to say and could not.

He was the one man with whom she could easily fall in love.

Clara reached out and took her hand as she wrestled with the realisation of the true nature of the danger he posed to her. For he was not the man with whom she *could* fall in love. Alan Cameron, the most dangerous man in Glenlui, was the man that she *was* falling in love with.

Thinking back, Sorcha understood now that from their first glance at their first meeting in the hall those weeks ago, the process had begun.

Then, as he wended his way into her life here with Clara and Jamie, it had strengthened and become something real. She smiled, remembering the gentle way he had with the bairns, even scooping up Wee Clara and soothing her when she'd fallen and scraped her knees.

Their earlier encounter in the field simply rushed it along.

Worse, she'd spent hours in the dark of night thinking about him and how he would be a man she could… she could love.

'I must leave.'

That was it. She must leave and make her way to Skye now, before things got even more mucked up than they were already. And there she would spend her days praying for forgiveness for her stubbornness and lack of humility. For thinking she could outwit and outmanoeuvre her father and all his plans by lying and drawing in these innocent people.

'I will send word to my cousin on Skye on the morrow and declare my intentions,' she said. Neither Clara nor Jamie had said much so she looked at them now.

'If that is what you wish to do...' Clara began. 'But I would urge you to give yourself more time.'

'Alan will not push himself if you do not wish it,' Jamie said.

Though meaning to ease her worries, it increased them. For she wanted him. She wanted Alan to follow through with his whispered promise that he was not done kissing her. And she feared he would do exactly that and chip away at any resolve she might put forward.

'And, Sorcha, I would not break your confidence to him or to anyone. Worry not that I will share anything you have said or any knowledge I have of your identity.' Jamie's hand covered his wife's and Sorcha's then.

'I trust you both,' she said.

'What about Alan?' Jamie asked.

'I think it best if I avoid him until I depart for Skye.'

The words were spoken with an assuredness she truly did not feel. Avoiding him was the only way to put a halt to something that could not and would not ever be possible. Better to avoid him and save her heart from nothing less than complete destruction.

* * *

The rest of the day had gone quietly by and by the next morn, Sorcha remained convinced of her decision to move on from here and to elude Alan and any attempts to spend time with her. Or to kiss her. Or…

Unfortunately, no one had informed Alan of her plans or her resolve.

Chapter Fourteen

He turned up sometimes in the most expected and sometimes most surprising places at the most unanticipated times over the next days. And, as he'd promised or threatened, he stole kisses regularly. He always checked to see if someone would see, but there were several times when Sorcha thought they might be caught.

Quick kisses. Leisurely ones. Tempting her on and making her want more. Dangerous in so many ways, as was the man himself.

Then there were the gentle soft touches and whisper-soft caresses when he was near. A touch on her thigh when he sat next to her at table. A caress across her neck as he passed her in the corridor of the keep on some task or another. The intense gaze that seemed to tease her skin to a sensitivity she'd never knew could be.

'What was the name of the priest who instructed you in Latin?' Father Diarmid asked. Sorcha looked up from her plate and wondered how to respond to his question. More importantly, had the priest or anyone noticed that she'd been lost in her own thoughts?

Seated here at the laird's table with the lady, the priest and others, Sorcha tried to gather her scattered thoughts carefully before answering. Luckily, on this matter, she could say the truth of the matter.

'Father Euan was my teacher,' she said. 'But he passed more than five years ago.'

'Was this priest a MacPherson then?' the lady asked.

'Nay, my lady,' she said, shaking her head and placing her spoon and eating knife down by her plate. She clutched her hands on her lap where none could see them. 'He was of the MacNeills.'

'And your husband allowed this?' the priest asked.

Of all those at table and listening to her words, only Alan's regard worried her. She could feel his gaze on her skin and the blush that rose into her cheeks. Her husband…?

'My husband's duties took him away and he permitted my study because we had not the blessings of children.'

Lady Arabella smiled and nodded. 'Children are a woman's focus of life, Saraid. 'Tis sad you did not have any with your husband.'

She nodded then, unable to gather words. This meal, like the three before she'd been summoned to with the lady and various people, was an exercise in self-control and thinking quickly. Lady Mackintosh managed to bring up a dizzying mix of topics, but they all came back to her. Her upbringing. Her decision to enter the convent. Her relatives. Her marriage.

That was the worst for her. Asking about a husband who never existed. Sorcha found herself speaking of a husband who could not exist—one with infinite patience, an openness to learning, one who allowed her the freedom she wanted and needed.

Yet, when the lady's questions grew too many, it was Alan who would interrupt to stop them. Never openly. Never forceful. He seemed to ken how to draw his cousin's attentions to different topics and away from her.

Because he chose, many times, to ask his cousin about something personal, Sorcha learned much about him and his place here. She learned of how he'd been sent to find his cousin when Brodie had kidnapped her during the struggle for control of the Mackintoshes. And that he spent his time divided and got several glimpses into his life here and about his parents. Though he tried to keep the banter light and lively, Sorcha recognised a profound hurt and a longing she could not identify within the depths of his stormy gaze. It reminded her of what she'd felt when she'd listened to him describe her own disappearance and death. Something lingered within him that would not be soothed or eased. And, damn her, she wanted to find the cause and rid him of it!

At those times when he deflected attention from her she wanted to offer her thanks to him, but she did not. From the intense gaze of his eyes, she understood he did it on purpose and for her. Sorcha sensed that there were many, many more questions he wished to ask of her, but did not…or did not yet.

'Bella,' Alan said, 'are felicitations owed you and Brodie?'

Everyone at table paused then and looked to the lady for confirmation of such a blessed event, though Alan bringing it up so was unexpected.

'Aye,' the lady said after smiling at her husband who was seated at the other end of the table for now. 'If, pray God, all goes well, we will welcome another child in the spring.'

The announcement drew everyone in the hall forward and the laird to his wife's side. As though alone, The Mackintosh pulled the lady to her feet and into his arms. The kiss was nothing less than thorough and scorching and something Sorcha had never seen done before others in this manner. If Father Diarmid was alarmed or offended, it did not show. Unable to look away, Sorcha could almost feel Alan's mouth on hers tasting her deeply. Now knowing what that felt like, she could not pull her gaze away from the sight of them.

'Come now, Brodie,' Alan called out as he stood. 'We know how it was accomplished and there is no need to demonstrate it here!'

The bawdy words brought on loud laughter and calls for more. Others climbed the steps to the dais to offer their good wishes to their laird and lady. Sorcha took it as a chance to escape. Skirting the growing crowd, she made her way through the corridor and out through the kitchens. Pushing open the door there, she rushed faster and faster until almost running towards the gate and the path to the village.

'Saraid!'

She heard his voice above the noise of the yard and slowed her pace. Turning, Sorcha watched as he trotted across to her. In her attempts to avoid him, she'd ended up spending more time in his company these last few days than she had before.

'Does the lady wish me to return?' she asked, brushing her palms over her gown. 'I had thought her busy with other matters.'

'Nay, she is seeing to her husband's pride over his ability to father bairns right now.'

Something made her stop then and speak the truth to him.

'You did that to draw her attention from me,' she said, stating what she'd observed him doing these last days. His eyes widened just the tiniest bit before he nodded. 'Why?'

'I can tell when Bella is set on a course to discover someone's secrets.' He reached out and grabbed her shoulders as she felt all the blood in her body rush to her feet at his admission. 'She'd been wheedling you these last days and I could see how wearing it was on you.'

His words struck fear in her heart and yet spoke of his having a care for her in a way no one ever had. Sorcha leaned in his direction and he slipped his arms around her shoulders, holding her at his side.

'Are you going back to the village?' he asked.

'Aye.'

'I will walk with you,' he said. 'I need only return by supper to speak to Brodie.' They had passed through the gates before he spoke again. 'Bella told me you are leaving soon.'

'I think it is for the best, Alan,' she said quietly. His arm yet lay on her shoulders though it was more comforting than she dare admit. 'The longer I remain here...' she began.

'The harder it will be to leave,' he finished her words.

Sorcha did not say anything more, for it was true.

Every day she spent here was a day she regretted her choices. Especially when it came to this man. Oh, she understood that there was no chance for them together, more than he did, but it did not mean she did not wish it could be otherwise for them.

With him.

And with all the knowledge she had gained about him—his past, his boyhood, his choices—it made it that much harder to think about leaving him.

If she told him the truth, his honour would demand a certain course of actions in loyalty to his clan and his uncle. If she left, at least he would never know the depths of her deceit. Sorcha would find some way to warn The Mackintosh of the perfidious nature of Gilbert Cameron and Hugh MacMillan, if only as a way to thank him and his people for their hospitality.

Nay, her own honour demanded that she reveal the truth and protect these people who protected her.

How long they'd stood in the shadows off the path, she kenned not. But one moment she was lost in her thoughts and plans and then the next found her wrapped in Alan's arms, held tightly against his muscular chest once more.

'I was wondering if you'd notice.'

'Notice?' she asked, inhaling the scent of him as he gathered her even closer.

'That I have taken you into the forest to have my way with you, lass.'

His mouth curved into an enticing smile that both promised and teased her. He leaned down and kissed the sensitive place just below her ear, sending ripples of pleasure and awareness through her body as he whispered against her neck.

'May I, Saraid? May I have my way with you?'

No! her mind screamed. *Not him!* her reason said. *Not now!* Every bit of sense and restraint cried out to stop him and to stop him now. But it was her heart that answered.

'Aye.'

He pulled back to search her face for the truth of it and she smiled at him. The kiss was fast and hard and demanding as he touched their lips and laid his claim. Sorcha reached up and slid her hands into his hair, holding his head close to hers as he opened his mouth and beckoned her tongue inside.

At some moment, he lifted her into his arms and carried her further away from the path and into the shadows. She was breathless and aching by the time he put her back on her feet and lifted his mouth from hers. Gasping for breath, she looked around and kenned they were far enough away that no one would see or hear anything that happened now.

Instead of worrying her, she felt safe with him. Sorcha did not doubt that he would have his way, as he'd said, but she also kenned to a certainty that he would stop if she told him so.

Right or wrong, in this moment now, she did not wish him to stop. She wanted a full measure of what she would be giving up once she left him here to go to Skye. She wanted him to be the first man and the only one to whom she gave herself. Sorcha reached up and tugged the laces of her cloak loose, allowing it to fall around her on the leaf-covered ground at her feet.

Then, offering him her heart and her trust, Sorcha held out her hand to him and waited for him to accept.

* * *

She gazed at him with such faith and trust that Alan lost his breath. As though this was more than a simple bout of pleasure between a man and a willing woman. As though she offered him more than just her body. Yet he kenned she planned to leave him and the rest of the world behind soon. Whether manly confidence or simple hope, Alan wanted to be the one to change her mind on that matter.

Pulling his belt free, he lifted off his plaid and added it to her cloak on the ground, making a place for them there. Taking her proffered hand, he brought her back to him, embracing her as he took her mouth. The innocence was still there, on her tongue, in her movements, in the way she waited for him to begin.

With an arm around her, he guided them to their knees and then to lie on the bed of cloaks. Holding her close, he used his free hand to ease open the laces of her gown and then her shift, kissing a path from her mouth to her ear and then on to her neck. The sighs she uttered spurred him on, lower and lower. When he kissed and bit the slope of her breast gently, she arched against him. Her legs grew restless, sliding against his own until he caught them between his.

Easing his arm from beneath her, he leaned up on his elbow and watched her eyes when he slid his hand inside her shift and on her naked skin. With each inch his fingers moved closer to the tip of her breast, her eyes widened and her mouth opened. Her breaths were now shallow as he touched the now turgid nipple. Gasping with each movement he made, Saraid closed her eyes as her body pressed into his grasp.

'Lovely, Saraid. You are lovely,' he whispered.

He cupped her full breast and lifted it free of the cloth that yet covered it. With his gaze still on her face, he licked the dark-pink flesh and then drew it into his mouth as he had her tongue. Her eyes opened on a loud gasp as she looked at him. Slowly, teasingly, he released the tip and did it again as she watched. And again, enjoying the way her body shuddered under his touch and the way her eyes filled with pleasure at each kiss.

Tugging the laces, he pulled her gown and shift open, exposing her to his sight. Her breasts filled his hands—pert and plump and perfect for him. Now caressing both, he slid his rough thumbs over the nipples until she gifted him with those gasps. He teased and licked and suckled one and then the other, readying her for him even as his flesh grew harder.

Lifting his leg, he released his hold on her legs so that he could touch her there. With his mouth still on her breast, he slid his hand down and gathered the length of her garments in his palm. Easing them up, he pushed them out of his way and touched her thighs. Clenched together tightly, he caressed them until they trembled under his touch. Alan lifted his head and kissed her on the mouth.

'Open for me, lass,' he whispered against her lips. When her mouth opened, he felt her legs relax just a bit. He moved his hand between them and kissed her again.

'Your legs, lass. Open your legs.' A momentary hesitation and then she opened for him. Smiling, he kissed her again as he let his fingers slide into the place he wanted most to touch. She was wet and hot there. Wet for him. But her body remained tense. When he met her gaze he recognised that there was fear there.

'Kiss me, Saraid. I pray you, kiss me.'

Whatever he had expected, her reaction was not it. If he had thought her reticent or fearful, the way she took hold of his face and kissed him now destroyed that notion. She claimed his mouth, tasting him as he'd tasted her, thrusting her tongue deep into him and swirling it. When his tongue met hers, she suckled it as he had her nipple. His cock grew harder against her hip as he thought of how her tongue would feel on his hardened flesh.

Alan flexed his fingers then, sliding between her legs and deeper into the cleft of her woman's flesh. Rubbing his finger along it, he brought the moisture to the tight bud hidden there. She arched and bucked against him at his touch. A little pressure on that raised flesh of hers and she gasped against his mouth. Sliding one finger inside her, the tightness there surprised him. Her kiss became frantic now, her tongue more forceful, with each caress between her legs.

At first, Alan thought it arousal, but soon he noticed the way her body tensed as though she was fighting for control. He stilled his hand and lifted his head from her.

Fear.

Fear in her wild gaze.

Fear in the tightness of her body. Not arousal. Not pleasure. Almost as if she did not know what he would do. As if she feared him, feared this…

'I will not hurt you, Saraid,' he whispered. 'I want only to give you pleasure.' Alan eased his hand from her and waited on her reaction and to see if the fear receded or increased. He had never forced a woman, by word or by deed, and he would never do anything without Saraid's permission.

Then he realised what a fool he'd been. Was this the first time she would be with a man other than her husband? He wanted to smack himself for his stupidity. She was a virtuous woman, anyone could see it in her manners and her ways. He was the first man to touch her so since her husband's passing and she was nervous and fearful. In spite of any willingness on her part, there had to be some hesitation to accepting another man into her body.

'Forgive me for not thinking,' he said. 'This must be difficult for you.' Alan settled back on his elbow. She slid a scant foot back and did the same.

'Difficult?' Her voice trembled on speaking. Was it from his caresses or her fears, he kenned not.

'To take another man to you, since your husband's passing.'

The fear left her eyes, but was quickly replaced by first surprise, then confusion and then, worst, loathing. For him or herself, he could not begin to guess. Alan sat up and waited as she righted her clothing, watching as she covered herself from his sight.

The moment of passion and desire had fled and Alan wondered at the cause of it and its demise. Was it mourning over a dead man or something else? She glanced away as though embarrassed by what *had* passed between them.

'Alan, I...'

'No need, lass,' he said, waving off whatever words she was about to offer. He stood and held out his hand to help her to her feet. 'You owe me nothing.'

She startled as though stung by his words, hurt darkening the blues and golds of her eyes. Although she took his hand and stood before him, she no longer met his gaze. Struck by the differences in their size then, he stepped back to allow her space.

'Come, I will take you back to Clara's,' he said, waiting for her to walk past him without touching her. 'And see to Brodie's call.'

An excuse, nothing more, to let her escape. He wanted her more than he had any woman before, but something stood between them. The obvious thing would be her dead husband, but Alan doubted that man was the reason for her reaction. He searched his memory and realised that not once had she used the man's name.

'What was your husband's name?' he blurted out. She blinked several times before speaking, a conspicuous delay now that he was noticing such things.

'Micheil. Micheil MacNeill,' she said. 'Why do you ask?'

'I wanted to know the name of the man who stands in my way.'

They walked in silence all the way back to the path and down to Clara's as he thought of his words and plans. Something was not right here. Something more that he could not figure out. It teased the edges of his thoughts—bits and pieces and words and images that floated in disarray as they did at the beginning of a search for him.

He bid her a quiet farewell once they'd reached the smithy and walked back to the keep. By the time he reached it, his purpose was clear in his mind.

It was not until the middle of that night, when he awoke in the darkness of his chamber, that the reason was clear to him.

Saraid MacPherson, wife of the late Micheil Mac-Neill, was both more and different from what she seemed to be.

That much he'd known for some time. Something about her story and her bearing and her education and knowledge did not make sense to him. The real surprise, the one that woke him in the night, was something else entirely.

He needed to know her secrets because he was in love with her.

And, in order to claim the woman he loved, he would have to know whatever she was hiding before his uncle could discover them and destroy her the way he had destroyed others he'd loved.

Chapter Fifteen

'I need to act on your behalf,' Alan said, watching Brodie closely as he spoke. Brodie stopped in the middle of taking a mouthful of wine and put the cup on the mantel of the hearth of his chamber before facing him.

'Should you not be acting on your uncle's behalf? As his man here in Glenlui?'

'Do not be an arse, Brodie. Your spies ken more about my uncle and his actions and intentions than I could ever tell you of him.' Alan drank down the last of his wine and crossed his arms over his chest. 'This is not about my uncle.'

'Everything you do is about your uncle, lad,' Brodie said. Smiling grimly at him, he continued. 'About your loyalty to him. To your clan.' Alan cursed and the foul words echoed across the chamber between them. 'Been listening to Rob, have you?' The chieftain laughed and put his hand on Alan's shoulder.

''Tis the way of things, Alan. Every man must decide his place in the scheme of things and if he can live in it.' Releasing him, Brodie picked up his cup once more and filled it from the jug there on the table. 'I have watched you walk this impossible path between our clans for years. Since you grew hair on your b— well, since you became a man.'

Irritated by Brodie's ease in seeing the pattern of his life, Alan cursed again and held out his own cup for more. 'And? So?'

'I wonder if 'tis time for you to make your stand with him.'

Since the words mirrored his own thoughts, it was difficult to argue with them or the man who spoke them now. Brodie had known him since he was but a boy and had provided a shelter to him when he needed it. His debt to Alan was long settled, but Brodie had never taken back his support. Some would say, and some had, that it was just to keep pricking at Gilbert. Some said it was just to use his abilities as a tracker. Alan kenned the truth—Brodie was an honourable man and stood by those he called friend.

'It is coming sooner than I'd thought it would,' he replied, accepting that knowledge for the first time.

'Does this mission you undertake on my behalf have to do with the lovely and accomplished Widow MacPherson?'

'Aye.' One word spoken and he'd made his claim. He needed Brodie to understand the rest of it. 'She is hiding something.'

'Does not every woman do that before she trusts a man?' Brodie asked. Arabella, Alan kenned, had hidden many things from her future husband. Not strange considering that Brodie kidnapped her from her own wedding and held her prisoner. ''Tis the telling and revealing of those secrets that sometimes lead to love.'

'My uncle cares not for love or trust, Brodie. You

ken him. I need to find out what she hides before he can discover it and destroy her.'

'As he did Agneis?' Brodie asked. Alan nodded. 'The problem there was that *you* were her secret and she yours. Your uncle found two weapons in one and wielded them expertly. Will he do that once more?'

Alan threw the cup before he'd even thought to do so and it crashed into the wall just above Brodie's head. To hear his past put so coldly into words made him want to rage and strike out.

'You have swallowed your uncle's insults and injuries for a long time, Alan. What makes this woman the one for whom you would go to war with him?'

That was what had kept him up these last nights. He kenned that something was different in the way he felt about her from their first meeting. Mayhap it was because he kenned she was the one worth fighting over? Or that this was a perfect mix of the woman, the love he felt and his own readiness?

'Simply put, Brodie, she is the one who makes me want to do just that.'

Brodie did not speak immediately. Instead, he saw to the cup on the floor first, giving that declaration time to sink into Alan's mind. Did the young man he thought of and treated like his own son know the importance of those words? Did he understand what would come his way?

The widowed Saraid MacPherson was not the only person with secrets to be withheld or revealed in this. Confidences were held, actions covered over and old wounds to be torn open if Alan followed this path. Brodie could not tell him the right or wrong of it, for it was not his place to say such things. But, at the same time, he would not mind Gilbert Cameron facing his past and being found wanting.

'Have you asked her for the truth? Have you told her about your own past?'

He could tell from Alan's expression that he had not. Someone with Alan's skills was more adept and experienced in finding out and gathering knowledge about another than in sharing his own.

'Speak to her first, before seeking out anything else about her,' he suggested.

'And if she holds her secrets to herself?'

'Then, 'tis up to you.'

He did not say more, for the fact that Alan understood his choice lay there plainly on his face. Brodie had fallen in love with his Arabella knowing she kept secrets and betrayed him. And Bella had loved him in spite of believing Brodie had killed her brother. Their love, born in the fires of hell, was the strongest kind of love—one tested and toughened by the obstacles they'd had to face and overcome. It had never been easy, but every moment of it was worth any pain he'd paid to claim her.

'If your uncle summons you, what should I tell him?'

This journey was going to happen, Brodie had no doubt of it. From what he'd seen of Alan and the widow, the love was there already. The only question was could it survive the coming challenges. When his Arabella offered her counsel, she told Brodie she believed it would. She'd stated confidently that Saraid MacPherson would not spend one day inside the walls of a convent.

But his beloved did not ken the depths and darkness of her uncle as Brodie did. Looking at Alan now, Brodie knew the young man was strong enough to face his uncle, he just did not know if he was strong enough to face and survive the coming revelations from everyone else around him.

'That I will return soon and will answer his call as quickly as I am able.'

Alan held out his hand to Brodie and Brodie took it, clasping him tightly. There was more he would like to say, but Alan must discover many things on his own and it was not Brodie's place to interfere right now.

'Try not to start any new feuds in my name,' he did advise.

'Brodie,' Alan began. 'I would...'

'There will time enough to speak on matters of all kinds later, Alan. Seek her truth and yours.'

Alan nodded and turned to leave. He paused at the door after lifting the latch and Brodie thought he'd speak more, but he did not. He listened to Alan's footsteps leading away from the chamber and down the stairs with a heaviness in his heart.

One way or another, the young man who left here today would not be the same one on his return to Glenlui after his search.

Saraid looked up from the chair near the hearth to find him there at the door. He had made no sound, so she had no idea for how long he'd been there, just watching her sew. Clara, Jamie and the children had gone to visit their cousins for the day and so Saraid had taken advantage of the quiet and solitude. The door was ajar to let in the unseasonably warm breeze as she worked.

Clara had known something was not right since Alan brought her back here the other afternoon, but Saraid could not find the words to explain the situation and the problem. How could she tell her cousin that she despised herself for the story they'd made up to protect her? How could she say that she wanted nothing more than to remain here and be with him?

How could Saraid stay and live the lie while knowing the wrongness of it? Nay, the growing feelings she had for Alan forbade her from putting him in the centre of something he had little to do with or little say over.

She'd wanted to lie with him in the forest that day. Saraid wanted to give herself to him and take with her the memory of such a time in the arms of a man she loved. But, at the last, as he pleasured her in his embrace and in intimate ways she'd never dreamt of, she could not. He thought it was because of a dead husband when it was simply the conscience within her finally speaking.

'May I speak with you?' he asked when she did not greet him.

Saraid stood and nodded, inviting him to the table in the centre of the room.

'Walk with me?' he asked. 'To the bench?'

She followed him outside and around the cottage to Jamie's work area. The bench gave them some privacy, but was in plain sight of anyone walking the lane there. He stepped aside and waited for her to sit. Clenching her hands together, she knew she must say something about her behaviour.

'I would ask your pardon for the other day,' she said softly, not able to meet his gaze as she spoke. 'I did a terrible thing and you did not deserve such a thing.'

He frowned, his brows gathering close, and his eyes darkened as he studied her. 'A terrible thing?'

'Aye.' She nodded, watching some leaves moving around near her feet in the breezes. 'I…led you to believe that…I…led you on…' His hand, gently lifting her chin, stopped her words and forced her to look up at him.

'Do not lie to me, Saraid,' he whispered. 'Just answer me this—did you want to lie with me?' She hesitated for several long moments before replying.

'Aye.'

'You wanted me to make love to you, did you not?' he asked. Not letting her look away, he continued. 'You wanted me and offered yourself to me in that way.' He sat at her side then, leaning down towards her. 'Then why did you stop?'

She wanted to deny his words and to protest his declaration, but she could not make her sins even worse by doing that now. She had kept the lies alive and added to them that day. Now, the weight of all of them pressed down on her and she wanted nothing more than to scream out the truth.

She loved him.

She wanted him.

She wanted to stay with him.

Letting out a sigh, she reached out and caressed his cheek before adding more lies to her ever-growing pile. The strange thing was that her answer to this was not a falsehood at all. She could never be with him.

'Fear. Fear stopped me.'

He cupped her hand against him and tilted his head to gaze into her eyes then. 'Tell me what you fear, Saraid. Tell me how I can rid you of it.'

'There is nothing to be done, Alan. I cannot remain here. I cannot be with you.'

Alan stood then and pulled free of her touch. It was better to have some distance between them for it made it less likely that she would fall into his embrace and give in to the longing she felt for him. Still, she mourned it.

'I think I began falling in love with you that first time I saw you in the hall. Standing with Clara and speaking to Jamie and the others. I sensed a kindred soul within you even then and have found so many things about us that make us companionable.' He paused then and stared at her. 'Tell me, I pray you, why you must leave behind any chance for us? Tell me what you fear, what haunts you so that you must flee to a convent.'

How easy it would be to pour out her story to him now. To tell him that she'd felt the same magical connection to him even in those first moments. To beg him to make this all right for them. But her mother's words echoed in her thoughts, her heart and soul then.

Loyalty. Honour. Courage.

The first two were about him—he was honourable and loyal and he would be forced to turn her over to his uncle if he knew her identity. The third was for her—she must have the courage to stay with the plan her mother had begun to save her from exactly that.

'I do not flee to the convent, Alan. I go there willingly to seek a place away from the world in prayer.'

She'd expected him to argue with her. Even to yell out his anger. But, when he nodded and walked away in silence, she was stunned. He'd taken several paces towards the road when he abruptly came back and took hold of her shoulders, pulling her to her feet in front of him.

He stole her breath and her thoughts with a searing, possessive kiss, slanting his lips over hers and thrusting his tongue deep into her mouth. As quickly as it had begun, he ended it, tearing his mouth from hers and releasing her.

'I leave in the morn to see to something for The Mackintosh. If you have need of anything while I am away, seek him out. You can trust him and Arabella, even if you cannot trust me.'

When she would have argued his words, he turned and disappeared down the road towards the keep. Sorcha dropped back on to the bench, out of breath and confused. She wanted nothing more than to trust him. But that would place him in an impossible situation and give him no choices over his actions.

Her cousin returned some hours later to find her still sitting there on the bench, staring off down the road. Sorcha blamed it on exhaustion and a sleepless night—another lie added to her ever-increasing roster of them. If she wanted to press for more, Clara gave no sign. Instead, she took Sorcha inside and made tea for her that would aid her in sleeping.

By the time Sorcha had risen the next day, the sun was halfway across the morning sky and most of the tasks the two of them accomplished by midday were done. Over the next few days, she found herself hoping for his return. Hoping that he would grab her from behind and kiss her. Hoping that he would sit next to her at table when the lady began her questions. Wishing that his voice would interrupt her walk from keep to village.

None of that happened for he was gone. Though no one spoke of his specific task for The Mackintosh, the lady let one detail slip when Sorcha mentioned his absence.

He'd gone south on some business for The Mackintosh. South.

Knowing her days here were at an end, Sorcha understood that she would need help to get to Skye now. She could wait or delay no more. When she met with Father Diarmid for prayers that day, she asked if he would arrange a private meeting with Brodie Mackintosh. By the day's end, she stood before the laird and lady's chamber, knowing that everything would be different when she left here later.

As she knocked and lifted the latch when beckoned, she left the widow Saraid MacPherson behind and stepped into the chamber as Lady Sorcha MacMillan once more.

Chapter Sixteen

Sorcha walked before the laird and lady with her head held high and the confidence of the young woman she'd been raised to be. Though The Mackintosh's titles were more elevated than her own father's and though Lady Mackintosh was the daughter of a chieftain, their position in the scheme of things was similar enough that she need not curtsy to them. But, she did. From the way their eyes widened in surprise, she knew they noticed the difference in her demeanour and understood what it meant.

That she'd been an impostor in their midst.

Not for a moment did Sorcha fool herself into thinking they'd been convinced of her disguise. The lady's recent and relentless questioning under the guise of casual conversation at meals revealed her suspicions. And Brodie Mackintosh did not reach and retain his position over a mighty clan and federation by missing the details or believing the false trails before him.

'I wondered when the truth would out,' Brodie said quietly.

'I would like to make a bargain with you and the lady,' she said.

Her plan was to offer the knowledge she had about her father and The Cameron in exchange for their help—not only for her escape, but also to protect Alan. Then and only then would she reveal her identity. His next words destroyed all that.

'What, Lady Sorcha, could we offer to a dead woman?'

Courage, her mother whispered in her heart. Sorcha kept her gaze on the chieftain while answering his question.

''Tis more about what a dead woman could offer you, Laird Mackintosh.'

He blinked then and let out a loud laugh, as she and his wife watched and waited. Lady Arabella studied her in silence, but Sorcha kenned the woman missed little even if she did not say so.

'And that would be…?'

'Knowledge of a grave weakness in your alliance with several clans.'

'Certain knowledge or rumours and innuendos?'

He stood then and walked to her, looking down from his great height for a moment. No doubt he wanted the difference in their size and power to intimidate her. The problem for him was that she kenned him to be an honourable man, one trusted by Alan and everyone living here. Brodie Mackintosh would never use his size and strength against a woman. But, she must never underestimate his power or his intelligence. Try as she might, she was not as calm as she was attempting to be. Sorcha entwined her fingers to keep them from trembling.

'I was witness to several conversations in which specific arrangements were discussed, certain promises made and bargains sealed.' The epithet that The Mackintosh hissed out made her and Lady Arabella wince.

Her father never dreamt a woman would plot against him, certainly not his wife or daughter who lived in fear of his every word and deed. Hugh MacMillan paid no heed to the words she and her mother overhead in his talks with Gilbert Cameron for Sorcha's marriage to the chieftain. He'd never worried over a mere woman listening in on the treasonous negotiations that led to an agreement of support and marriage of his daughter.

Sorcha noticed that the lady paled now as betrayal was mentioned and wondered if it was her delicate condition or her family connection to the one whom Sorcha was about to implicate in a plan against her husband.

'My lady, do you wish to hear this in…your condition?' Sorcha asked, trying to be mindful that Arabella had extended every kindness and welcome to her during these last weeks. When Arabella sat up a bit straighter, Sorcha wondered if her words were misconstrued. 'I mean no insult, lady. I have long been accustomed to the truth of my father's nature, but I do not presume to ken your knowledge of your uncle's.'

'And I hold no pretences about Gilbert Cameron,' the lady said. 'Let us be frank amongst ourselves since you have come with an offer of information.'

'And a demand for a bargain, Bella. Forget not that part of it,' The Mackintosh said.

The lady rose then and walked to her husband's side, touching his arm as if to draw him back. Their gazes met and Sorcha could not help but long for such a look from a strong man such as this one. Her heart stung then as she realised Alan had looked at her with the same expression of love in his eyes…just before she sent him away. A tear trickled down her cheek and she wiped it away quickly, hoping they'd not seen it. She could not take the risk of appearing weak now.

'A woman is wise to bargain when she has the power to do so, Brodie. You ken that as I do. Come, let us sit and discuss this quandary and the threat to our families.'

The chieftain stepped aside now and walked with his wife to an alcove where several chairs sat. After the lady sat down, he nodded to Sorcha who did the same. Only then did he sit. Thoughts and words raced through her mind as she attempted to find the right place to begin her plea. Instead, her curiosity won out.

'How long have you kenned?' she asked, looking at him. He did not pretend not to understand her question.

'I suspected when my wife began asking her questions. Her suspicions are usually well grounded, but I ken more of my family's connections than she does.' His wife sputtered at his words, but he laid his hand over hers to ease her insult. 'When I thought on the connections between the MacPhersons and the Mac-Neills, I remembered my father's cousin Erca who would be known to Clara. Then there was your letter to your cousin in the convent…'

Sorcha gasped as he unveiled the extent of his knowledge. She'd placed both her mother's cousins in a terrible place of being exposed to this man.

'You opened my letter?'

'Aye.' No apology, no explanation, would come from

this chieftain. The lady's expression confirmed that she'd read it as well.

'My lord, I pray you not to hold Clara responsible for my transgressions. She felt the duty owed to kin and I...'

'Worry not on that, Sorcha,' the man said with a shrug. 'I do not begrudge her helping you. But I am interested in what brought you to my village and to her door.'

'Pure happenstance and accident,' she admitted. 'None of this was supposed to happen. If everything had gone according to the plan my mother made—'

'Life rarely follows plans,' Arabella whispered.

'What did your mother have in mind? Why the convent?' he asked quietly.

Sorcha did not miss the importance of his question, for it would bring up kith and kin and expose many secrets. She realised she must not reveal everything until she had Brodie's agreement to her terms. She would help him protect his clan if he helped her protect... Alan.

'You *must* promise me first,' she said.

'Although my wife thinks otherwise, lady, you actually have little power right now in this. Now that you have confirmed your identity, there is nothing to stop me from contacting your father and your betrothed with the happy news of your survival. They would both be beholden to me for my aid to you in your time of need.'

Her first reaction was purely physical—her stomach roiled and threatened to heave up its contents. Then, her body urged her to run, to run fast and far, to run now. Tremors shook their way through her as she fought for control. She could not allow everything to be ruined now, not when she understood she must walk away from the man she loved in order to protect him. This was too important for him. She cleared her throat and placed both hands flat on the table before her in an attempt to calm herself.

'Unlike my father and unlike the lady's uncle, you are a man of honour, Brodie Mackintosh. Alan told me I could trust you and I will.' The two exchanged some glance, one that seemed to say she'd confirmed something they suspected. 'And, if you send the news that I am alive, they will simply wait and find another way to break the treaty and destroy all you hold dear.'

He made a sound like an exhalation but it carried in it some acceptance of her words. At his nod, she continued.

'My mother and I kenned I would have to disappear and not be found. There were not many options in that regard and the convent seemed the best place for me.' She paused and took a breath. She must be controlled. She must leave her emotions out of this for now. 'I confess no true vocation, but a life of quiet contemplation is not unappealing.'

Now it was the lady's turn to let out a protesting breath. Her husband gave a visible squeeze to her hand that he yet held under his.

'I did not mean to show up here and involve you. I meant to make my way to Skye and enter the convent and no one would ever hear the name Sorcha MacMillan again.' She shook her head at how wrongly things had gone. 'My mother chose a friend to help me escape. Actually I kenned nothing of her plans until he arrived that night at my tent to take me away. I followed him, making our way through the storm and to the west. When he died, I had no choice but to seek help from kin.'

She stopped then, not certain what else he wanted to hear from her. Glancing from one to the other, she waited.

'And the bargain you wish me to make in exchange for the knowledge and details you hold?' he asked.

'A simple one—help me disappear. Aid me in getting to the convent and I will provide you with the information you need to ensure the safety of your people.'

'And you do not think that knowing what I ken now is enough for me to do that? Now that I am aware of the threat—'

'There are always suspicions and nebulous threats between any and every clan in the kingdom, my lord,' she interrupted. From his surprised expression, he was neither used to being interrupted nor had expected it from her. 'All I'm asking is an escort to Skye.'

'What about Alan?' the lady asked softly.

'Lady?' she replied.

Plainly put, all of this centred on him. Sorcha needed to get away before he returned with the truth. For now, though, it was all speculation. As long as he did not bring back someone who actually could identify her, she could deny it all.

''Tis ironic somehow that you should end up in the same place and in love with the man so linked to your *death* and your escape.' Sorcha could feel herself blanch at the words. 'And the one man who could seek out the truth of both matters.'

'I cannot put him in the position of choosing his honour over me, my lady. If he kens the truth, he has no choice but to tell my father and his uncle. 'Tis why I must leave before he returns.'

Now, their gazes at her softened, as though her admission had eased whatever their concern was. Sorcha had decided, in those long nights of contemplation before coming here, that she would not deny her feelings for Alan to them.

'And you give him no choice in this matter? No chance to make his own decision after finding out the truth of you?' The Mackintosh asked.

Courage, her mother's voice whispered once more.

'I am a coward, my lord. I cannot face him after the lies.' Sorcha looked away, staring at the window on the wall there so she did not have to see the expression of disappointment at her admission.

'Your actions say otherwise, lady,' he said, drawing her attention back. 'I ken a few, a very small number of, well-born women who would be able to survive as you have, first with your father and then on your own, using your wits to make it from day to day.'

She noticed he tightened his hold on his lady's hand then and the tears that spilt down Arabella's cheek at his words that were high praise indeed. Then, he lifted his wife's hand to his lips and kissed it with a reverence that nearly undid her last vestige of control.

'I suspect that he will continue his search for you if he finds you gone when he arrives,' he said as he stood once more. 'But I agree to your bargain, my lady. With a few modifications.'

'What changes?'

'The first place he will seek you out will be on Skye, so I will send you to kin of mine in the north. After he gives up on his search, then I will see that you are escorted to your chosen convent.'

It made sense. If Alan felt towards her as she did for him, he would not meet the news of her departure well and would try to find her. Especially with the unanswered questions she kenned he would have. A man like Alan did not give up easily once his interest was roused.

'Very well,' she said.

The Mackintosh retrieved cups and a jug and filled one for each of them. He sat back down and waited for her to do the same. The time for reckoning had come.

It took some time to reveal her knowledge and to answer the dozens and dozens of questions that the laird and lady asked. At first, she thought that Arabella did not believe her words about her uncle's plans, but it soon became clear to Sorcha that the lady had a full understanding of her kin.

When a servant knocked on the chamber's door summoning the laird below-stairs, Sorcha was exhausted and empty. As he left to see to the matter, Brodie Mackintosh turned and faced her once more.

'I cannot order you to wait for him, but the lad deserves to hear the truth from your lips, just as you should hear his from him.'

He was gone before she could reply. His words, not the ones about staying but those about Alan's truths, struck her. With their conversations and hearing about him from the lady and from Clara and Jamie, Sorcha felt that she knew him well. Only now did she think how there must be reasons for his estrangement from his family, his almost-exile by his uncle, and those things in his character or life that drove him to search for all manner of things and people lost. She turned to face Arabella Cameron.

'You understand why it can be never be more between us, do you not, lady?' Surely the woman of breeding and experience understood her dilemma. 'So many would pay a price for my actions. He would be in an impossible situation.'

'Sometimes, Sorcha, I think it best to let a man decide his own fate.'

'I cannot stay here and risk recognition when The Cameron comes to pay a visit. Or, God forbid, my father comes here.' Sorcha shook her head. 'We both know that as close kin to the chieftain, Alan cannot marry at will. 'Twill do us no good to continue with any hope that there is a way for us to be together, lady.'

The tears would not stay then, so Sorcha stood and curtsied. She needed to leave.

'I pray you to send word when your husband has made arrangements. I would like to leave as soon as possible.'

She stumbled out the door even as the lady called her name, grabbing on to the railing on the wall to make her way down the stairs. Without looking left or right or pausing, she made her way out of the keep and out of the gates. Caring not for her destination, she walked and walked and walked, somehow ending up this time in front of Clara's cottage. Lucky for her, since Alan was not there to search and find her if she got lost now.

A messenger from Brodie came the next day and told her to prepare to leave Glenlui in two days' time. Even though she kenned she must, Sorcha understood that she would be leaving a part of herself behind in this village. A piece of her heart and her soul would remain with Alan Cameron for ever even if she could not.

As she bade farewell to Clara and Jamie, even the words that gave her comfort and strength did not work. But loyalty, honour and courage were all she had left in her life, for she left her love behind with the people who had helped her so much in her need.

And with the one man who could never be in her life again.

Chapter Seventeen

Alan cursed the weather, his stupidity, his fate and various other things for the hundredth time that day. The sun had long ago hidden itself behind the thick, swirling clouds and Alan suspected his luck as a tracker had run out days ago. It mattered not now, for he'd discovered what he'd set out to find and was on his journey back to Glenlui.

Somehow, Sorcha MacMillan, the only daughter of Hugh MacMillan of Knapdale, had not died that night in the storm. She'd not been washed away in the torrential rains. She'd not died in the rushing river and had not been dragged along for miles in its storm-swollen rage. Indeed, Sorcha MacMillan had been spirited away by a man, led west towards Skye only to find herself alone and lost.

He laughed then, bitterly, as he remembered his words to her on another stormy night. She need not worry about being lost, he would find her. Instead, this ill-begotten plan of a dead woman had led Sorcha straight to him and he'd never seen her coming. He'd never realised their connection because why would he search for a dead woman?

Rubbing his hand over his face, he pushed his wet hair out of his eyes and then tugged his plaid back up into place. Alan was lucky the road had not washed out in this area where the river flowed into the loch. It would take another day of riding to get to the Mackintosh village. Then what, he had no idea.

Taking refuge in a thicket of trees, he saw to his horse and ate some of the last of his supplies before seeking the driest place he could find. Alan wrapped the extra plaid around him and leaned against a tree to sleep.

His search had taken longer and taken him further south than he'd expected. Although some details were still missing, he had no doubt that the widow Saraid MacPherson was Lady Sorcha MacMillan. When he tracked her path backwards from Glenlui, he recognised details he'd missed before. Hell. Once convinced the girl was dead, he'd overlooked signs the likes of which he hadn't missed since his first days tracking.

Brodie would have a fine laugh at this failure of his. But, kenning the Mackintosh chieftain, Alan did not doubt that the man suspected more than he'd let on to him.

As the night passed, the anticipation grew in him at the thought of taking the truth back to her. His uncle's betrothed. The woman he loved. He laughed then and the horse snickered in reply. Now that he knew who she was, her actions and words made more sense to him.

She had not been fearful in his arms because she missed a dead husband—the distress in her expression and in her body's reactions was a virgin's natural reticence at her first experience. She had not been distraught over her husband's death, but over her mother's and her protector's. She had not refused him because she did not want him, but because she was to be his uncle's wife.

Sorcha was trying to prevent him from making a grave error, one that could have serious consequences if anyone discovered her true identity and her connection to this uncle. She'd understood the gravity of the situation and tried to protect him from himself.

So, now what? What was his next step in this? He loved her. He wanted her. But his honour demanded that he tell his uncle of her existence and give her up to him. His body reacted immediately at such a thought.

Never. Never would he give another innocent into his uncle's rough and deadly care. And never would he walk away from the woman he loved.

But what were his choices?

Sorcha, if he believed her words, was intent on avoiding the matter by entering the convent. That part of her story and her plan matched the truths he'd discovered all his journey. He'd tracked down her mother's companion and long-time servant who, after fainting in shock at the news that Sorcha was alive, was happy to speak of her lady and her desire before passing away to help her daughter escape the same fate she'd had.

Apparently, his uncle's reputation had made it to Knapdale. Alan smiled grimly at that for, with the power of his position and the wealth he controlled, Gilbert Cameron would never have a problem finding another man willing to sell off his daughter or sister for the amount of gold he could offer and the alliances he could promise.

The winds quieted over the next hours as he turned this over and over in his thoughts. Gradually the rains ceased once the clouds thinned. Though exhausted from the hard riding of the day, Alan found that his thoughts would not quiet enough to allow him to sleep.

What would her reaction be when he returned on the morrow? Had she guessed why he'd left? Did she fear him now? Would her gold-flecked eyes fill with dread at his approach? Dear God, he prayed not! He wanted to see the frank desire there that he'd glimpsed when she'd told him that he could have his way with her.

Considering her reaction now, and the tightness he'd found, Alan could not figure out how he'd missed all the signs that he was not dealing with a married and widowed woman, but a noble-born virgin.

Love.

He would blame it on love. And on his pride, too, for he'd convinced himself of her death and no matter his hesitation or doubt in the signs he'd found. He was so desperate to keep the young woman out of his uncle's control that he'd done the one thing he warned others about doing—overlooked his process and the warning in his gut.

By the time the sun rose into a calm, clear sky, Alan was no closer to sorting out his possibilities or in deciding what he thought Sorcha would do. Would she insist on leaving? If she agreed to stay with him, where would they go? If he denounced his uncle without proof, it would ruin his honour amongst most of his kith and kin.

Since Sorcha was the one who could prove Gilbert's guilt in planning to act against the clan's interests for his own, Alan would never ask her to do so. For that would put her in Gilbert's power if Alan did not succeed or if Alan died in his efforts to unseat his uncle.

Alan had no doubt that Brodie would stand by him and welcome him, but Alan's presence could cause problems that rippled out to other alliances and put the truce in jeopardy. Another consequence to his actions.

So, did they leave together and make their way to another place? Assume new names to avoid the trouble that would follow Alan Cameron, disgraced nephew to The Cameron? The worst part was the worry over how his parents and younger brothers would bear this. He did not have to guess how his uncle would treat them over this, he'd already seen the disdain and disrespect borne by his father for years.

How much more could his father withstand?

In the final few hours of his journey into the mountains south of Loch Arkaig, Alan felt gratitude in a strange way to the lass who'd tried to keep this from him. Sorcha, daughter to a chieftain, understood the consequences of choices considered and choices made and she'd clearly tried to keep him from having to make this one. He now thought that her reason for doing that was the same one that was making him question his next moves…love.

Though he wanted to enter Brodie's domain with his decision certain, he approached the road to Glenlui with no such frame of mind. Nay, he would speak to Sorcha first and seek Brodie's counsel before taking any action. He must not allow his temper to choose his path this time. No matter the rage he felt when he thought of Sorcha being his uncle's bride. No matter when he remembered Agneis's sad words about her coming marriage to his uncle and the results of that.

Though late in the evening when he arrived, late enough that the gates were closed for the night, Alan rode straight to Clara and Jamie's cottage. Having a care to be quiet and not wake the bairns, he knocked softly on the door and waited. He could hear Jamie's path through the darkened chamber within and smiled when his friend opened the door to him.

'I am sorry for the late hour, Jamie,' he said, glancing past his friend to see if Sorcha was there. 'I would speak with *Saraid*, if you could wake her.'

Jamie shrugged and shook his head in one motion. He pulled the door open wide enough for Alan to see only Clara there. A very sick and burning feeling began in the pit of his stomach at their expressions. He kenned he was not going to like whatever words they had to say.

'She is not here,' Clara whispered over her husband's shoulder.

'Where is she?' he asked.

'She left two days ago,' Jamie said. 'Brodie's man brought a message to her and she was gone a few hours later.'

'The convent on Skye? Is that where she went?' That was her goal from the first time he'd met her. Had Brodie arranged for her travel there?

'She did not say,' Clara answered. 'She said her farewells and was gone. She did promise to write when she was settled, but said that would be some time so not to worry.'

'Alan,' Jamie began, stepping between him and

Clara. 'Come, let us talk outside. Clara, I will see to this.'

For the first time in a long time of watching them, Clara did not argue or naysay her husband. Instead, she nodded at Alan and closed the door behind Jamie as he walked outside. They walked around to the smithy and Jamie turned to face him—the truth in his friend's eyes.

'You kenned the truth, did you not?'

'Aye.'

Torn between anger and his own stupidity, Alan realised he could not be truly angry because Jamie had been protecting Sorcha—even from him.

'From the beginning? Even when I spoke to you of Sorcha MacMillan?' He was trying to sort through the way it had happened. Jamie motioned to the bench and they sat down.

'I only kenned she was kin to Clara when she arrived. But Clara told me the rest of it once she learned it from her cousin.' Jamie leaned back against the tree and narrowed his gaze. 'Was I wrong to take her in? Wrong to keep her secret?'

Alan thought on his friend's question. Would he have done anything differently? Would he have turned away a helpless young woman in her hour of need—no matter who it had been?'

'Nay, not wrong,' he admitted.

'She had planned to be here only days, but was in such a state that Clara convinced her to stay longer. To give herself time to recover from her ordeal and to contemplate what she would do.' Jamie shrugged. 'I thought that she might stay once things…well, once you two began circling each other.'

'You never thought to tell me?'

'If I thought she was a danger to you or to our people, I would have spoken. You made it clear to me that your uncle and her father had moved on and her death was over and done.' Jamie reached over and slapped Alan on his shoulder then.

'Your uncle is a right bastard. She escaped the fate that she would face as his wife. Why would I ruin that for her?'

'Honour? Loyalty?' Alan spoke the words that most haunted him now.

'Ah, but I have no loyalty to your uncle. And my honour is not in question,' Jamie replied. 'If I'd thought there was a danger to my clan, I would have brought it to Brodie's attention. Which is unnecessary now since he clearly kens and is aiding Sorcha.'

Alan stood and paced a few strides away and back, thinking on Jamie's words. His friend spoke first.

'When you mentioned her, you were more upset by your uncle's plans to marry again. You were tormenting yourself over the same things you always do and allowing him to control you and your future. Does this, does kenning this young woman's identity, that she escaped him and is now gone from your life, change any of that?'

At that moment, Alan had no answer for his friend. First, he must find Sorcha and speak to her. Offer himself and his own secrets to her as he should have done before. Offer his heart and see if she would accept him.

'You have my gratitude for protecting when I could not or was too stupid to realise the need for it.'

He turned and walked away then, knowing that only Brodie could tell him where she was. He knew The

Mackintosh well enough to ken that Skye and any convent on it would be the last place to which he'd send her. And the chieftain had learned much since that time years ago when Alan had found his camp in the mountains. He kenned how to cover his trail better than anyone Alan could think of.

Without his help, Alan would spend weeks and possibly months going in circles and getting nowhere. And no one in this area, save for his uncle, would dare to help him if Brodie had not given permission to do so. Again, something Alan should have noticed.

It took some persuading for the guards to allow him entrance after the gates had been closed. If this was a usual night, Alan would spend it somewhere in the village and wait until morning. But there was nothing usual about this night or his quest to find and claim the woman he loved. Now that he'd made up his mind to do that, he would brook no more delays.

If Brodie was surprised by his arrival at his chamber door, he did not show it. He stepped out into the corridor there and pulled the door closed behind him.

'Bella needs her rest,' he said softly in explanation. 'She is not carrying easily this time.' His cousin Bella had been blessed with three children, but she'd lost several others. So this time in her pregnancy was always a concern to Brodie, who cared not who might ken it.

Alan walked with him down to the lower floor and to that small chamber off the kitchens where he conducted his business. Once the door was closed, he waited for Brodie to speak first. The infuriating man met his gaze without flinching or speaking. Alan chose a different topic.

'Is she well?' he asked. There had been similar signs in the pregnancies that ended sadly for them.

'She said it feels different to her this time,' Brodie said, thrusting his hands into his hair and shrugging. 'Sick, but not that way. I pray God…' His words drifted off.

'So do I, my friend. So do I,' Alan added.

Nothing was more dangerous for a woman than carrying and giving birth and Bella had braved it many times to give her husband his heir and other bairns. Alan walked to a side table where a jug sat and poured some of the ale in the cups there. Handing one to Brodie, he asked the question that bothered him the most.

'When did you figure it all out?' he asked.

'Before you did, but not much sooner,' Brodie admitted.

'So, where is she? Jamie said your men took her away two days ago.' Brodie snorted then and drank some ale before answering.

'The lady asked for my help and I gave it,' he said. 'My men escorted her, they did not take her.'

'Where, Brodie? Just tell me where she is.'

Brodie did not answer right away and Alan was not certain if he was making Alan wait or deciding whether or not to tell him at all. The laird drank the rest of his ale and put the cup on the table. Crossing his arms over his chest, Brodie glared at Alan.

'The lady is intent on entering the convent,' he began. 'But Bella convinced her that she should speak to you first. That leaving the world behind when so many lies and half-truths lie between you is not the right state of mind or grace to enter such a place.' Alan would be grateful to Bella for yet another thing now, but he begrudged her not. 'You may thank my wife for her soft heart later.'

Within an hour, Alan was on his way to the secluded cottage at the edge of Glenlui village where Sorcha waited.

Chapter Eighteen

Sorcha grew restless. With a thick, woollen blanket wrapped around her shoulders to keep out the chill of the night air, she wandered around the perimeter of the chamber. Every sound outside the cottage seemed to startle her, but then she *was* waiting and listening for his approach.

She'd agreed to remain here until Alan returned and to speak to him at Arabella's behest and against her own judgement. After leaving Clara's, she'd been brought here to this cottage on the far side of the village, near the drovers' road. Away from everyone, it gave her the chance to calm her thoughts and prepare for the journey and life ahead.

Though her first stay would be in a village much further north, in the heart of the lands controlled by the Chattan Confederation outside the royal burgh of Inbhir Nis, she hoped that Alan would not follow her once they'd had a chance to speak. If he relented, then she could travel to Skye as she'd planned much sooner than the time needed to wait him out. Sorcha needed to convince him, if her dishonesty had not already, that there was no way they could be together.

The cleaner and sooner she broke from this life and moved on, the better she would feel. This way, agreeing to meet with him, was certain to lead to more tears and heartache but she owed him that much.

How could she bear the look of disappointment when he looked at her knowing how deceitful she'd been? When he discovered how she'd lied and run away rather than facing her duty as the daughter of a nobleman. When he'd professed his love and she'd let him, nay pushed him to, walk away.

It was for the best, but what man wanted to hear that from a woman? Especially from a woman who'd lied with every breath she took and word she spoke? He'd always seemed reasonable, slow to anger yet capable of fighting his own battles. She prayed the reasonable man was the one who came to her door.

With little to do while waiting, she'd spent her time walking in the area around the cottage and reading the books that Arabella had allowed her to borrow. It was a joy to meet a woman so well educated and well read as Lady Mackintosh. And, though the lady was quite strong-minded, she did not overstep, even when Sorcha made a decision different from the one Arabella wished her to make.

Two days she'd waited for him. Two days was the length of time she'd told the laird and lady she'd wait before setting off north. Now, as night had fallen and she'd prepared for bed, Sorcha found herself unable to sleep. Why had he not come? Brodie was quite exact in his estimate of Alan's return, as though this was something he had experienced many times.

Then, a noise caught her attention and she turned to find Alan there before her. So lost in her thoughts had she been that she had not heard him enter.

He looked exhausted and haunted. He looked angry and determined. He looked…wonderful to her. His boots and breeches were muddied from travelling and his long hair was pulled back away from his face, exposing the masculine lines and angles. A short growth of beard covered his jaw and gave him a dangerous appeal. She began to reach out to stroke his cheek, but stopped herself. Surely he would not welcome her touch until he'd said what he came here to say.

'Sorcha,' he whispered into the space between them. Hearing her own name spoken by his deep voice sent chills through her. 'Sorcha MacMillan.'

A strange tension grew within her, making her skin prickle and her heart race. Part of her wanted to deny it, to say he was wrong, but the dark expression in his eyes told her he kenned the whole truth of her and denying it would do her no good. Part of her wanted to finally embrace her identity to someone, to him.

'Aye.'

That one word freed her. Freed her from the guilt of needing to lie to him. Freed her to be herself. He took three long strides and stood before her, staring at her mouth, her eyes and her hair.

'I never noticed the similarities in your eyes and his,' he said. 'Oh, not the colour exactly, but the shape of them. Or your height. He'd even pointed out that you were only this tall…' Alan pointed to the place on his chest where her head reached when she stood close to him. 'I just never put it together, thinking you, Sorcha, were dead.'

It was he who reached out and touched her then, sliding his hand along her cheek and then into her hair that lay unbound around her shoulders. He lifted several strands and let them curl around his fingers.

'Anna said your colouring is your mother's mark.'

'You spoke to Anna?' she asked, her spirits rose. 'Is she well?'

'Once she recovered from fainting at the news, aye, she is well.'

She took a deep breath and met his gaze then. Now, instead of the anger and exhaustion, she felt only desire and a need she could not identify there.

'Alan,' she whispered. 'I lied about so many things to you.'

'Did you lie when you told me you wanted me?' He lifted her chin up and kissed her lips quickly. 'Did you lie about that, Sorcha MacMillan?' She could feel the heat of his breath on her face and his fingers tangled more in her hair, holding her close.

'Nay, Alan Cameron. I spoke the truth about wanting you.' She could not move or breathe then. Her body ached and felt as though she would die if he did not touch her soon.

'And I spoke the truth about loving you, Sorcha.'

Tears gathered at his declaration. It made her leaving so much harder, but his words could not make her stay. They changed nothing for them, but it made one thing very clear to her.

'I must leave in the morn, but I want to spend this night in your arms, Alan. Give me this night, I pray you.'

He stilled and searched her face, a glimmer of hope in his gaze then. She did not tell him otherwise, for she

wanted this night with him so she had it to remember
for ever. Alan looked as though he would argue for a
moment before nodding his answer.

'Aye, Sorcha. I want this night,' he whispered
against her mouth before he took it.

In spite of the calm and quiet manner in which he'd
entered the cottage, all of that disappeared as he tasted
her then. His tongue sought entrance and she opened
to him. His hands slid up behind her head and he held
her tightly to him, slanting his face and kissing her over
and over again. She grabbed on to his arms to keep herself standing and felt the blanket slip off her shoulders.

The bedgown she wore was thin and provided little cover. The chill air made her shiver. Or mayhap it
was his kisses that did that? Soon his hands released
her hair and moved down over her shoulders, along
her back until he cupped her bottom and pulled her up
and to him. Sorcha gasped as their bodies touched, her
soft curves against his hard, muscled thighs and chest.

With little effort, he carried her so across the cottage
to the pallet in the corner. Kneeling, he let her down
on to the bed and followed her, pushing himself into
the cradle of her thighs, against the place that ached
the most for his touch. She watched as he leaned back,
releasing his hold on her and tugging the belt that held
his plaid in place free, then tossing it away. His plaid
and then his shirt were next and she watched as every
inch of his sculpted chest was exposed to her.

Her body heated and, without hesitation this time,
she reached up and outlined the edges of those muscles.
He shivered then and she felt powerful when she realised she'd caused that reaction in him. She flattened
her palms against his hot skin and caressed him, from

his chest down towards his waist, watching his eyes close and hearing the shallow breaths he exhaled. She hadn't known she'd laughed aloud until he opened his eyes and spoke.

'Enjoy your power now, for you will soon be under my touch.'

The passionate words promised something that she did not fear. Indeed she wanted to feel the rush of desire and wanting race through her as it had before at his intimate touch. But, she took his words as an invitation to do as she would. And she did.

Sitting up, she reached out and loosened the laces at his waist. He inhaled sharply and held his breath as she slipped her hands inside the border of his breeches and tugged them down. Every inch of his body was more beautiful than the last. Her fingers touched the curly hair below his waist, but that did not stop her.

Bolder now and ready to claim what she wanted, Sorcha moved her hand deeper until she felt his hard flesh against her palm. Encircling the thick rod of him with her fingers, she watched as he gasped at every movement of her fingers over him. He aided her access by shoving his breeches down further and she watched as his erect flesh sprang free of the clothing.

Sorcha stopped then and stared at it, at him. This part of him would be inside of her soon, deep in a private place and changing her for ever. How it would happen, she could only guess.

'Do not lose courage now, lass,' he whispered. 'Learn me.' He leaned closer and kissed her, plunging his tongue inside her mouth. As he would his flesh into hers soon. 'Touch me, Sorcha. Touch me.'

He knelt there before her, exposed, rampant, wanting her to touch him. So she did. Without his breeches to block her, she used both hands to explore him. She'd seen a man's privy parts before, but did not expect them to feel as they did under her hands. Hard. Hot. Smooth. Throbbing in her grasp.

Every touch, every sensation of her fingers on him echoed in her own body and she found herself panting as he did as she cupped her hands and held him in her palms. He moaned as she stroked up and around the length and width of him. Her breasts grew tight and her own flesh throbbed as she learned him. When a small bead of moisture gathered at the opening at the top of his flesh, she leaned over to look more closely at it. She was wet between her legs and this seemed his body's reaction.

Another moan echoed in the silence around them as he guided her hands to capture him and to stroke up and down in quicker movements. He thrust then, his hips pushing forward and bringing him even closer to her face. What would it be like to kiss him there?

'Nay, lass,' he whispered in a ragged voice. 'Have some pity on me.'

Sorcha did not ken exactly what he meant by that, but she drew back and instead slid her hands down over his strong thighs, enjoying the way he tensed under her palms. The differences between their bodies fascinated her and she moved her hands around until she could touch his buttocks. Again his hips thrust forward as she massaged and stroked his firm muscles there. Was there no part of him that was not hard and muscular?

He'd held himself in check, barely, but now he needed to touch her and explore her body as thoroughly as she did his. Alan eased back out of her grasp and leaned back on his heels.

'Take off your gown and lie back, love,' he urged.

Alan saw the momentary hesitation as she heard his words. He wanted to see every inch of her. He wanted to touch and taste every part of her body before he finally let himself find satisfaction. He saw the tiniest glimmer of fear in her gaze when she saw and felt his size, knowing he would join with her by putting that part into her body. Now, he wanted to show her such pleasure that it would wipe out any fear between them.

She gathered the length of the bedgown in her hands and tugged it up over her head. The movement brought her breasts, her lovely, pink-tipped breasts, up and out, begging to be touched. Whether she'd pulled her legs closed on purpose or not, she presented him with the most perfect pose as she tossed her gown off the pallet.

Her hair flowed around her, cascading down and swirling over her breasts and her hips. As she moved, the lengthy curls did, too, teasing him and gifting him with enticing peeks at her creamy flesh. If she thought it gave her some measure of protection from his gaze, she was wrong. He reached out and caressed her ankles, easing them apart so he could crawl up between her legs. As he did that, she leaned back until she lay spread before him like a virgin sacrifice to the ancient gods.

But she was his virgin. His to take. His to love.

His cock grew even harder as he watched her slide her hips down on the pallet. His fingers itched to touch the soft curls now before him. Alan reached out and stroked the inside of her legs, watching as she trembled with each inch he moved closer to those curls. He caressed gently, up and up and up, stopping just before he touched them. Her body arched each time as though trying to make him finally reach his goal. Now, she pulled her knees up and her legs fell wide enough that he could see the glistening flesh there, plump and wet and aroused for him.

But he wanted her ready for him when he would enter her, to ease whatever pain there might be in their joining. The last time he had rushed his caresses to the most sensitive flesh but now, knowing she was untouched but for him, he would take his time and pleasure her before that last intimacy.

'Sorcha,' he said, sliding back so he could lean down between her legs. 'Look at me.' She lifted her head and stared at him with glazed eyes. 'Do not look away.'

She nodded and he dipped his mouth to kiss the inside of her thigh. Sorcha gasped and her legs fell open more. Alan followed with more kisses, open-mouthed, suckling kisses that moved ever closer to his goal. He never took his gaze from hers as he reached the curls there and placed his mouth right on the plump and heated flesh. She moaned and began to close her eyes.

'Watch me, Sorcha,' he said. When her gaze was back on his, he slid his hands under and around her thighs, pulling her against his mouth and spreading her even wider. 'Feel this. Feel me tasting you.'

He licked in long strokes, parting the folds with the tip of his tongue. Her body blossomed beneath his mouth, swelling and growing wet until he lapped at her essence. He felt the moment when she lost herself to the pleasure, falling back and gasping over and over, no longer able to keep her focus on him.

Alan laughed and felt it reverberate through her as

he relentlessly pushed her on to more pleasure. Her body arched against his mouth, accepting his tongue as it dived inside her woman's channel. Tight. She was so very tight and he kenned he was the first to touch her here. He reached his hands over her legs and stroked her there, teasing her with lips and tongue and teeth as he touched her and found her own little, hard bit of flesh waiting for him. She grabbed his hair then and her body bucked against him.

'Easy now, love,' he urged. 'Can you feel it?' He licked in a long stroke from her core to that bud. 'Something inside you is pulling tight.' Another finger plunged in to join the first one deep inside her flesh. 'Let me show you where it is.' He rubbed against the sensitive place within her core and was rewarded by a keening sound she moaned out. 'Do you feel it there, Sorcha?' He moved his hand, adding a third finger, and she screamed out. 'Rub against me now, love. Feel me inside you…here…and here.'

Alan moved then, his hand pressing deep within her, until he could kiss her breasts. Now she was completely enthralled, matching the rhythm he'd set with his fingers with her hips, arching and relaxing, faster and faster until he felt everything within her release. The tips of her breasts tightened against his mouth even as her flesh within her throbbed, spasms tightening her inner channel around his fingers.

He could not help but smile as he watched her reach her peak. For several minutes, her body responded and shuddered against his hand, pouring the moisture that would ease his way on to his fingers. Then he knew the moment when she went limp, when her satisfaction filled her and her body relented. As he eased his hold on her and eased back on to his heels again, he nearly came at the sight of her then.

Like the famed goddess of love, she lay open and glistening before him, her body relaxed in that way that complete satisfaction causes. Her hair lay around her, pooled in places that made him ache to touch and outlining her curves in a silken cloud. Her quick and shallow breathing slowed and became even. Alan waited for her to open her eyes, confident that he had brought her to pleasure for the first time in her life.

'Alan?' she whispered as she met his gaze. Her hips shook then as another pulse of pleasure raced through her, an aftershock of sorts to what she'd already felt. 'What happened?'

'That was pleasure, my love,' he said, easing to her side and gathering her close.

'Are we done then? she asked. 'I thought you had to…' She glanced at his still-rampant flesh before she looked back at him.

'Nay, we can have pleasure without joining.'

'Oh,' she said, her well-kissed lips forming the perfect shape that would haunt his dreams for ever. He pictured those luscious lips around the head of his cock and his hips flexed against her, letting her know he was not done yet. 'Oh,' she repeated.

'Not done at all.'

'When will we…?'

Taking her question as an invitation, he began to show her how pleasure could be shared again and again. And that there was so much more to show her.

Chapter Nineteen

If he'd given any indication that he was surprised or ashamed of the way her body became a thing unknown to her, the soft chuckle that he uttered then dispelled her fear that she had acted unseemly. She'd waited for him to enter her until he drove her mad with pleasure and wanting. He seemed to know what he wanted for his touch was exact and with purpose.

She lay there feeling as satisfied as when she ate too much at the Christmastide feast. But this was fullness and satiation of a different kind. One that made her feel as though she could do this again and again and still want it…again. All it took was his hand sliding along her hip towards her breasts to make her body want more.

'Will you put it inside me now?' she asked. Even knowing about the pain to come, Sorcha forgot as the magic of his touch roused her body once more.

'Aye.'

His hand cupped her breast and lifted it so his mouth could cover its tip. He suckled it and gently bit the nipple, before drawing it out from between his teeth.

When the tip slid out, she moaned at the exquisite sensation of pleasure that was almost pain. Would he do that again? Would he put his mouth on her flesh and do that again?

'When, Alan? When?'

She could barely form words to speak her wants and her need as her body arched then. Her legs moved in some restless pattern against his as he took her other breast in his mouth and did the same thing. An unearthly sound escaped from her, for words would not form for her then. He laughed at her and she kenned in her heart that he was enjoying what he did to her and her reaction to him.

'Soon,' he promised, putting his hand against her mound and pressing there.

It both eased and worsened the ache deep inside and all she could do was let her body respond. As one finger slid within the sensitive folds between her legs, she arched against his hand. She wanted him there. She wanted him to bring that pleasure, that ache, that need, back. Sorcha needed to make him hurry, so she reached out and took hold of his hardness.

He laughed then, thrusting against her palm. Her mouth watered then and she wondered what that part of him would taste like. But when she pushed herself up, he covered her body with his and lay between her splayed legs. Now, his erect flesh was against her and, when she lifted her hips, it slipped along her cleft. She could feel the wide head of it touch there. Need and desire took over then and she begged him. She wanted him there. She wanted him inside. She wanted him…

'Now, Alan,' she urged, grabbing on to his buttocks so he could not move away. 'Fill me.'

All it took was a slight shift in his hips and he pushed himself inside of her. His hardness slid within her softness, pressing and then stretching her until it was almost too much for her.

Almost.

Then he eased back a scant inch before pushing further. She gasped at the feeling of it. Just when the burning would begin, he would ease back and begin again. His expression was intense above her as he found a pace that left her gasping and moaning. Filling her, then leaving, thrusting deeper before withdrawing, every stroke of his flesh easing his way back in.

An overwhelming sensation raced through her body then. Invaded, aye. Filled, aye. Stretched, aye. But it was not enough. She wanted more. She wanted something. His soft words, more promise than threat, were the only warning she got before he moved.

'Now, love. Now.'

He guided her legs up and around his hips and began thrusting faster and faster. No pausing now, he led her into a primitive rhythm of giving and taking, of full and empty, of need and want. Her body rose to meet his, taking him in so deep he touched her womb. His flesh grew with each stroke until she could not take more of him. Sorcha needed to tell him to stop, but her body opened for him, allowing him in even more.

She could not breathe. She could not think. She wanted to scream as everything within her came loose and shattered around him. Alan threw his head back and groaned loudly as she felt his seed spill inside her. Over and over, more and again, he stroked her deep and hard until every hot drop had been milked from him by the tightening spasms of her flesh. Sorcha lost herself then, giving up to the overwhelming pleasure, as Alan collapsed on her, tucking his head against her neck and breathing heavily.

'Done,' she thought she heard him whisper against her skin.

It took some time before either of them could breathe or speak.

Completely awed by what had happened, Sorcha lay without moving and waited for him to rouse. This feeling, this satisfaction, was bone-deep and permeated her body and soul. She did not want it to be over. She did not want it to go away. It was then, when he moved ever so slightly, that she realised he was still inside her.

She winced at the discomfort there until he slid his flesh out of her. Then she wished he had not. She was empty in a place she'd never kenned was there. But now, she wanted him back inside. She was about to ask him if that was possible, when he lifted his head and stared at her.

'Did I hurt you, lass?' he asked. 'I ken I was rougher than I should have been with it being your first time.' When he began to sit up, she clutched at his shoulders.

'I pray you, do not leave yet.' She feared that once away from her, he would never return. That the night would be over and she would have this emptiness inside her for the rest of her life.

He settled back down and eased to his side, holding her against him as he drew a blanket over them. Cocooned with him, Sorcha leaned her head against his chest and kissed him there. She could feel his heart beat against her mouth and savoured this closeness for she kenned well it would not and could not last.

'You did not answer my question, Sorcha. Did I hurt you?'

She smiled against his skin and shook her head. She'd heard about the pain a woman suffered on her first time with a man, but none of that came close in describing what she'd felt.

'You did not,' she said. She let out a sigh and he began stroking her back under the blanket. 'It was… quite pleasant.' She swore that he growled as he turned her on her back and climbed over her.

'Then I did something wrong,' he said. A kiss followed that robbed her of her ability to think. How could he do that? 'Pleasant?'

Sorcha would have offered him words to soothe his displeasure over her description, but one kiss led to a caress and to a stroking and then touching and then… well, then to another joining that was so slow and gentle she cried softly when it was finished. They seemed to be one body, breathing in and out together, as their flesh became one.

It might have been an hour after that before she could speak. But talk she kenned they must, so Sorcha forced herself out of his embrace while he slept to sit on the pallet near him. Collecting her bedgown, she folded it and placed it in a satchel that sat by the hearth. She took out a shift and gown and stockings and dressed while listening to him snore softly. It made her smile, but tears followed when she realised she would never hear this sound again.

She would never feel his touch on her skin and become one with him when he entered her body in such an incredible way. It was a sin, what they had done, but she found it difficult to come up with the proper amount of guilt she should feel at something so…sublime. Wiping the tears from her eyes and cheeks with the back of her sleeve, she sat and watched him sleep for a short while.

The rays of a watery sun began to pierce the darkness of night and Sorcha understood that her time here and with him was done. Her courage fled her then and she was tempted to leave before he woke.

'You look as though the weight of the whole world is on your lovely shoulders.' He was awake and watching her. 'Your lovely and overly dressed shoulders. Come back to bed.' His invitation was issued in a voice that was husky with arousal. One she could see when he rolled to his back.

'I must go, Alan.' Plain. Simple. Direct.

'What do you mean?' he asked, pushing the blanket back and standing. 'You cannot leave now. We will seek a life together elsewhere. My uncle will never ken that you survived.'

'I make no claim on you because of what we shared,' she whispered. Though she felt as though they had branded each other by touch and caress and kiss, there could be no more than that and the memories she would carry with her for the rest of her days.

He cursed then, an angry and bitter tirade of words that told her so much about him. Not one word was about her. Not one word condemned her or what they'd done. All of it about his uncle. Interesting. She let him finish before even attempting to speak. Though her father could never be approached when his fury rose for fear of life and limb, Sorcha felt no such danger here now.

'Would you cause war and destruction between your clan and Brodie's, then? When your uncle discovers the truth of my existence and our involvement—as you ken he will—do you think he will ignore it and ignore the insult?'

Alan glared at her then, pushing his hair out of his face and trying to sort through the words he should say now that he'd got the worst out first. Damn it all to hell!

Waking this morn should have been a joyful one with her in his arms and another bout of bedplay when he could bring her pleasure and show his love for her. Then they would plan their future and begin a life together. Instead, she was intent on walking away from him.

'We can find a way through this together, Sorcha,' he said. 'Brodie will support me, support us, in this.'

'Which will put him in conflict, open conflict, with your uncle as well as other clans in our extended families.'

Why did she have to sound so calm and reasonable when he wanted to rage against the fates and anyone else who had a hand in this?

'I will find a way to prove his betrayal of the Camerons. The proof that he is negotiating with other clans to form an alliance that will destroy the Mackintoshes.'

She paled at his words and he knew now what he'd suspected before—she was the proof. Sorcha MacMillan kenned the why and the when and how his uncle and her father would move against Brodie. And Alan understood that he was not willing to draw her into the battle between him and his uncle. Gilbert Cameron must stand or fall without Sorcha being in danger.

'Now I think you understand why there is no choice in this, Alan,' she said. 'Too many lives rest on our actions. I cannot risk those who have helped me or given me shelter.' Sorcha walked to him and took his hand. Placing it against her cheek, she rubbed her face against his palm. 'Or ask the man I love to give up all he is and can be when that would destroy him.'

'Damn it, Sorcha,' he said, moving back. Even though he loathed the distance between them, he must not let it grow. 'We will find a way.'

His words rang hollow and wrong even to him. Alan simply did not want to face losing her completely and for ever. Losing her and allowing his uncle to win… again.

''Tis better this way,' she whispered.

The sound of footsteps outside drew his attention. He grabbed his sword and pushed her behind him. But he realised from her calm manner that she was not surprised to hear them. He lifted the latch and looked outside. Rob and a small group of men stood there.

'Rob, what is this?'

'Lady, if you are ready,' Rob called to her instead of answering Alan's question. Alan slammed the door, tossed his sword aside and met her gaze.

'They are my escort from Brodie.'

'Taking you to the convent?' He could not stop the bitterness in his voice as he faced her leaving.

'Soon.'

She walked to him and he took her by the shoulders and dragged her to him, kissing her as though it was

their last. Because, no matter how much he would protest or fight it, this was the last time for them.

'I beg you not to follow me, Alan. Let me go.'

He felt his soul tearing in two as he could only nod
at her. How could he deny her anything? But how could
he let her walk away? She did just that, though, lifting a leather satchel from the floor, opening the door
and walking out of his life. She spoke just before she
closed the door.

'I will pray every day of my life that you will find it
in your heart to forgive me. For lying. For loving you
when I had no right to do so.'

And she *was* gone.

The door closed almost silently as she pulled it and
he wanted to howl like the wounded animal he was at
her departure. Only when he heard the movement of
horses outside did he act—pulling his shirt on and running outside before she left.

Rob and Magnus, one of the biggest men he'd ever
seen, stood there blocking his path. Along with four
other warriors he kenned were Rob's best men, they
formed a wall that kept him from going after her.
Something dark roused within him and he flung himself at the men, asking for a fight, a fight they gave
him. Later, as they tossed him up on his horse to take
him back to Drumlui Keep as they'd been ordered to
do, Alan was honest enough with himself to accept that
they had not given him their best fight.

No matter that for it still took him two days before
he could piss without seeing blood. His jaw was swollen, forcing him to drink his food for two days past
that. Everyone in Drumlui Keep and Glenlui village

steered a wide path around him, giving him both the silence and the time he needed to think.

Not follow her?

There was no chance of that. He had told her that he could find her and he would. No matter where Brodie sent her and no matter how long it took, he would claim her as his and his alone.

But first, he had to deal with his uncle and make certain no one else would suffer because of his self-serving treachery. As though waiting for this moment his whole life, Alan understood that, at long last, it would come down to him and his uncle.

And only one would be left alive.

A week and three days after Sorcha left him, Alan left Glenlui for what he thought would be the last time and went off to settle things with Gilbert Cameron.

Chapter Twenty

Alan was not rash or ill tempered. He did not rush forward in a task without a plan, without a process. For this one, he took his time and thought long about how to first approach and then challenge his uncle. To run in and throw allegations in his face would end exactly as Alan had always feared it would—with his death and his parents disgraced and exiled.

So, to battle a man such as Gilbert Cameron he must be deliberate and prepared. He must have evidence and he must somehow make Gilbert confess his plan before witnesses. He had already tracked down enough of the story to ken the whole of it and Alan would reveal it bit by bit, goading Gilbert's temper and waiting for him to play his part in his own downfall.

The most difficult thing would be not involving Sorcha—not by word or whisper. Her name must remain out of it or her safety would be threatened. Her life would be at risk. A thing he simply would not risk. For if he failed and left a trail to her, his uncle would destroy her as surely as he lived and breathed.

Brodie did not approach him or offer counsel during

those days. He showed up in the yard when Alan was training and fought him with sword and staff and targe, teaching him without saying a word. Brodie moved in a different way in the training yard than most others Alan had observed over time. He had gained his knowledge through battle so Alan tried to absorb as much as he could.

For Gilbert Cameron had learned his skills in battle, too.

But it was Gilbert who gave him the perfect opportunity for his plan when he summoned Alan back to Achnacarry the next week. Clan business, the messenger said, which was the way Gilbert ensured Alan would not ignore his call. This time, though, Alan was pleased to be beckoned home. Pleased to finally take this step and claim his life as his own and free his clan from Gilbert's treachery.

The messenger's words gave a day and time of the gathering—four days hence—but Alan would not wait for his uncle to get his pieces and pawns in place and walk in to find himself the only one not ready for this game. He packed and left that night, bidding Brodie and Arabella a private farewell before he walked out of the keep alone, into the dark.

He kenned his uncle had spies there in Glenlui, probably as many as Brodie had at Achnacarry, so he made it appear as though he was going to the village when he left. No horse, no supplies, no weapons. Those waited for him at the cottage where he'd spent that glorious night with Sorcha. He would retrieve them under cover of night and be hours away by morn. That would give him the opportunity to examine and study Achnacarry and its approaches and to see more of Gilbert's plan before walking into it.

It was part of him, this process of tracking. He'd begun when barely out of childhood for it gave him something to concentrate on during the dark days of the clan feud with the Mackintoshes. Then, it made him feel important and valued to the Camerons even while being a vital service to his uncle, the then chieftain Euan Cameron. Arabella's father had led them through the last battles and seized the opportunity to seek a lasting peace and end to the mutual destruction of both families.

Once Alan's reputation as a tracker was in place, he used those skills to take him far and wide, out of Cameron lands, even all the way to Edinburgh and the Lowlands. And though Gilbert had sent him out to help other chieftains or allies of his, it gave Alan a chance to be away from his uncle who was now in the chieftain's seat at Achnacarry.

A chance to avoid watching his father be belittled and harassed by a younger brother unworthy of the position he held. A chance to ignore the thinly disguised contempt his uncle had for him. A chance to pretend his life was as he wanted it. Now, in spite of his father's hesitation to act, for some reason known only to him, Alan would.

He arrived in the middle of the night two days before the time the messenger gave him and hid himself in the thick forest that surrounded the castle near Loch Arkaig. And he sat back and watched and waited to learn the true intent of Gilbert Cameron's plan for him.

* * *

Sorcha stared at the note in her hand once more. Reading it for the first or for the twenty-fifth time made no difference to her understanding of it. It was not that she could not read its meaning, but rather that she could not believe the information there and what it meant.

He goes to our uncle.

The message came from Arabella, though the man did not say her name as he handed the small piece of folded parchment to her. Though Brodie had assured Sorcha that no one else but he kenned her location, she did not doubt for a moment that his wife could wheedle any secret she wanted out of him. Or discover it on her own.

The piece of parchment proved that. Sorcha thanked the man and asked him to wait for a reply. When he'd left, she collapsed into a chair and began to tremble.

Picking up the bad habit that Rob was known for, she whispered out the harshest words she could think of in the moment. Nothing close to what she'd heard uttered by that man or even Alan or Brodie, but it made her feel better for a short time. Glancing at the message again, she closed her eyes and tried to come up with a reply.

She had brought this about. She had caused Alan to go and confront his uncle about the plans the chieftain and her father had made. With no proof, he would be, at best, laughed out of his clan or, at worst, executed as a outlaw. Cold chills pierced her body and soul at the thought of his death.

Sorcha had been convinced that her leaving solved

everything. She would disappear and no more thought would be given to the still-dead Lady Sorcha MacMillan. No one would link her to Alan or Brodie or think anything about the distant relation to the late Erca MacNeill who bought her way into the prayer community in the north-west of Skye.

Life would be as her mother had planned—she would be free of her father and his machinations and live out a quiet life. Of course, Erca MacNeill never dreamt that her daughter would meet a man along that path and fall in love with him. Erca never considered the many flaws in her plan, but then, her mother was sick and dying when she'd concocted this. Her only hope was to save her daughter from a life like the one she'd suffered through.

So, running away and walking away had not worked. People she loved and cared about were still in danger. The man she loved would face his own demise because of his desire to prevent his uncle from ruining another life and trading the security of his clan for his own aims.

Loyalty. Honour. Courage.

Sometimes she wanted to curse her mother for teaching her those values. For instilling in her the belief that those traits were just as important in a woman as in a man. For giving her the desire to live those qualities in memory of all her mother had sacrificed to see her free.

More so, she wanted to be a woman of loyalty and honour and courage.

Putting the note into the flame of the candle on the table, Sorcha watched it burn. Then she sought the leather satchel in the trunk and packed her clothing

into it. Pulling open the chamber's door, she waited
for the man to approach.

'I will take my answer back to the lady myself.'

He sputtered a bit, clearly unprepared for such a
thing, but he did not argue it. The man must be used
to serving Arabella Cameron for he did not try to dissuade her from her decision. Instead, he stepped back
and directed her out of the cottage and to the yard
where the horses were kept.

Within an hour of receiving the note, she was on the
road south and back to Glenlui.

Two days later, she walked into the lady's solar and
curtsied to Arabella. Though the lady seemed to expect
her arrival, the laird did not. Sorcha forced herself not
to take a step back when he rose, growling his displeasure. It was not Sorcha's name he spoke, but his wife's.

'Bella!' he yelled out, as he faced her. 'Why must
you meddle in everything?' Sorcha swore the costly
glass panels in the windows of the chamber rattled at
the intensity and fury of his voice.

Sorcha watched as a silent battle raged between
these two strong people. Both of them loved the other
without bounds and it made them even stronger together than separately. If he thought to convince her
not to go to Alan by his behaviour with his wife, he
would fail. For, in spite of the ear-shattering loudness
of his words, she needed only to look at the love that
was visible there between them to know her choice
was the correct one.

'She has the right to know what he's doing, Brodie,'
Arabella said in a calm, soft voice that was the perfect

counterpoint to his angry, boisterous one. 'This is her battle, too.' The bluster drained from him in an instant and he nodded, first to his wife and then to her.

'I do not like you being involved. The worrying is not good for you or the bairn,' he said as he reached out and took hold of her hand. As he kissed her there, Sorcha tried to ignore the whispered words of love and concern she could not help but hear.

'The bairn will take hold or not, my love. 'Tis the Almighty's plan, not yours nor mine,' Arabella said in a resolute tone. 'But He will find me lacking if I stood by and allowed our cousin to face his enemy without friends at his side and our love at his back.'

'Must you make so much sense, Bella?' he asked, clearly hating the answer he already kenned. 'There is one thing, Wife.' The chieftain who was used to commanding hundreds of men and loyal kith and kin faced a far stronger foe here than any of them presented. 'You will remain here.'

Sorcha watched as Arabella struggled with this order from her husband. When she capitulated quickly, Sorcha understood the seriousness of her condition and the danger she faced. The lady feared for the bairn she was trying to carry.

'Promise me you will stand by him, Brodie.' It was not a question, but an order of her own that brooked no refusal. 'No matter what.'

Brodie did not answer her demand directly, but did by dismissing Sorcha from the chamber.

'We leave at first light,' he said through clenched teeth. 'The servant will take you to a chamber and see to your needs.'

'I will be ready, my lord,' she said. Then she turned and left the two alone in their chamber as they wished to be.

The storms that greeted her at dawn somehow seemed appropriate. As they rode from Drumlui Keep, she watched the way the clouds swirled in greys and blues above their heads, promising rain and reminding her of Alan's eyes.

Brodie waited for the young woman to leave before facing his beloved. He should have kenned what she would do. It was not the first time she'd overstepped and overrode his orders and he was as certain that it would not be the last time.

'I wish you had told me, Bella,' he said, pulling her to her feet and wrapping his arms around her. Things felt better, felt right, when he could feel her against him and listen to her breathing.

'You would have warned me not to interfere and I would have interfered.' He kissed her lovely mouth at the truth she told.

'So you thought to skip those steps and get us right into the thick of it then?'

'Sorcha has the right—'

'Sorcha MacMillan is dead!' he said sharply, releasing when Bella pushed against his hold. ''Twould be better for her to remain that way. For all concerned.'

'You would let Alan face down that bastard without her?' Bella asked, staring at him. 'Come now, Brodie. You do not allow your men into battle without their weapons.'

'Battle is the key here, my love. For more than the

last ten years, there have been none between our families or in this area that we control. All of that will change when Alan accuses Gilbert of his crimes.'

'Then you ken him to be guilty?'

'Certainly he is that. I had suspicions of it long before that lady stepped foot into my village or hall. Gilbert has been dealing behind our backs since before he took the high seat. Indeed, even in how he took it over instead of Robert. But that does not mean this will not lead us back into the depths of the feud.'

She shuddered then and Brodie took her back into his embrace. Nuzzling her hair, he inhaled the scent of her and knew he would do whatever was necessary to keep her and their loved ones safe. Even if it included standing by a young man who had no idea what he was walking into and the young woman who loved him.

'All will be well, Bella. I swear it to you.'

He did not leave her side until he slid silently and carefully from their bed the next morn. Brodie did not doubt that she was awake and aware he was leaving. But it was not her way to make a situation worse by speaking of dangers or more. They had faced everything together and he had no doubt there was more left for them to do.

Still, it did not lighten his spirits when he mounted his horse and saw her staring at him from their chamber. He nodded at her, confirming everything he'd said to her in that one gesture. He gathered the reins in one hand and motioned for their group of warriors and a woman to follow.

But he could not fight the need to take one more look at his wife as they rode through the gates.

Chapter Twenty-One

Tensions were high in the great hall as the low and the high of Clan Cameron gathered there at their chieftain's command. The sick feeling in his gut told Alan he kenned what brought them there, but he hoped and prayed that was not the reason. Would another young woman be sacrificed to appease Gilbert's insatiable need for more?

Not if Alan had anything to do with it…and he planned to have something to say on the matter if, when, it arose. Glancing around, he saw his parents and brothers enter then. The same expression of surprise lay on his father's face when he caught sight of Alan there. Alan made his way through those present and kissed his mother on her cheeks before greeting his father and brothers.

It had been nigh to a year since he'd seen either of them. Young Robbie, who looked like a younger version of their father, had been living with the powerful MacLerie Clan, already betrothed to the chieftain's second daughter. Tomas, younger still, was being fostered with their mother's brother, laird of the MacSorley clan in the south.

'You were summoned as well?' he asked once they'd got wine and were waiting for Gilbert to arrive.

'This cannot be good,' his father warned. 'You two, be on your guard and stay with your mother,' he ordered the younger boys.

'Father,' Alan said. 'I must speak with you now. Before this goes any further.' Alan had already witnessed the arrival of a young woman who was being kept in a private chamber until Gilbert made his announcement. 'Come.'

His father said something to his mother before following Alan out into the corridor. Alan strode up the stairs, heading for Gilbert's chamber, kenning there was little time left to him.

'What are you doing, Alan?' his father asked as they turned the last corner and approached the chamber.

''Tis time for me to do what I should have done long ago, Father.' His father grabbed his arm and pulled him to stop.

'Why, Alan? Why now and why you?' he asked. 'Have you thought this through?'

'I have done nothing but think on this matter and the time has come for our family to choose a path. I found proof of his treachery and his plans against the truce—'

'Have you, now?'

Alan and his father turned to discover Gilbert and the council of elders standing there listening. His uncle crossed his arms over his chest and lifted his chin at them.

'And where did you find this proof?'

Many of elders fidgeted and shifted on their feet.

Alan knew that they were not unified behind Gilbert's leadership, but none would speak out first or be openly supportive of one who brought a claim as he did now.

'You do not deny that you plot against the treaty with the Mackintoshes and Chattan Confederation?'

Murmurs and questions rippled through the growing crowd. Many of those who'd been below stairs came to see what was happening there and watched now. Even his mother and brothers had followed the crowd and stood there listening.

'The treaty has outlived its usefulness,' his uncle claimed. 'I have been looking into our options and opportunities.'

Alan walked towards his uncle, leaving his father a few paces behind him. Gilbert's smirk spoke of his confidence in this matter. Certainly he would be confident if he kenned that the only witness was a dead woman.

'Opportunities that benefit you while destroying more of our kith and kin,' Alan challenged. 'The peace has been good for all of us.'

'Peace is for weak men,' Gilbert snarled out the words. 'Like my brother and like you.' He shook his head at them. 'Weaklings who would seek the favour of our enemies and allow the Camerons to be thought of as followers instead of the leaders we are.'

Gilbert strode towards him and Alan waited for him.

'Weaklings who take the dregs left by other men and are not worthy of being called a Cameron.' His father lunged past him and grabbed at Gilbert then, surprising everyone including Alan.

'You bastard,' his father yelled as he threw a punch at his brother's jaw. 'I supported you all these years.'

Alan watched as his father was thrown back by his uncle. Confused by their exchange, he pulled his father to his feet.

'Camerons do not betray their own,' Alan said quietly then. 'Camerons do what is best for the clan and we expect our chieftains to uphold that.'

'Are you challenging me, boy? You? Are you certain you wish to let him do this, Brother?' his uncle yelled. When a few of his closest allies tried to calm him, he pushed them away and nodded at Alan. 'This is about that whore I married, is it not? The one you thought was in love with you and chose me instead?'

Alan understood his uncle's aim—to break his concentration and make him doubt his purpose. Hearing Agneis spoken of like that disturbed him, but it would not change his mind. He had to keep himself under control or he would lose this before it began.

'You wanted her, but she left you the moment I showed interest in her and called her to my bed,' his uncle boasted. 'Why settle for a worthless boy when she could have a man? A chieftain with the power of life and death.'

'And you killed her!' Alan called out to him. 'Used your fists like she was a beast of burden instead of your wife.'

His uncle's reaction to that was to laugh. Stunned silence filled the corridor as Gilbert laughed loud and hard. Even Alan could not fathom the cause of it.

'It is about her. She tried to tell me my rights and my duty. I showed her what hers was. Even a stupid beast could learn the lesson sooner than she did.'

His sword was in his hand before he thought of

drawing it. The gasps and outrage spiralled around those watching.

'You would challenge me over that dead piece of arse?' his uncle asked. Now, his voice was cold and controlled, as he was. 'Or do you think you should be chieftain instead of me? That is it, is it not? You want to take the seat from me—for your spineless father? Nay, for yourself? Think again, bastard, if you think you can take it from me.'

'I will stop you from killing any more women whose only sin is to find themselves in your control, Uncle.' He shifted the hilt of the sword in his hand, finding its comfortable place, and grasped it strongly.

'Uncle?' Gilbert asked, mockingly. 'Robbie, have you not told the boy the truth? He has no place here other than what I give him, like the stray mutt he is. He has no right to challenge me—'

'We have an agreement, Gilbert,' his father said in a quiet voice.

Though not loud, the import of it carried across the area and drew all the attention. Alan glanced at him and then his mother and saw the shame and dread in both their expressions. When she tried to push his brothers behind her, Alan kenned it would be bad.

'An agreement? Oh, aye, we did. But I warned you that I would end it if you did not bring him to heel.'

A sick feeling rose in the pit of his stomach and Alan looked to his father for some explanation. Let him speak it before Gilbert did. But his uncle began laughing again and the sound of it made Alan's blood run cold in his veins.

'Gilbert.' There was sadness and shame and a plea

all in one name, but his father's mistake was in thinking that there was some mercy in this man.

'You should hate the Mackintoshes more than I do, boy. Robbie and I came upon three of them having their way with his betrothed. During one of the last battles. Three Mackintosh warriors, fresh from the fight, found her and took her. Used her right there in the road. Killed her maid and her guard while she watched.'

Everything around him stopped in that moment.

Was he saying that…? One glance at his mother's pallor told him it was true. She had been raped. Violated by three men. And he was the product of that attack.

'I see you understand now. You are nothing more than a mongrel Mackintosh bastard, raised by a man too soft and weak to put her aside as he should have. No man who takes a soiled woman like that in marriage was worthy to be chieftain.'

No one spoke. No one seemed to breathe or move.

'And no one will accept you because you carry no Cameron blood at all in your veins. My brother knew it and took the shame in exchange for his place as my steward.'

His uncle laughed again and a nervous titter ran through those listening to the shocking disclosures.

'He took whatever I would give him in exchange for me allowing you and your soiled mother to live with among us. 'Twould have been better if we'd put you both down the day we found her in the road, covered in her own blood and their seed.'

It made everything so clear to him. Every slight against his parents, every mean and crude gesture, every insult and demeaning action—they all made sense now. Though he was horrified to learn of his mother's past and to hear her exposed before everyone she kenned, it lightened his heart and gave him new purpose.

He was not beholden to this man. He was not related to him and held no oath of loyalty to him. He was not honour bound to uphold his commands. In good conscience, in good faith, for those who had died meaningless deaths at the hands of Gilbert Cameron and for those betrayed by his actions, Alan was freed from any constraints now.

'Mayhap you should have, Gilbert,' he said quietly as he rolled on the balls of his feet to get his balance. 'But you may have another chance to do that right now.'

'You have no standing here. You are the bastard of some nameless Mackintosh warriors who we killed when we found them over her,' Gilbert said, pointing at his mother then. 'And you have no proof with which to accuse me of anything.'

'He may not, but I do.'

A voice he never thought to hear again whispered across those gathered. The crowd parted to allow her through. Sorcha MacMillan walked to confront Gilbert Cameron with his crimes.

Dressed in the fine raiment of a lady of high standing, she nearly glowed. Jewels on her hands and at her neck. Costly gown and tunic. Her hair had been arranged in swirls around her head before the length of it cascaded down her back, the fine golden chains woven through it sparkling in the light of the candles around the chamber.

'You cannot be here,' Gilbert yelled. 'You are…you

are…dead.' He lost all the colour in his face and wobbled unsteadily on his feet at the sight of her.

'I would be if I had not escaped.'

'Who are you?' Alan's father asked.

'This is Lady Sorcha MacMillan,' Brodie said as he stepped to her side. Spread out behind him were the same Mackintosh men he'd faced that morning when she left him. 'She has some things to say that you all might find interesting. Especially you, Colum, and you, Duncan.' He'd spoken the names of two of his unc—two of Gilbert's most trusted cronies. 'Your days are numbered in his plans as well.'

'No woman will ever betray me,' The Cameron said, grabbing a sword from the nearest guard and running at Sorcha.

Alan was too far and Brodie was unarmed and under truce. He screamed out her name and watched as Gilbert lifted the sword to strike her.

'Nay, Brother, you will not!'

The man who'd raised him as his beloved son stepped in front of her, sword raised and held, and protected her from the death blow. Two years older and just as skilled, he pushed back against Gilbert's frenzied attack on her as Brodie pulled her to safety.

Now, it was up to Alan.

Whatever he'd expected this moment to feel like, this was not it. Instead of anger and fury filling him, a cold calmness flowed through him. This man who had struck down his friend Agneis and who tried to kill the woman he loved just now must die. For shaming his mother before all there. For all the innocents who'd died at his hands and all of their kith and kin who would fall in his vainglorious attempts to destroy the Mackintoshes, Alan would strike him down. Gilbert regained his footing and faced Alan.

'Come then, mutt,' he goaded Alan. 'If you think you can…'

Alan did not wait for the taunt, he attacked. He took the man on his own terms, determined not to let him set the pace or path of this fight. But he did not fool himself that he would win other than by wearing the older man down and killing him.

The crowds moved back, giving them room to move, and Alan became a relentless force against the man. Some cheered for one or the other, but Alan ceased noticing anything but his quarry. When Gilbert moved to the left, Alan spun and met his blow. When he feinted right, Alan struck with the strength of his sword. He kept the man moving, pushing, kicking and shoving with his elbow and body to tire him out.

With grim determination, he used every move that Brodie had taught him and he could tell from his lack of counterattacks that Gilbert was not expecting them. Alan could not help the smile that lifted his mouth then. He would defeat this man who would bring dishonour and death to everyone about whom Alan cared.

When Gilbert's laboured breathing signalled that the contest was nearing an end, Alan did not play or draw it out any longer. With a kick, he crushed the man's knee, sending him to the floor. Hardly winded himself, he shoved The Cameron sharply on to his back and pressed his sword to the man's neck.

But before he ended this miserable cur's life, he looked to those who mattered most to him in the room. To make certain they knew, no matter the outcome for him, they mattered. His mother. His father. His brothers.

Sorcha.

She met his gaze unflinchingly and a slight smile lifted the curve of her lips. He kenned what those lips felt like on his skin and against his mouth. He smiled back.

When Brodie placed his hand on her arm, telling Alan she would be protected no matter what happened, Alan looked down at the man under his sword.

'Burn in hell.'

He leaned his weight down and thrust the blade through the place where a man's heart should be. A gasp and then a long hiss of breath escaping was the last sound the man made before dying. The silence erupted then, with screaming and yelling as Gilbert Cameron died before them. Releasing the hilt of his sword, he left it in place for all to see.

'Take him.'

Alan did not know who called the order, but he found himself grabbed by many hands and dragged down the corridor. He would face the consequences of this act, but he would never regret ending the man's life and his reign of terror. Never.

And, even if Sorcha could never be his, she would not be Gilbert's either. She was safe, Brodie would see to that and no one would naysay The Mackintosh in that. Alan did not fight back and found himself not harmed as they locked him in a small chamber along the hallway there.

Some time passed with many people rushing along the corridor past the chamber. He heard bits and pieces, names whispered and yelled, as the commotion raged there. Well, he had killed their chieftain, so he expected that there would be confusion and questions about who would lead them. He was not certain if his actions would speak to his father's fate. Or the man he would always call father.

Alan was standing by the door when it opened. Of all those who it could have been, she was not the one he expected.

'Alan,' his mother cried as she rushed to him. 'Are you injured?' She began rubbing her hands over him, seeking any wounds.

'Nay, I am well, Mother.'

The enormity of the things they needed to speak about was crushing and they stood looking at each other for some long moments.

'Mother...'

'Alan...'

He took her in his arms and held her, wishing he kenned the words that would ease the terrible shame and choices she'd faced for him. And now, everyone had heard the tale.

No matter that she had been faithfully married to Robert Cameron and bore him two other legitimate sons. No matter that she had raised the child born of violence and horror with love and caring. No matter that she had suffered such a thing and had to face the scorn of those closest to her. Alan worried that none of those qualities and manners be remembered now and only. Gilbert's shocking words would be.

'Thank you,' he finally whispered. 'I just wish that you did not have to suffer such a thing.

'Robbie gave me the hope I needed,' she said, wiping her eyes as she leaned her head against his chest. 'His love never let me lose heart. He taught me how to love.'

'You must have hated me.' Surely, a woman who'd suffered such an attack and then borne a child from it would have harsh feelings for the result of her shame. And yet… He'd never had a clue of his origins from either her or his father.

'You were mine, Alan. Always first in my heart. And he claimed you before everyone as his. Neither of us ever felt anything but love for you.'

'I would speak to him, to Father, before…'

He did not ken what he faced, but he hoped he would have a chance to make his peace with the man who'd raised him. So much made sense now and he had questions that no one else could answer. But the sound of a number of people approaching the chamber made Alan wonder if his fate was now at hand.

Chapter Twenty-Two

Hours passed and still the questions came. She answered each one as carefully, completely and truthfully as she could. Some of the elders did not want to believe her words. Others nodded at her revelations and knowledge. Brodie remained at her side, watching over the interrogation and asking his own questions when she missed some bit that she'd told him already.

Her back hurt and her head throbbed by the fourth hour. Her voice grew hoarse from talking so much, but if that was what Alan needed to defend his actions and prove The Cameron committed treasonous acts against his clan, she would continue.

'The lady has agreed to remain here to provide you with what you need, but she is exhausted and needs food and time to rest,' Brodie announced then. 'She has travelled many miles for some days to bring her evidence before you.'

'There is a chamber for her,' Colum offered. The man nodded at one of the servants who scurried off to prepare it. 'And the food and drink will be waiting for her there.'

'I would like the chamber next to hers,' Brodie said. 'I have sworn to safeguard her and will not leave her alone until this is done.' She thought him done, and thorough at that, but he had one more condition. 'A serving woman of my choosing will see to her care.'

He'd just accused the Camerons of any number of deficiencies in their hospitality and their manners and insulted them, yet they simply nodded in acceptance.

'Lord Mackintosh?' A tall, young man stepped closer to Brodie then. 'I am Davidh, Malcolm's friend and Ailean's brother.'

'Davidh,' Brodie said, nodding at the man.

'Ailean is here if you would like her to see to the lady.'

Sorcha had heard Eva and Arabella mention the lady's cousin Ailean who had served as her companion for many years before returning to Achnacarry recently to care for her ailing mother.

'Aye, Davidh. That would be fine.' The chieftain nodded.

Within a short time, Sorcha found herself in a comfortable chamber with a very nice companion who had much to discuss with her about Arabella and everyone at Drumlui Keep and in the village. But, tired and in need of rest, she bid the woman a good night and sought the comforts of the rope-strung bed with thick and warm covers.

She'd just fallen asleep when the door opened slightly, throwing the light from the corridor across the chamber. Sitting up, she pushed her hair out of her face and stared at the man standing there.

'Alan?' she whispered, fearing that she was awake and dreaming.

'Aye, 'tis me, Sorcha.' He closed the door quietly and crossed the chamber to her. He leaned against the bed and just looked at her.

He did not look injured in any way. As she'd watched the fight, she thought he'd been punched several times and once she swore that Gilbert's sword sliced through his shirt, drawing blood. But now, he seemed hale and whole as he stared at her.

'How? Why?' He sat on the bed next to her, just watching her.

'How? Brodie, of course. I wonder when the Camerons will realise he is manipulating them the way his bairns play with their toy horses and dolls.' She reached out and touched his hand. 'Why? I could not allow the man I love to die for my honour.'

There was worry in his gaze as he pulled free of her caress and walked away. In silence, Alan stood before the hearth with his hands held out to its warmth. She slipped from under the covers and walked to him, sliding her hands around him and leaning against his strong back. She'd never thought to see him again, let alone be able to touch him. The tension in him was something she could feel beneath the tips of her fingers as they lay on his chest.

'What is it, Alan? Tell me.'

'You heard it all.'

'Heard what?' Then she realised the issue. 'About your parents?'

'All of that. The way my life began.'

She moved to his side and touched the side of his face. When he gazed down at her, she saw the shame there.

'You had no choice in it, Alan.' She stroked his

cheek. 'Your mother is a strong woman to have survived her ordeal and she loves you.'

He smiled then and touched her face.

'She said the same thing about you,' he admitted. 'That you are strong and that you love me.'

'I am not certain about the strong part, but, aye, I do love you.'

He picked her up in his arms then and carried her to the bed. Standing there, he waited.

'What about Brodie?' she asked, knowing the chieftain was sleeping in the next chamber.

'He is in the hall, holding up his reputation against all comers.' She frowned, trying to think of what kind of reputation. 'Chess. He loves a good challenge in the game.'

'So his request for the next chamber was…?'

'Simply a ruse to give us some measure of privacy as we discuss our plans.'

'Our plans? I spoke to Brodie and he said…'

She gasped as he dropped her back on the bed. Turning to face him, she slid up to the pillows. This bed was a luxury considering what she'd slept on over these past weeks and months. From the look in his eyes now, she understood that his plans included more than she'd hoped for. When he tugged his plaid loose and dropped it to the floor, her body responded to what she knew would follow. His shirt and breeches and boots followed and then he climbed up next to her.

Sorcha kenned she should object. That now that her identity was revealed she had no choice in what came next. That she could not make a commitment until she sorted it all out, with Brodie's help and his protection, if needed.

Alan sat without saying a word, as though not completely aroused and ready to join with her. As though she had not noticed this amazing, naked man at her side. As though she would refuse him. But she could play along with whatever ruse this was and make her decisions in the light of day. The next day…or the next one.

'So, tell me of your plans,' she said.

Before he could speak a word, she reached out and touched him. His flesh was hot and hard and the ache deep inside her began immediately. She was too new at this to pretend to be unaffected by his nearness, by the feel of his flesh under her touch. In her hand.

'Brodie suggests that we make our plans quickly.' He spoke as though in pain, but she kenned he liked the way she caressed his length. 'I told him by morning we would be ready.'

'Ready? By morning?' She tried to jest, but could not help laughing. She gave up the pretence. 'Alan, I am ready now.'

He laughed then as he pulled her on top of him and guided her to sit across his legs. She gathered the bedgown up so she could straddle him and moaned as he rubbed along her cleft.

'Aye, love. You are ready,' he said. He pulled her face to his and kissed her, mimicking with his tongue what he would soon do with his flesh. Then, holding her face in his hands, he spoke. 'We have two choices.'

How could he keep speaking rationally? How could she concentrate on his words when one of his hands slipped between her legs, searching for…something. She tossed her head back when he found it, that place where her ache was the strongest, and she rode his hand as he made it worse…or better.

'Two choices?' she asked, her voice deep with arousal as she thought of the myriad of things they'd done before. 'I remember six or seven choices.' Proud of her ability to speak at all as he did those things to her, she lifted her hips and rocked against him, wanting him inside of her.

Now.

'No more talk,' she said, taking his mouth and taking his breath with a searing kiss then.

Alan lifted her up and guided her body down on his shaft. Her breathing stopped as he filled her, inch by inch, until she had him completely within her. In this position, he was deeper than he'd been and she shifted to feel all of him there.

'He will see you to the convent and you can take your vows.'

Her head spun and all thoughts escaped as he moved beneath her, sliding her down until she was sitting on him, riding his body as she would ride a horse. She ignored everything until she found the rhythm that felt the best. Alan moaned as she slid up along his length and back down. With her knees down and his hands under her, she could move faster and faster and feel every inch of his hot, hard flesh between her legs.

He reached up and gathered the length of her curls together, tossing them over her shoulders so that they pooled on his legs behind her. Another moan told her that he liked the feel of her hair on his skin. Then, he slid his hands up to cup her breasts, teasing the tips with his thumbs until she could feel her body growing tight from within.

'Or you can marry me and we leave in the morning for Mackintosh lands.'

The words swirled around her in the echoing sounds of passion and made no sense to her. She was far into seeking her release and the pleasure she kenned that waited for her. When he slipped one hand into the folds of flesh between her legs and stroked her there, she felt everything begin to shudder and tremble. From deep inside to her skin, she tightened and then fell apart, moaning as she felt his seed spray against her womb.

Sorcha fell then and he caught her, easing her down on top of him so they lay chest to chest, his flesh still filling her. When she could breathe again, she lifted up and met his gaze. 'I had no idea it could be done that way.'

'Oh,' he said against her hair. 'I can think of many more ways it can be done.' He stroked her back then, holding her close. He whispered several things to her she had never considered either before sighing. 'If only you were not intent on that convent.'

She looked at him and let the laughter flow then. He was purposely misunderstanding her words in an attempt to tempt her into marriage with him. He continued to make suggestions, all of them carnal in nature and each one piqued her curiosity. Could a man and woman truly join in those positions and find pleasure?

He rolled then and now looked down on her. His flesh grew harder within her and he moved just enough to glide further within before he kissed her. Was this his attempt to tempt her even more? This time, though, it was his words that convinced her rather than his actions.

'You should ken that I will find you, Sorcha. Wher-

ever you go. I will find you and bring you back to me.'
He took hold of her hand and lifted it to his lips. 'I love
you. Hell, I even like you and so does my mother,'
he admitted. 'She said you'd be perfect to keep me
from all my bad habits.' Then his eyes turned into that
stormy mix and he kissed her hand again.

'In all seriousness, love, will you marry me? I promise to let you read your books and help Arabella with
her tasks. You can be learned or sew all your days. I
will be more lenient with you and a better man than
Micheil MacNeill ever was.'

It was nigh impossible to concentrate on this vital
conversation when he was so deep within her body.
When he covered her with his weight and strength and
heat. But he clearly would not relent or finish until they
did speak of it.

'What of my father when he learns I am alive?' She
ignored his jest about her non-existent husband and
worried over the real danger to their happiness. Her
father was her biggest concern. Her father still controlled her life.

'I think that is Brodie's reason for suggesting we
choose quickly. If you are legally wed by the time he
learns of your survival and arrives to find you in Brodie's protection, I think his demand for your return
would fall on deaf ears. Brodie is high in the favour of
both the king and the Church.'

'He really does manipulate people, does he not?'

'He learned quickly that finding and using a person's weaknesses and strengths was the way to survive. Brodie is a master.' She'd watched him during
the questioning and agreed. 'Not to lean too heavily on
his methods, but my parents did truly ask if we would

marry here before we leave for Glenlui.' He moved just enough then to take her breath away and to remind her what would happen when the words stopped.

'Are you certain of this, Alan? Do you truly wish us to marry? I ken you have many questions yet to seek answers to about your parents and your life.'

'Aye, my love. I have never wanted something or someone so much as I do you. No matter what else I seek in my life, I want you at my side.' He paused and stared into her eyes. 'In my heart. In my life.'

'Aye.'

They did not speak words for the rest of the night. Within minutes they confirmed their choice and then allowed caresses, kisses and their bodies to speak of their love. By morning, she realised what she had already learned—that she had found what she'd always wanted in her life in Alan. A strong man who would protect her and love her and find her when she was lost.

Alan helped her dress and then led her down to the great hall where his parents were waiting. Brodie had negotiated with the elders over his fate while he had been in her bed and Alan was pleased with the arrangements his long-time friend had made for him.

With Sorcha's knowledge of details and bargains made, Gilbert's supporters seemed to fade away, some even disappearing from the castle while confusion reigned after the fight. Now, those who stood to lose the most from Gilbert's treachery were safe, thanks to Alan and Sorcha. Any talk of charges against Alan quickly turned into accolades.

Robert Cameron took his place as chieftain of the clan with his son Robbie named tanist. Alan did not begrudge his father or brothers this and understood now why his father had not done it at Euan's death. For him. For him and his mother. Now, Robert would lead the clan and the peace would be in place for years to come.

Within an hour, they'd spoken their vows before his family. After breaking their fast, Alan and Sorcha left Achnacarry with promises to return once Robert was settled in the chieftain's seat and the elders who supported the new chieftain were in place on the council. Rob and Magnus accompanied them back to Brodie's lands and his wife. Someone had to tell her the news that she'd missed their wedding and Brodie did not wish to be that person.

And over the months and years, Alan would often think on how he'd found the woman he loved by accident and in spite of the fact she did not wish to be found. Sometimes, his skills as a tracker left him unable to see that which was right in front of him all the time.

Epilogue

'The midwife said you should remain abed,' Sorcha
warned as she entered Arabella's chamber and found
her standing at the window.

'I will scream if I have to lie abed any longer, Sorcha.' But Sorcha noticed that the lady did sit in the
chair there instead of standing.

'Here, place your legs on this,' she said, tugging the
cushioned stool from the corner and helping Arabella
get more comfortable.

'I ken that you are handling me,' the lady said. 'You
have been watching my husband too much.'

'Aye,' she admitted. 'I thought him so different from
my father when I first arrived here.' Sorcha pulled
the other chair closer and sat down, her own body's
increase in size making her ungainly as she moved
around now. And she tired more easily. And she wanted
strange combinations of food. And she wanted…more.
Her thoughts drifted away from Brodie to her husband's attempts to appease the other appetite that had
recently increased during her pregnancy. Arabella's
knowing glance brought her back to it. 'Brodie gets

what he wants, but uses completely different tactics to accomplish it.'

'Beware, my friend, for Alan is his able student and he will use those same tactics on you soon.'

Almost as though called by Bella's words, Alan entered the chamber. Both of them laughed and then again at his confusion. He kissed her and whispered a promise in her ear that made her blush and grow hot.

'A letter from my mother,' he said, holding out the folded parchment. 'Would you like to read it to me?'

Elizabeth's letters came regularly now and were filled with bits of information about Alan's brothers and the changes in Achnacarry since Gilbert's death. His mother had an amazing sense of humour and imbued her letters with it, leaving Sorcha laughing so hard that sometimes she cried from it.

Sorcha understood now that it was that sense of humour and inner strength that had seen the woman through her terrible ordeal those years ago. Now, no longer in fear of disclosure or retribution by Robert's brother, she was a different person.

'I would love to,' Sorcha said, opening the parchment and flattening it on her shrinking lap so she could read the words. But, before reading it aloud, she quickly read bits of it to herself.

'That is interesting,' she said after seeing one part of it.

'Interesting?' Arabella asked.

'Elizabeth speaks of a witch who lives on Cameron land north of Achnacarry.'

'A witch?' Alan asked, peering over her shoulder.

'There have been stories of a witch who lives near the falls there.' Arabella smiled at some memory. 'Aunt

Devorgilla used to tell us about her, but the details always seemed to change. In one story, she was old and wizened and in another she was young and comely.'

'Us?' Sorcha asked, looking at Alan who shook his head.

'My brother Malcolm and I.' A sadness entered her voice then, but Arabella shook free of it. 'He was my twin.' She brushed a tear away quickly, but Sorcha noticed it and realised of whom she spoke. 'He used to claim he would find that witch and chase her from our lands. It was a challenge made to all the young men in Achnacarry—find the witch and be a hero. He was determined to be the one.'

'And did he? Find her?'

''Twas just a story, Sorcha. There was no witch.'

Sorcha began reading the letter then and Arabella smiled when she reached the part that mentioned the rumours of a witch, shaking her head again at the fanciful idea.

But at that very moment, near Caig Falls on the lands of the Camerons, a woman looked out of her small cottage hidden deep in the woods. She whispered words that rhymed as another Cameron warrior climbed the rocky sides of the falls seeking her. When he slipped, his grasp on the wet stones not strong enough to hold him, and when he fell down into the deep pool that gathered below, she smiled.

That should scare him off for a while.

So, for a time, she would be safe from discovery and her secrets would remain hidden there with her.

* * * * *

Cord knew she was watching his every move, assessing him, judging him. Eleanor resented his presence in her kitchen, rooting around in her pantry and in the cutlery drawers. But she wanted an apple pie, didn't she? If there was one thing he'd learned in this life, it was that you don't get something for nothing. No rooting around in a pantry, no apple pie.

He worked on, trying to ignore her, and trying to ignore the undercurrent of pleasure he felt knowing that her eyes were following every move he made. It made his chest feel as hot inside as he felt outside in the stifling kitchen with the roaring fire in the stove heating up the oven.

While the pies baked, the children drifted out the back door to play in the yard and Cord warmed up the coffee, poured two cups and carried them into the parlor, where Eleanor sat.

She looked up at him with a strange expression on her pale face. He sucked in his breath and waited.

"You're not just a hired man, are you?" she said. "I mean, that's not what you did before I hired you, is it?"

"I'm a hired man here," he said carefully. "I'm not sure what I'd be somewhere else."

She reached for his offered cup of coffee, then glanced up again. "Do you have plans for 'somewhere else'?"

He gave her such a long look that she lowered her eyes.

"I was planning to go to California, to the gold fields."

"What stopped you?"

He didn't answer for a long time, just focused his gaze out the window on the apple orchard. "To be honest, I wouldn't have stopped here if I hadn't been so hungry, even though I'd seen your advert in town. But then I came up on that little hill and saw all those apple trees covered with lacy white blossoms. Kinda made my heart feel funny, so I stopped and…well, you know the rest."

She paused with her cup halfway to her mouth. "How long will you stay?"

"It's April now," he said slowly. "I thought I'd give it five months, say till August, before I move on."

"Very good. Doc Dougherty tells me I should be completely well and strong long before August."

"Yeah? You gonna chop wood and hitch up the horse and drive that wagon to town and muck out your barn by yourself? You need some help out here, ma'am. Even if I'm not going to be here, you should have a hired man to help out."

She gave him a half smile and sipped her coffee for a full minute before she spoke. "I chopped wood and mucked out the barn before I fell ill, Mr. Winterman. I have been on my own here for almost seven years, ever since Molly was born."

Cord studied her. Her cheeks were getting pink. "It's too hard for a woman alone. That's most likely why you got sick."

"That is pure nonsense. I got sick because I fell in the creek while I was chasing the cow and took a chill. A week later it turned into pneumonia."

He stood up suddenly. Dammit, he didn't want to concern himself with her well-being. He didn't want to like her kids, and he didn't want to like her. But he did. And he had to admit it scared the hell out of him.

"Think I'll check on the pies," he growled. He moved into the kitchen and bent over the oven door, and when he returned he brought the coffeepot and filled her cup. He didn't look at her. But he did ask the question that had been niggling in the back of his mind.

"Do you and your husband own this place free and clear?"

"I own it. I removed Tom's name from the deed when he…when he left home to go off to war. It's been seven years now, and he is considered legally dead."

"You said you had a hired man before you hired me."

"Yes. Isaiah. As I told you, he didn't do much."

"Why'd you keep him, then?"

"He needed a place to stay and I needed someone to help about the farm. Molly was just a baby then, and Danny was too little to be much help."

"How'd you manage after this hired man, Isaiah, left?"

"I managed," she said in a quiet voice.

"And then you got sick," he observed drily.

She took a swallow of her coffee. "Well, yes, I did. Doc Dougherty came, and he sent a woman out from town, Helen, I think her name was, to nurse me and take care of Molly and Daniel. She stayed until I was strong enough to get out of bed. I am growing stronger with every day that passes."

"Mrs. Malloy. Eleanor," he amended. "Seems to me you're just hangin' on by a thread. You've got two kids. You owe it to them to take better care of yourself. That means no more milking and no chopping wood."

She pressed her lips into a thin line but said nothing.

Cord studied the rigid set of her shoulders and the white-knuckled grip she had on the handle of her china cup. "I get the feeling you don't take orders too well."

She gave him a wobbly smile. "You are most likely correct. I was a great trial to my parents."

That made him laugh out loud. "I bet you're still plenty stubborn when it comes to doing things your own way."

"Oh, maybe just a little." Her cheeks turned an even deeper shade of rose.

"Maybe you're more than a little stubborn," he said. "Maybe a lot stubborn."

"Oh, all right, maybe I'm a lot stubborn." By now her cheeks were flushed scarlet. "Now that you're here, I will take better care of myself. Especially," she said with a little bubble of laughter, "since you can bake an apple pie. Which," she added with an impish grin, "you have quite forgotten is still in the oven."

Instantly he wheeled away from her and strode into the kitchen. The pies were not burned, as he had feared, just nicely baked. He grabbed pot holders and lifted them out of the oven. Oh, man, they looked just right, golden brown on top with rich juice bubbling out the vents he'd slashed in the crust. They smelled wonderful! He was damn proud of them.

Eleanor followed him into the kitchen, cup and saucer still in her hand. "Who taught you to make a pie? Your mother?"

"No," he said shortly.

She looked at him with another question in her eyes, but he ignored it. Best not to dig around in those long-past years. No good ever came from opening a wound that had healed over.

He set both pies on the open windowsill to cool and stacked the mixing bowl and the paring knives in the sink for the kids to wash up after supper. Eleanor returned to the parlor, where she curled up on the settee and gazed out the front window.

"You don't like talking to me, do you?" she asked suddenly.

Whoa, Nelly. How'd she figure that?

"Why is that?" she pursued, her eyes on his face.

"Guess I haven't been around many ladies lately."

"Silence is perfectly all right with me," she went on. "I spent years and years not being talked to."

She closed her eyes against the late-afternoon sun's glare, and that gave him a chance to really look at her. Her lids were purplish with blue-black smudges shadowing her eyes. She might not be sick anymore, but she was obviously exhausted.

So even if she was as stubborn as three ornery mules, now she had a hired man to help her. He drew in a long, quiet breath. For the first time in longer than he could remember he felt needed.

And that, he thought with a silent groan, made him nervous.

Don't miss
The Hired Man *by Lynna Banning,*
available September 2018.

www.Harlequin.com

HHEXP46758

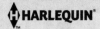

HARLEQUIN

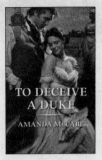

TO DECEIVE A DUKE

AMANDA McCABE

Save $1.00

off the purchase of ANY

Harlequin® series book.

Available wherever books are sold, including most bookstores, supermarkets, drugstores and discount stores.

- ✂

Save $1.00

on the purchase of ANY Harlequin® series book.

Coupon valid until September 30, 2018.
Redeemable at participating retail outlets in the U.S. and Canada only.
Limit one coupon per customer.

52615867

5 65373 00076 2   (8100)0 12376

® and ™ are trademarks owned and used by the trademark owner and/or its licensee.

HHCOUP46758

Earn points on your purchase of new Harlequin books from participating retailers.

Turn your points into **FREE BOOKS** of your choice!

Join for FREE today at
www.HarlequinMyRewards.com.

Harlequin My Rewards is a free program (no fees) without any commitments or obligations.